Paper Sons and Daughters

MODERN
African
Writing
from Ohio University Press

This series brings the best African writing to an international audience. These ground-breaking novels, memoirs, and other literary works showcase the most talented writers of the African continent. The series also features works of significant historical and literary value translated into English for the first time. Moderately priced, the books chosen for the series are well crafted, original, and ideally suited for African studies classes, world literature classes, or any reader looking for compelling voices of diverse African perspectives.

Welcome to Our Hillbrow: A Novel of Postapartheid South Africa
by Phaswane Mpe
ISBN: 978-0-8214-1962-5

Dog Eat Dog: A Novel
by Niq Mhlongo
ISBN: 978-0-8214-1994-6

After Tears: A Novel
by Niq Mhlongo
ISBN: 978-0-8214-1984-7

From Sleep Unbound
Andrée Chedid
ISBN: 978-0-8040-0837-2

On Black Sisters Street: A Novel
Chika Unigwe
ISBN: 978-0-8214-1992-2

Paper Sons and Daughters: Growing Up Chinese in South Africa
Ufrieda Ho
ISBN: 978-0-8214-2020-1

The Conscript: A Novel of Libya's Anticolonial War
Gebreyesus Hailu
ISBN: 978-0-8214-2023-2

Ohio University Press, Athens, Ohio 45701
www.ohioswallow.com

First published in 2011 by Picador Africa
An imprint of Pan Macmillan South Africa
Private Bag X19, Northlands
Johannesburg, 2116

To obtain permission to quote, reprint, or otherwise reproduce or distribute
material from Ohio University Press publications, please contact our rights
and permissions department at (740) 593-1154 or (740) 593-4536 (fax).

First published in North America in 2012 by Ohio University Press
Printed in the United States of America
Ohio University Press books are printed on acid-free paper ⊗ ™

20 19 18 17 16 15 14 13 12   5 4 3 2 1

Library of Congress Cataloguing-in-Publication Data

Ho, Ufrieda.
 Paper sons and daughters : growing up Chinese in South Africa / Ufrieda
Ho.
     p. cm. — (Modern African writing)
 Originally published: Johannesburg, South Africa : Picador Africa, 2011.
 ISBN 978-0-8214-2020-1 (pbk. : acid-free paper) — ISBN 978-0-8214-
4444-3 (electronic)
 1. Ho, Ufrieda. 2. Ho, Ufrieda—Family. 3. Chinese—South Africa—
Biography. 4. Chinese—South Africa—Ethnic identity. 5. Chinese—South
Africa—History. 6. South Africa—Race relations. 7. South Africa—
Biography. I. Title.
 DT1768.C55H6 2012
 305.895'1068092—dc23
 [B]
                                    2012020804

Paper Sons and Daughters

Growing up Chinese in South Africa

Ufrieda Ho

OHIO UNIVERSITY PRESS
ATHENS

Contents

For my mother and my father

Acknowledgements

There's an exquisite alchemy in how this book became real. My deepest gratitude goes to the people and mysterious synchronicities that offered up their magic to the process.

I have been privileged to be a custodian of the stories that have been passed to me from my grandparents, parents and my relatives. I am grateful to the many people in my community, the Ah Buks and Ah Mous and others, who have shared their anecdotes, narratives, reflections and insights through the years. I acknowledge with respect the academics, authors and researchers whose work has given voice to the Chinese community and has given me the courage to free my voice for this story.

Thanks and love to my friends (you are too numerous to mention by name but you know who you are) and those who have taken an authentic interest; you are my blessing and have held this book with gentle hands.

Maureen Isaacson was a champion of this book when it was only a few thousand words on newsprint as my journalism project for the Anthony Sampson Foundation Award. A thousand thank-yous for believing and for not letting me get away from penning a formal book proposal.

To the Pan Macmillan team, thank you for keeping me going and getting the nuts and bolts in place with such good humour. Sally Hines, thanks for being a kind wizard of an editor. To Andrea Nattrass, who survived my multi-coloured versions and drafts, you've pushed at the right times and have been a pillar to lean on at other times; always you've encouraged me and shown sensitivity to this story. You are a true professional, thank you.

My thanks to Anfasa for their generous author's grant and support for a book about a minority community in South Africa.

Shaun, thank you for loving me through this book, listening to confused thinking out loud, my long ramblings, my rages, even the tears, and always urging me on because you know this is a project of my heart.

To Ma, Yolanda, Kelvin, Unisda, Jo-Anne, Alexandra and Jordan, you have shared so much of this journey. We walk on, joined by our bond of blood, kin and love.

Pinky

I lie on the lap of a giant pink teddy bear and stare up at a galaxy of full stops in the perforated canopy of my dad's old Cortina.

My nine-year-old self starts to count the dots but my stop-start conversation with my dad in the driver's seat keeps bringing me back to number one. We lurch towards another traffic light and my counting is distracted again as I grip on to the Cortina's fake leather seats with their exhausted stitching that has long ago surrendered to outbursts of foam.

I work through the dots again. I do not mind because my father is in a good mood, so I am in a good mood. Dad is happy and Pinky is the trophy to prove it. We have bought her at a roadside stall along with two smaller teddies holding their breath inside puffed-up plastic bags. Among the gifts there is a round leather ottoman, dubiously shaped by a rustling straw inner. My mom is going to be delighted with her gift and so will my brother and two sisters.

But these are more than just gifts – Pinky, with her curly blue bow and large flat eyes, is a triumph of dad's success at the fahfee banks today.

My father, my Ah Ba, is a fahfee man, the mm-china or ma-china of the townships, a so-called *ju fah goung*, as we say in Cantonese. Fahfee is an illegal betting game with 36 numbers and wonderfully curious connections to dreams, to superstitions and to luck and chance; the dirty gambling of the townships.

In South Africa fahfee has evolved from its recreational gambling roots and has been transformed into an economic survival strategy. It can endure in South Africa's socio-political space where segregation is so well worn it is like an involuntary impulse to separate, to categorise, to divide. It is South Africa in the 1980s and there is no place for a yellow man, especially not one like my dad who is uneducated, who is not savvy to the social rules that make up polite white society and who is prohibited from even trying to fit in.

It is to fahfee that he turns and the townships far from the mainstream of middle class. And it is what my father does for the biggest chunk of my memory. Fahfee, when the gambling gods will it, brings fortune, good times and even the likes of Pinky. It pays for my school fees, treats at a roadhouse and eventually an assortment of second-hand cars as we climb the ladder to middle class.

All the time, what turns up in the numbers makes real the superstitions of the old country: the mysterious what-ifs that connect the realm of the explained with what cannot be known. And in the dreamtime, the fahfee man's beliefs and impressions thread together a place far, far east to the golden mountain of Johannesburg, glorious with the nostalgia of when the yellow metal did line the streets.

Fahfee is about sweat and drudgery. It is about toil on the periphery of society where it stays hidden, out of sight and secret. It is about what luck brings and what risks you are prepared to take when you stand to lose everything.

In my family, fahfee means we stand to lose a lot.

Here be Dragons

I grew up in Bertrams, in the east of Johannesburg, in the 1970s and 80s. I am the third of four children. We lived in a semi-detached house along a wide road that pulled apart the suburb for the cars advancing towards the shopping centre and highway exchange that over the next three decades would become the massive mall of Eastgate and the throbbing clot of the N3 interchange.

This was a so-called grey area, where Chinese people were mostly ignored for living in these spaces that were still legally reserved for whites in apartheid South Africa. No one cared really that a few Chinese lived here because these were not the fancy suburbs where people worried about backwashing swimming pools or keeping appointments at the doggie parlour. Like dragons in fairytales, we were left to become the demons of people's theories, mysteries and loathing. As long as we stayed in our lairs and did not breathe out fire, we were pretty much left alone.

Of course, I did not know then that things like pool maintenance separated and defined people. I did not know that being Chinese made me different, like I did not know what fahfee would come to mean for my family, and especially for my father.

This gambling game practised in hidden places was never spoken about openly to outsiders. Fahfee was always sullied, polluted somehow. It was associated with the working class, with transacting with the poorest of the poor. And so fahfee was something people skirted around even to community insiders and completely so to outsiders. It remained a practice of humiliation and secrecy, which turned into a practice of shame and stigma.

I did not know these things in the 1980s when I was growing up as we were a part of living these shadows and scars. We were a society full of cleavages; we shared a country, but we were not a nation. Separated in delineated living spaces, we stayed in our boxes of stereotypes, convenient prejudices and simmering tensions.

I was blissfully unaware of all this as a child, a bit like the small fertile patch in our garden that showed happy oblivion or maybe it was quiet rebellion, growing with abandon against expectation and convention. Where there should have been hydrangeas and pansies, the small patch of soil became a vegetable haven of downy winter melons, smooth green Chinese spinach and eruptions of spring onion – the vegetables you could not find in a local greengrocer in South Africa in the 1980s, but which were the staples on a Chinese family's daily menu.

Most Chinese we knew used whatever land was around them to grow food. No one really moaned about the fluttering strips of plastic bags that stood in for scarecrows because this was a crumbling bit of suburbia.

Further down the road lived a Chinese woman and her adult son. She raised chickens on the small property and sometimes we walked down to her corner house to buy a freshly slain bird.

The old aunty disappeared behind the backyard door, closed it and told us to wait. There was a muffled squawking, the sound of someone moving quickly. We sat in the kitchen in silence, imagining the poor chickens darting across their small pen hoping not to be the unlucky one. She reappeared some minutes later with a limp bird, some of its white feathers wet where the first blood of its death had been rinsed off. The chicken was placed into a double-bagged, blue-grey plastic bag and we walked home with its still-warm body knocking against our legs, ready to be paired with our winter melons on the dinner table.

Outside the stout walls of our house an oak tree's trunk burst out of the grey pavement. It was the pavement where the old brown Cortina was parked, because there was no garage or driveway. There was no grass around the old giant, just a scattering of its leaves and acorns; the rest was tarred. I liked to collect the little nuts, pop off their hats and peel off their hard casings until my fingernails were split and sore. The pain was worth it to treat the squirrels that I believed lived in our neighbour's tree. My older sister Yolanda (I called her Kaa Jeh or Kaatch) convinced me that my furry friends did appreciate my efforts, so I happily peeled away in pain, but there were no squirrels in suburban Joburg. Yolanda kept up her poker face and I believed her, thinking that the more I peeled, the more grateful the squirrels would be and then I would surely see them.

I did my growing up with Yolanda, who is the eldest. She was short, cheeky and always hatching a plan to get her way and to get us to be at her side when it happened, just in case things went pear-shaped. My older brother Kelvin was the only boy, all stringy and weedy when we were growing up. He tempted us to join in his invented games and we could not help being his participating audience for his card stunts and magic tricks, begging him to show us how to do them, but of course he revealed nothing. He was the brother who offered to 'operate' on a pair of talking teddies. He said he would open their voice boxes, tweak their wires and electric chips and they would greet us again with 'Hello, I am Teddy the bear, the one who is always there'. We believed him but once their little voice boxes landed in his surgeon hands, our bears never greeted us again. Perhaps they just needed a fresh set of batteries. The baby was Unisda. She was quiet and mostly went with the flow, scooped off her feet by the waves of her older siblings. Unisda and I were so close in age we became like twins relegated to the bottom of the pecking order.

Together we made up the generation of Hos born on South African soil, here in the eastern suburbs of Johannesburg. We have Chinese names, too. Mine is Chiu Ngaan, which means colour. In Chinese your surname comes first. My sisters are Chiu Yeng and Chiu Saan. Chui is the common name for us girls and it means jade. My brother is Beng Leung; it means bright, and Beng is a common name he shares with all the other second cousins in the extended family. My parents realised that in South Africa we needed to have English names, too. I thought I had a strange English name; for years until I was well into my teens I resented the unusualness of my name. Not only did I almost always have to repeat myself, but I also had to think up explanations that I had no answers for.

Even Ho is strange. People always wait for more, like surely I mean to say Hough or Home or maybe at least the addition of an 'e' and I have to say: 'That is it, just H.O.' There is not even an ordinary animal I know that starts with U, as in Betty the Bear, David the Donkey or Helen the Horse.

My mother's uncle was entrusted with the role of giving us English names, because my parents did not trust their own English proficiency. My theory is that this grand-uncle, whose English was also a little dodgy, managed fine with Yolanda and Kelvin – both being reasonably ordinary names. But by the time I came along I think he believed some creative licence had been earned. My younger sister also got a 'U' tagged on to the start of her name and she became Unisda. At least we both had Us and that horseshoe letter looped us together as we grew up. I always laugh when I imagine what would have happened if my parents had had a fifth child who would probably have been subjected to a concocted 'U' name, too.

In my family we call each other by our Chinese names. I respond to Ah Ngaan and we used an old-fashioned address of calling older siblings not by their names but by something that translates as 'my family sister' or 'my family brother'. With only a year or so between me and my younger sister, Unisda took to calling me Ah Ngaan when we were children. I was too little to think that it was not proper but my parents kept trying to drum into Unisda's head that I was Yee Kaa Jeh (second family sister) not Ah Ngaan to her. It did not work – I am still Ah Ngaan or Ngaanie to her today.

We were squashed into a less-than-six-year age gap from youngest to oldest so it made for a riotous growing up in our household.

We three girls shared a bedroom painted in a peachy pink. It was topped with a naked light bulb in the centre – there were no extras like fancy light fittings – that cast gently swaying shadows over the walls and floor at night when there was a bit of a breeze.

Unisda and I shared a bunk bed in the room, while Yolanda was pushed up against the opposite wall. For years we switched between taking up the bottom and the top bunk. We liked to push our feet up against the soft steel frame and irritate the person who was on the top bunk.

'Hey, stop it man,' the top-bunker whined as the bottom-bunker pushed harder against the diamond mesh of the bed frame, bouncing the top bunker a bit.

But the top bunk was also a refuge. With every few feet from ground level the lucky top-bunker got to escape the general madness of the congested shared space that was our bedroom.

The assortment of furniture in our room collided with patterned homemade curtains, dark, practical carpets and rugs and the rainbow frenzy of smiling teddies and toys that shared our beds.

We also made a mess, a lot of it. Clothes we never folded and never put away made ever-growing, crumpled mountains. And mom and dad's moans and threats could not keep up with the neglected dust balls we were supposed to clean up.

Across the passage my brother fought off the dolls and girly saturation with train sets and Lego. As the only boy he did not have to share a room but he did have to give up some of his domain for storage space in the form of locked wardrobes, canned food and toilet paper bought in bargain bulk.

Sometimes my parents opened up the wardrobes to air out a winter coat, lined and heavy, or to retrieve a satin-finished, heavily encrusted evening bag replete with sparkling beads and tassels. These were the outfits and accessories reserved for weddings, an 80th birthday or some other dress-up event. When my parents did open up the wardrobes, the strangely comforting smells of mothballs, old wood and dark places filled my nostrils. It was the release of these otherwise intangible treasures, the moment that these items of whimsy and wonder were temporarily let loose to interrupt the ordinariness of a normal day.

Normal days for us children were made up of the bliss of turning the passage that dominated the small semi into our playground. It was full of potential for hide-and-seek, which we played often, and games of fantastic make-believe.

An old record player had its home in the passage, wedged into a corner behind the front door that had a frosted glass panel in a design resembling a flower and was complete with an ankle-high letter flap that said 'Letters/ Briewe'. My father had won the record player in a community raffle years before he met my mother. For a long time it was the only fancy thing he owned that was not handed down, loaned or bought second-hand.

Even as it stood in our passage, it belonged to a different world, not the world of a fahfee man who worked long hours every day dodging authorities, arguing with grumpy gamblers or becoming grumpy himself on days when the gambling gods turned the tables on the ma-china. He did not have the luxury of turning to a music box for pleasure.

I do not remember my father ever pursuing a proper hobby all his life, just the distractions of his own gambling, or on the odd occasion being the master chef of a cook-up of a special dish like crispy deep-fried pigeon or garlic and ginger crab, all creepily alive, scratching in the boxes punched with small holes or in shallow buckets of water, waiting for my father to come home for the big slaughter.

The record player flanked a wardrobe filled with sheets and homemade curtains. My mother never threw anything out; a worn sheet was cut down the middle and sewn together again where the fabric still endured. Even when its life as a sheet was finally over, it was reincarnated as a patterned floor rag that found itself useful again on the kitchen floor.

The record player was the princess in this sea of sensible practicalities. It looked like an old-fashioned letter-writing bureau with its wooden legs and its curious flip-up lid. It had a revolving rubberised disc and a slow-moving mechanical arm. My mother kept a few records that were loaned from friends and family. They were mostly Chinese opera records or high-pitched sweetly sung folksongs, all dusty and housed in crumbling paper sleeves. When my mother plugged in the record player and set it into life, it never failed to fascinate us as its mechanical arm shifted across with fluid precision and dropped exactly as a vinyl flopped gently on to the revolving disc. It broke into the squeaky opera songs and we mimicked the singers and then put our hands over our ears as the records squealed on. My mother, though, loved it. She did not have a singing voice but it did not stop her from testing out the tunes and the lyrics. We laughed and laughed, making faces at what sounded like pained cries and howling. The singing was mostly in old-fashioned Chinese and with the added high-pitched squeaks we caught very little of the storyline, even though mom tried to tell us what was going on as the characters wailed to each other.

The record player also doubled up as a counter top when we played shop. We lifted its lid, took in the smell of its wood, pushed the arm and turned the dials like it was a cash machine. If I was the shopkeeper, I got to stand by the record player. Unisda was my customer most of the time, picking up her 'purchases' of bits of tea set, teddies, pencils and crayons before coming to the 'pay-point'. I pretended to ring up her goodies, pushed the buttons and the dials, then packed her purchases into a plastic bag and said 'thank you' and 'goodbye and see you again'.

Later on I learnt the dials were for record speeds and we drew out the comedy in the records by making them yelp at chipmunk-speak speed. Sometimes the record player was simply a place to sit and swing our legs when our mom and dad were not looking.

The old semi had pressed ceilings and old-fashioned chair rails. The chair rails created a split wall effect that convinced my ever-practical mother to paint the walls in an odd contrast of midnight-blue and creamy white in a paint that had a shiny finish. It was shiny because the oil paint finishes were easier to wash, my mom said. She chose midnight-blue on the bottom half of the wall, so the dark paint disguised our grubby handprints and our wax crayon art that proved to be stubbornly permanent – a little like the lingering sting of a whack on the bum for making the drawings in the first place.

We were punished quite harshly if we were naughty, misbehaved or were disrespectful. There was no thinking-step, time-out or negotiations; that is all the stuff of 21st-century parenting. In our household you could count on a tongue-lashing and a hiding. We might also be banished to our rooms or locked out of the house for a few hours, threatened with no dinner and told to ponder our actions on the *stoep* (veranda) – or rather to wait for my mother's seething finally to evaporate. If my mother was really mad she would wait until my dad came home. If he thought what we had done called for a second round of punishment then we would see a replay of my mother's rage, acted out by my dad and maybe even a whip or two from one of his belts.

One day, though, when I was about nine or ten, my dad said he would never hit me again because if I had not learnt my lessons by then no amount of hidings would teach me to be the wiser. It scared me more, thinking I would have to live up to the expectations of my parents rather than deal with a stinging bum.

But we did not fight with our parents much; we dared not. Chinese children, at least as far as my parents were concerned, did not negotiate, did not backchat. Filial respect was not an option for Chinese children. There was a Confucian thread that ran through our childhood of honouring your parents, of trusting their word even if you disagreed. I believed my parents were harsher than other parents. As I grew up, I thought them old fashioned, conservative; now I know that they were exactly as they had to be.

The old ways were ever-present in our house. Sometimes we were scared into good habits with old wives' tales and the superstitions, myths and rituals that were bred in a closeted place in China but were never far away. If we left grains of rice in our bowls, we were told that children were starving, that each grain could grow into a plant and we had wasted its potential. Other times my mom said it meant we would find an ugly spouse. If you sneaked food from a chopping board, she said it would mean we would be cursed to be damned for things that were not our fault.

Over time, the superstitions were infused with my mother's personal concoctions, too. We did not wash our hair on the first day of new year or on our birthdays or each other's birthdays because the word for prosperity, *faat*, sounds like the word for hair and washing your hair on these luckiest days would rinse away prosperity. My mother also believed that if you broke something on the last day of the old year, you took the same clumsiness and misfortune into the new year ... very unlucky. My gawky child's co-ordination dribbled food on my clothes and often relieved cups of their handles so I spent most New Year's Eves terrified of a slip-up.

Superstitions slipped directly into my beliefs, too, even though I eventually acquired enough common sense to doubt their actual power to manifest doom and gloom or to alter destiny. I understood that superstitions gave people something to hold on to. They helped them to contain the unexplained and they gave some order and hope when none existed. Still, I was not immune to these forces.

One day I was playing around in the house with Unisda and I accidentally bumped a stand where the porcelain statue of Kwun Yum took pride of place. One year my granny had bought each of us grandchildren a figurine of the most important deities that rule a Chinese home. Kwun Yum is the goddess of mercy and goodness, and she was Unisda's figurine. She rose out of a lotus flower with a flowing robe, a beatific expression, pure and so good. I literally decapitated this 30-cm saintly deity as she fell backwards. It was a clean break right across her slender neck and as I held her head in my hand I could peer down through the hollow core right to the small hole at the base of the porcelain goddess's lotus pedestal.

Terror gripped me as I imagined how angry my mother would be when she found out. More than this, though, I was also horrified that I had invoked the anger of this mystical creature and that she would rain bad luck and evil on me or my family for my insult and my violation.

Unisda could only look on in relief that she was not the one who had crashed against the stand. I had to enlist her help and her complicity and we took Pritt, the paper glue stick, from our schoolbags to glue her back together. I smeared the glue around the clay-like rim and balanced Kwun Yum's head back on her neck. I almost breathed a sigh of relief when I saw she was still smiling and looked surprisingly whole, no visible chips or anything. Still, I clasped my hands together, almost involuntarily, assumed a prayer position and bowed three times in front of the statue, in that old respectful Chinese way.

Kwun Yum made it and even survived a house move years later. In fact, she still stands in my mom's house today, perfect bar the faint line above the beads that adorn her throat. What also survived were my sister's sneers. She reminded me even when we were grown-ups about my submission to superstition. It embarrassed my adult wish to snub silly superstitions, but actually I was happy Kwun Yum was still smiling.

I even once followed a very old Chinese custom of going down on your knees and offering a cup of tea as a sincere apology. It was like a dramatic scene out of a Chinese period film. Imagine the flowing silk robes pushed to the side as the person with the guilt drops to the ground with head bowed and two hands raised holding up a teacup. The person who must grant forgiveness gazes out of a rice-paper-filled window pane and sighs; and tears maybe then roll down the cheeks of the person on the ground as the teacup is taken and the contents gulped down.

On one occasion I played out this scene with my mother because I had made her so angry. I cannot remember now what I had done but it had been terrible and I was truly sorry. On top of this, my mother suffered from migraines and on the day I had made her so cross she was struck by one of these headaches. When the headaches came they scared me because she would get so ill she would have to take to her bed with the curtains closed and she would lie there in the darkness.

My mother – who could fix anything of ours that broke, knew instantly where to find our missing shoes, toys or whatever, even when we said we had looked everywhere, and was never late with a dinner or for picking us up after school – was diminished to a groaning patient with no one to take care of her. We could only watch, occasionally slipping into the darkened room and calling her softly, only for her not to respond. She would not feel much better even with the green and white capsules that were in huge supply in her drawers and even after tying thin slices of potatoes with a cloth around her forehead and smearing the Chinese *bak fa youw*, the menthol-smelling 'white flower oil', on her temples and behind her ears.

When a headache coincided with that terrible something I had done, I was horror-struck and sure that I had brought on the pain. I remembered the old custom of asking for forgiveness and how my mother had said it

11

was old fashioned but correct. So I brewed a cup of Chinese tea with a few dried leaves, throwing out the first seep then refreshing it with more hot water. I put a saucer under the cup and took it to my mother's room. I called her and she turned on the bedside lamp in the darkened room. I said my teary sorry as I dropped to my knees and I offered her the tea. She drank the tea; mothers always do, I guess.

The semi-detached house at number 62A was a treasure trove – to us children anyway. It was tiny but we grew up along its central passage that seemed perfectly long enough for my six- or seven-year-old self. It was a house with hiding places and unusual nooks and crannies. There was a small pantry and scullery attached to the kitchen. The pantry was like a science laboratory with shelves upon shelves of strange and wonderful things stored in glass Consol jars and tins with faded pictures of cherry blossoms and Chinese words. They were filled with dried wood fungus, dried wolf berries (now marketed as superfood goji berries that make it on to the ingredients list for smoothies and muesli), dried shrimp and dried sheets of crinkling, brittle tofu; there was pungent fermented tofu in jars of spicy brine and pickled lettuce and pickled salted fish. Sometimes when my mom was not looking, my father would sneak down a handful of dried shrimp from a shelf we children could not reach. Usually these shrimps were soaked until soft and added to other dishes like glutinous rice cooked up in sticky deliciousness or taro potato cakes dotted with these treasures in their sturdy slabs. To eat the small and salty, peanut-like morsels was forbidden – they were expensive delicacies that my mom tried to ration and use sparingly. Sometimes we would chew on these curled salty bodies, giggling in our secret pact.

When our games spilled out of the semi-detached house, we amused ourselves in the backyard. The backyard began with a long strip veranda jammed with a few chairs, pot plants and an outside cooking area that always left everything slightly greasy. Every authentic Chinese house needed one of these cooking spots. It was here that a fierce gas fire could be tamed into a cooking plate to make woks sizzle for gastronomic alchemy and it made easy work of even a three-tier bamboo steaming rack.

To get to the yard, you went down a flight of grey, concrete steps. The yard's uneven surface was filled with small, dark, coal-like flakes, not concrete paving or sand or grass. It crunched under our feet and was so loose and uneven you could not bounce a ball on its rutted dreariness. There were also two small hollowed-out areas under the house and the stairs. These cavernous structures spooked me. They were used to store coal in the house's previous lives when people still relied on coal for their stoves and fireplaces. In our house, though, the stained, larger hollow was filled with junk, mostly broken furniture and appliances that no longer worked but that my parents thought might be fixed and prove useful again some day. The smaller hollow became a dog kennel of cardboard and old blankets for the dogs that shared our lives as children.

There were also three smaller storerooms in the yard and an outside toilet. One was used as a storeroom with more old toys, broken appliances, wedding gifts never opened and saved for a special occasion and more toilet paper and soap bought in bulk that did not fit in Kelvin's room.

The second storeroom was turned into a pigeon coop on and off in the years we lived in Bertrams. When it was used to raise birds, the stifling dark room was filled with stacked old five-litre oil tins with pictures of sunflowers on the front. These were cut out crudely, folded back and filled with dried grass and straw for the nests. These pigeons were not pets. They were raised for slaughter. I did not like going into their room and the adjoining open aviary but we were expected to clean the coops, scatter the feed and change the water bowls. As the pigeons' cooing gave way to sudden flapping, I was always startled and felt like holding my breath among the dirty airborne down feathers and bird poop. I guess I also never liked the coop because I knew the pigeons' throats would be slit and their sagged bodies would be plunged into boiling water sooner or later. They would be plucked of the feathers that made them resemble the birds that were just moments ago pecking away at their corn and my feet. Then they would be deep fried to a crispy delicacy that my father was particularly fond of. I also liked them for many of my childhood years, I have to admit, but it became too sad to connect the dots to their death and then to my stomach.

Throughout our time in the Bertrams Road house, and even for a few years after that, my mother raised chickens and even a duck or two. We all eventually learnt not to get attached to them as they roamed around pecking corn and seeds that we scattered for them. I was never comfortable with the slaughter even when it was deliberately hidden from us children and sometimes we were simply told the birds had flown away.

Unisda (or Ah Saan as I called her by her Chinese name) and I also had two pet rabbits. Hers was snow white and her eyes looked reddish sometimes in different light. We called her Jane. My bunny was called Dick; we decided he was a boy because he was black and white. The names came from a book my sister and I had to read as one of our first readers, the iconic Dick and Jane series.

My mother built our rabbits a hutch, sectioning off a part of the charcoaled backyard for them and putting up chicken wire held together with scrap bits of wood nailed together. We fed them wilted Chinese spinach leaves, vegetable scraps and treats of juicy carrots wedged through the hexagons of the chicken wire.

My mom did not drive until I was about eight years old. So sometimes she let Saan and I walk to the local greengrocer a couple of blocks from our home to get food for Dick and Jane. We dragged home a big mesh bag of carrots for our bunnies. We loved to watch them hop close to the mesh and gnaw down at the sweet carrots, leaving small stumps once the sweetness of the sections of new growth were spent. I liked that we could pet them without fear that they would dart out of their hutch or retreat to a corner.

One day we arrived home from school to find an aunt we called Yee Gu Mah, a spinster and an older relative on my father's side of the family, had come to visit. It was a novelty that she had come over to visit on a school night and she said she would be staying for dinner. The break in routine was fun enough; it meant mom let up on the routine of homework and chores as she was distracted with Yee Gu Mah's visit. We changed out of our school uniforms, which my mother was always strict about, and went to feed Dick and Jane.

When we could not find them we rushed with alarm back up the stairs to tell my mom that the rabbits were missing. She said they must have burrowed out of the hutch and run away. We were heartbroken and crushed. That night, though, my chopsticks could not connect with the pieces of meat that were generously piled in my bowl. I did not know for sure then that our rabbits were the meal and years later I have never asked outright either. I guess it is because I have always known the answer.

As we grew up our games were made up of the mystical East and the reality of South African life. They were two different worlds that adhered together, contiguous and joined, and in places they fused in a weird but easy mingle. The copper-plated springbok ornament with mighty horns in relief was the epitome of 1970s kitsch decor. Ours was mounted alongside a fabric wall-hanging of an artist's impression of the precipitous drop of China's sheer mountains as they spiked into the mists of the old country.

A game my brother Kelvin invented one afternoon saw Unisda and I pretend to be the lion from the traditional Chinese lion dance. The dances are part of every Chinese celebration, chasing away bad spirits and welcoming new abundance. We were the head and the tail of the lion and Kelvin played the part of the *daai dou faat*, the caricatured big-headed man, who leads the menacing lion away from the village in a fable of triumph over evil, of bravery and community celebration.

To lead the creature away from the village, as the myth goes, Kelvin needed a magical wand, a chalice of sorts, as all good *daai dou faats* have. For that day's game he managed to smuggle a joss stick from the bundle that my mother kept locked away to light for the ancestors and the gods. They were lit for protection and prosperity on auspicious days or days of remembrance. We knew these fragrant incense sticks were not toys and playthings, along with all the other paraphernalia of pretend gold and silver printed papers that were folded into intricate paper ingots to be burnt for the dead, our revered ancestors. But which eight-year-old could resist something that burned and glowed and left a wisp of fragrant smoke in a tidy trail just long enough to be noted before it dissipated?

Kelvin had figured out that the small cupboard in the hallway where the joss sticks, candles, matches and papers were kept locked away was topped by a drawer that could be removed completely. If you slipped your hand carefully between the partition of the drawer and the locked door you could maybe fish out a prize like the joss stick he successfully captured that day.

Unisda and I took up our positions as the head and the tail of the lion under a brightly coloured blanket. The lions in the dance were always brightly coloured with bells and ribbon frills and my favourite – their fantastically long-lashed eyelids could be pulled along a pulley on the inside by the dancer to make the lion look like he was winking. In keeping with the festive shades of the lions we were so used to for these dances, the blanket we chose to use was one that had bright blooms on the one side, a soft cloth underside and a pleated ribbon edge.

We threw the blanket over our heads, Unisda bent and gripped my waist to become the hind legs and we peeped out to follow Kelvin's glowing joss stick as we danced around the bedroom, careful not to bump against the double bunk. As the joss stick glowed, we followed its seductive smoke coils, making up our own version of the rhythmic drum beat that accompanied every lion dance. 'Boom ba da boom, ba boom, ba boom, ba boom,' we shouted out. But in our manic twists and turns and our jokes and giggles, the joss stick dropped on to the blanket and its decorative flower prints proved to serve better as synthetic kindling. There were no flames, just an enlarging hole that spread at a speed outpaced only by our growing horror of what we could look forward to when my mother and father found out.

We would be punished for sure for this palm-sized hole we had created and for playing with the joss stick. We stamped out the rush of the burn but the hole stayed and the room filled with a chemical stench. And so, in the end, we decided to conceal the evidence of the now holey blanket. We said nothing and hoped to high heaven that we were never caught out.

Unisda and I had matching versions of this ill-fated blanket, hers with dominant blue colours and mine with stronger pink colours. As with so many of our things, from our clothes to our toys, they were identical or almost matching. Even our teddies and soft toys that have survived into our adulthood are twins or near twins and we named them similarly. We found tiny differences in our toys to distinguish ownership. Like 'Pinky Winky has longer whiskers and Winky Pinky has shorter whiskers'; we also had matching St Bernard toy dogs called Sweetball and Meatball, sausage dogs we called Dakin and Dalkin, and small teddies we called Blackey and Purpley. When we played Big Ears and Noddy, I was Big Ears and she was Noddy but we had matching orange knitted hats with multi-coloured pompoms at their ends made by my mother; my pompom was slightly bigger than her pompom, we decided, always finding the small differences of our twinned things.

It was a system that Unisda and I worked out and kept to quite naturally and it followed us into our adulthood. Many years later, my sister-in-law gave us beautiful classic bears after she and Kelvin were married. There were three bears for her new sisters-in-law and she asked us to choose. Two of the three bears were identical and as always Unisda and I chose the twin teddies simultaneously. Joe, my sister-in-law, could only laugh. 'Kelvin said that was exactly what you would do.'

Yolanda, too, had a favourite game that she made up when we were growing up – a completely South African one that she liked to play on cold days when we were stuck indoors. The game started with the four of us piling on to her bed. An old Sealy with wheels, it was my dad's bed from his bachelor days. Our backs faced the wall. In her scariest voice she told us that the bogeyman, the ghost of a man called Vorster, was going to come and get us if we fell off the bed. Much, much later I found out that Vorster was the prime minister at the time and he was indeed a bogeyman, but then he was a random name Yolanda had plucked from her imagination or maybe snatched from a passing conversation she heard from the adults. In her game, it was about who fell off the bed first. With her legs, which at that stage of her life (and about the only stage of her life) were longer than all of ours, she nudged the bed away from the wall, telling us the Vorster ghost was stalking us. Screaming in terror as the bed squeaked along the worn carpets and the floor, we scrambled around the bed, pushing each other to stay away from the edge. But inevitably one of us, usually Unisda or I, fell, or was pushed on to the floor and into the abyss of Yolanda's horror stories. We sobbed and vowed never to play the stupid game again, at least not until later that afternoon.

On hot summer days we wished into being the pale blue ice cream truck that said 'Roomys' on its side and, like the Pied Piper, cranked out a mechanical tune to lead the children into lactose heaven. We wished even harder that our mom would say yes to the treat of creamy ice cream swirls and the dubious ooze of pink syrup.

Occasionally she conceded and then we screamed down the street, waving to stop the van as its musical tune started to get softer and softer in the distance. My mom stood watch at the gate, purse in hand, as we chased the van, then ran back to her for a few shiny, solid discs that were the old R1 coins with their assured springboks. We raced back to the idling van, stood on tiptoe to watch the ice cream vendor push down the lever that made the ice cream flop in crenulated twirls into a coloured cone.

Mom did not have much of a sweet tooth, so she mostly shook her head when we asked if she was sure she did not want an ice cream, too. We returned to the *stoep*, walking, licking our ice creams. She told us to eat up quickly before they melted, but already the serviette wrapped around the cone was sticky and wet and so were our hands.

At dinner we crunched through fare of yummy delights of black wood ear fungus or savoured the rich grey mush of the yolks of 100-year-old preserved eggs. These were the foods of the Cantonese plate.

The kitchen was my mom's domain for preparing vegetables, steaming dumplings and creating slowly cooked rice soups, *congee*. There was always the sound of chopping, knives slicing vegetables into julienned perfection or mighty Chinese choppers slashing down into animal carcasses – all done on a prized dense round of tree trunk that even the sharpest Chinese chopper failed to penetrate. My mom also had a pasta-making machine, but in our house it was for noodles and wonton skins. It was hi-tech for its time with its shiny silver colour, its metal screw-on bracket to keep the machine firmly wedged against the kitchen top and its removable winding arm to slot into varying settings.

My mother kneaded the eggy dough patiently, turning it over again and again, slamming it against the table, anointing sprinkles of flour everywhere and then repeating the squish, squash action.

Cutting thick slices from the dough, she dusted them and set them through the machine to turn the dough into silky tumbles of noodles. She collected the noodles with her fingers and coiled them into little rounds that she laid out on a baking sheet with grease-proof paper. The wonton skins awaited small teaspoons of seasoned minced meat with water chestnuts and slivers of wood ear fungus.

The trick, my mother said, was not to make flabby wontons that would burst when they were dropped into the rapidly boiling water. But I struggled to mimic the consecutively neat parcels that were my mom's wonton origami. She allowed us to keep trying though.

Yolanda and Kelvin, as the older children, had the daily chore of rinsing out the raw rice grains and setting them to boil slowly in our hard-working rice cooker with its dim orange indicator light and convex viewing window on the lid. Rice was on our menu every night without fail. As the rice boiled, the lid rattled softly against the metal sides of the pot. Sometimes small bubbles escaped to the edges, then disappeared into a hissing haze of steam.

'Once you have rinsed out the rice two or three times you have to level it out in the pot before you add the water. You know you have put in enough water when the water touches just above your knuckles,' my mom said as it became my turn to take on more of the cooking responsibilities.

I have kept to the formula all these years, only now my rice cooker is a fancy upgrade with a multi-programme electronic brain and comes complete with coloured lights and warning chimes. There is no clinking lid to bounce against the sides of the pot and there is no little window to view the watery bubbles being absorbed by the rice grains. I only remember now and again that my hand is not the child's hand any more and the water level that my mom talked about should drop closer to below where my knuckles are.

Ours was not a home of breakfasts of yoghurts and Weet-bix or fry-ups of hash browns, eggs and grilled tomatoes. I only realised as a grown-up how little dairy there was in traditional Chinese foods or the fact that cornflakes and bran were not the universal breakfasts like they were portrayed with smiling, 'regular' people in advertisements. My parents raised us in a time before low GI, probiotics, live cultures and pariah status for trans-fats and tartrazine.

Mostly we ate the foods that tested the stomachs of many. We loved steamed fish, like Red Roman, with ginger and spring onion finished off with oil and soya sauce. But it was the eyeballs that my father liked to share with us as children. The big eye peered out from the plate and my dad offered the eye, plunging his chopsticks into the socket and dropping the squishy mess of eye on top of my scoop of rice. The gelatinous glob melted until just the hard little bead rolled over my tongue. My dad loved that I loved it just as he did.

Years later I watched an episode of *Fear Factor*, the reality TV show that in part challenges contestants' potential to hold down 'gross' foods. Next to hissing cockroaches and pigs' testes, they set out the good old 100-year-old egg. The egg is preserved with straw and a soy mix, which turns the egg pitch black and into a firm jelly consistency. Its yolk becomes ash-grey goo. I laughed so much at the retching faces and the absolute refusals to try the egg and I remember thinking how good the eggs would taste with a thin slice of preserved ginger and a tiny sprinkling of sugar.

Most days before school we had a quick breakfast of a steaming cup of tea and a slice of bread with some butter and jam or a stack of Marie biscuits that we dunked into the sweet tea, carefully counting the seconds to get a perfect tea-infused biscuit – not so soggy that the biscuits broke off and descended to the bottom of the cup as squishy pulp, but not so dry that you could still crunch through the biscuits. School lunchboxes were not simply sandwiches of peanut butter and cold meats. We also packed in thermoses of savoury rice and noodles.

On weekends we sometimes enjoyed breakfasts of *congee*, the delicious slow-cooked rice soups simmered for hours with any variation of beans, dried scallop, dried sheets of *doufu*, shiitake mushrooms, spinach or meat. And just as the heat is turned off, a few lightly beaten eggs are stirred in to become floating wisps of suspended protein. I loved to watch my mother's gentle stirring as the translucence turned into opaque morsels. Without fail, each time she reminded me how important it was to have the heat turned off and not to over-stir, but not to let the egg clump either. I could not wait until I was old enough to give it a try.

Food and eating in the Ho household was a hybrid of chopsticks and woks alongside braai tongs and toasters. It was two worlds rolled into one in our Bertrams home and all spiced up with our own Ho family brand, too. I think of it a bit like the common sweet sesame cake that is served up at so many Chinese gatherings, especially over Chinese new years. These *jeeng dui* balls are multi-dimensions of taste and texture, all crisply fried and studded with sesame seeds on the outside before giving way to a chewy, glutinous layer and a surprise ball of dark, sweet lotus paste in the centre. That is us, layers, unusual textures and the surprise in the middle, all in one tiny package.

A Long Way
from Here

Long before Marmite and *pap* and *wors* collided with my mom and dad's world, their lives were very different. Home in China was a place of steamed rice, pungent fermented *doufu* and dried salted fish in viscous puddles of rich oil. Their countrymen and women looked exactly like they did, their houses were similarly smoky, with small altars that burnt with incense for the ancestors and deities to protect and bless their home and families. The codes of being and being accepted were known, like birthrights.

I have never made it back to the villages where my mother and father were born. Even on the few trips I have taken to Hong Kong and China, I have never been so deep into the interior that I have been able to get to what remains of these villages. Some relatives, though, have journeyed to the old country and returned with a bit of these rural outposts caught in megapixels of today's digital photographic genius. From these images, I see that even the passage of time does not cover up the simplicity of lives that are still spare even in an era of growing capitalist consumption. The pictures match up with some of the images I have held in my mind for the longest time and confirm so many of the stories that my parents used to share with us.

The mod cons are there now, even in the villages. But modernity must still yield to old habits sometimes. TV sets and DVD players may blink digital numbers in standby mode but they are covered under thick, flower-patterned plastic coverings. The formal family photos of ancestors, some with the distinct studio touches of oval framing or sepia tones, share wall space with calendars sponsored by electronic stores and sellotaped blessings and prayers in the tradition of *fai cheun*, the Chinese calligraphy poems of only four characters written on sheets of lucky red paper.

The young people may wear jeans and branded sportswear, but the old women in the villages still get dressed each day in the traditional pantsuit made almost always from highly patterned cheap fabric and sometimes still with that skew 'y' closing typical of a mandarin collar cut. There is no dyed hair and shaped eyebrows for these women whose accelerated ageing is witness to harsh lives working fields in endless piercing winds and scorching days. In the biting winters, villagers wear the puffy coats and waistcoats that have not changed for decades. They are the garments of insulated padding dressed up in a reversible silk cover. Summers are characterised by men with shirt buttons undone and sweat-soaked vests. Woven grass fans shaped like fat leaves are put to work constantly.

My mom and dad were both born in Guangdong in China. They came from this southern tip of the mighty landmass of Asia where its inhabitants are mostly Cantonese speakers. Many Chinese early emigrants left from places such as Guangdong and Fujian, forming the first waves of emigration and planting the seeds of diaspora. It was probably because they were closer to ports and exit points compared to places farther north or deeper in the interior.

My mother, Fok Jouw Yee, called the county of Li Geou her birthplace and for my father, Ho Sing Kee, his birthplace was the small county called Shun Tak.

When we were growing up, we were reminded often that it was a disgrace not to know your father's village. It did not matter that we had never visited it, or that there was not a single photograph of that place on which to hang a mental picture.

'Where is your head? Have you lost your mind? You probably cannot even remember where your father's village is.'

It was one of my mother's favourite scolds when she thought we had done something foolish, frivolously indulgent or a stupid deed that she deemed we should be embarrassed about. We skulked off, too shamed to defend ourselves.

I only learnt years later that stating your forefathers' village is a way for older people, in particular, to focus immediately on 'whose people you are'. It is like the place of origin is a parent. It centres on kinship and trusted allegiances and also pronounces on sure hatred and well-worn grudges. It matters little in a changed world far from the old country. Stating your place of clan origin still allows people's memories to race back along a known path of order and unbreakable bonds. They can insert you where you belong like it is determined by what runs through your veins, that fusion of blood and kin.

And as a Ho, Shun Tak took on a mystical importance for me. It was a place I envisioned only in my imagination, pieced together by stories, anecdotes and memory. It was where my father's story began and so also where my own narrative finds its roots.

My mother was an only child, born to Fok Yat Gou and Low Wan Yuk. My maternal grandparents were joined as teenagers through a hastily arranged marriage. The Japanese were invading China and the young virgins were at risk of being raped or turned into concubines for the bastards, my grandmother would say in stories she would share in years to come.

Meeting Chinese nationals many years later, I understood how the old wounds of the invasion throbbed for the Chinese well into the 21st century. They waited for apologies that did not come, so in the long delay they held on to the stories of great aunties raped and killed, babies ripped from their mothers' wombs and those who were not saved by death but were forced to be 'comfort women' for the loathed *gaa jay*, a pejorative snipe for a Japanese person that is supposed to mimic the sound of the Japanese language as heard by Chinese ears.

Once, on an overseas training workshop with foreign journalists, I wore a skirt that had a huge print of a striking Japanese woman on it, all kimono-clad with clay-white skin and dark, expressive eyes. I liked the skirt and I liked the contrast of being a Chinese person wearing a skirt with a Japanese icon on it. On the course were two journalists from China. Each commented on the skirt. 'Nice skirt,' they started in our mix of Cantonese, English and Mandarin, remarking on its patterning that was unusual and bold, I suppose. Then the piece of cotton wrapped around my legs became political and historical all of a sudden. Both these colleagues, who looked like me, but were also so different from me, being Chinese nationals, started talking about the Japanese as old enemies with old cruelties and never-to-be forgotten barbarisms. I understood then that a nation's memory stays with its people. Even this becomes a kind of birthright.

To them, my being born Chinese, even though I was born in South Africa, linked me instantly to that memory and that historical allegiance. I liked that skirt, but I did not wear it again during the course.

Had it not been wartime, my grandmother's family possibly would have been able to marry my grandmother to someone who was a more equal match in social standing. But there was no time for such an indulgence, and wealth and even class snobbery were levelled out when everyone was left with less than they started with before the Japanese invasion.

My grandparents never got along with each other – at least not by the time I knew them. They never fought outwardly; instead, they fell into a life of silent rage and deliberate separateness even though they shared the same roof until they were well into the winter of their lives. Although they did split up and lived separately, they still ended up in the same government retirement complex until they died – my grandfather in 1998 and my grandmother in 2000.

When I was a child I wished every day that they would make up, reconcile and be a happy couple. My childish hope always was that the big love that each of them showered on us would be enough to reunite them. I longed not to hear them speak badly about each other and wished that we children did not have to split up our time with each of them on the occasions when we visited them in Pretoria and then later Johannesburg.

During our weekly visits, my grandad, my Ah Goung, Fok Yat Gou, would take up his position in the single bedroom in their flat in Lorentzville, a tatty little suburb made up of ugly flats and light industrial factories in Johannesburg East. My grandmother, my Por Por, who was born Low

Wan Yuk, would be staked out on her sofa bed in the living room. They hardly spoke to each other, leaving biting notes sometimes when a grunt or sarcastic retort was not enough. The notes were a triumph for my grandmother, who had the privilege of being better educated and had a better vocabulary in her arsenal. My grandfather's defence was the saving grace of not always knowing the full extent of what she had written.

A visit saw the four of us children split up in pairs and spend time separately with each of them and then swop over as the afternoon progressed. We sat and talked nonsense with them about school, about family or some or other thing that we had been doing or had seen that week. Then we repeated some of our stories as we swopped over. They shared their stash of goodies with us but hid them from each other. 'Pour yourself some cooldrink, from my bottle, which is at the back of the fridge,' one of them would say, careful that we did not drink some of the other's provisions. Eventually my grandmother got her own small fridge that she plugged in near her sofa bed in the already crammed flat.

When they visited us in our home they tried never to be in the same room together and even when we sat down for meals as a family they perfected the art of making the other invisible, even around a small dinner table.

My father loved his in-laws; he was the son they had never had. And I think he wished as hard as I did that his in-laws could love each other or at least have that spousal devotion and caring that would have made their lives so much happier.

One of the biggest thorns in my parents' relationship was the fact that my father could not take sides when my mother did. Once, when my grandparents had obviously reached a breaking point in their relationship, my father suggested that my grandmother move in with us. We could squeeze her in somehow because it was the right thing to do, my father said. My mother hit the roof with shouting and screaming and sulking. She did not speak to my father for days and I remember my dad saying: 'I cannot believe your mom has this attitude. It is her own mother, for goodness sakes.'

My mother's affection was for her father, and in her stubborn, intractable way she made little excuses for her bias. She often said it was about making up for lost time. Sometimes she would say it was because my granny was not a good wife to my grandfather. But it was not about favouritism skewed by making up for the years she missed out on having a dad close by. And I know she knew my granny never did anything that would make her a 'bad' wife. She had a bitter, abrasive relationship with my gran, and there was something deliberately evil about playing up her affection for my grandfather to hurt my gran. I resented my mother for this as I grew up. As for how I felt about my grandparents, like my father, there was no way to choose between two people I loved equally.

A gift my father bought once for my Ah Goung and Ah Por was a small statue of an old Chinese couple, beaming, holding hands. He said he had given it to them as a wish that they would grow older together happily: *bak tau dou lou* is a common wish for couples; it is a blessing to grow together until your hair is white. Like the blessing in the statue, I would wish that they could love each other, even just a little.

One day, though, I stopped wishing. I grew into the truth of my grandparents' history, their life stories and the reality of fractures that are made by a thousand disappointments and a thousand crushed dreams too severe to be healed even by the desperate hopes of a child.

My granny, the fine-boned flower, was born into a decent, quite well-to-do family in the 1920s. Her father was an official of some rank and was sufficiently statured to marry numerous wives, even though polygamy was not reserved for only the wealthy class in China. My great-grandfather was sent to Vietnam along with his wives and it was there that my grandmother was born along with several of her siblings and half-siblings. Her mother did not survive beyond my grandmother's first few years of life and she probably did not see her father all that often between his many wives and his official duties. When she was still a little girl, it was decided that she should be sent back to China to be educated there to stay true to her Chinese culture.

She was singled out for this important journey, but for my granny it was a separation from her family and she also hated that she had to leave the country of her birth, because it meant leaving her family.

She stayed with extended family in China and undertook to fulfil her father's wishes for her to be educated. Education was the basics of learning to read and write and to be schooled in the teachings of what prepares young girls to be good wives one day. That education was enough to be the lifelong treasure that no one could take from my granny. In later life she could escape into books, she could write to family back in China without having to find someone to dictate the letter to, and in this way she could stay connected to the China of her memory when she had become a South African citizen. I am not sure who she wrote to all those times, apart from some of her extended family, but she did write and often she was asked to help people pen a few words home and then to slip them into the very important looking airmail envelopes. Education set her apart from many of her peers, including her sisters, who were not as interested in learning as she was, or were never given the same opportunity. And it set her apart from my grandfather.

My grandad grew up to be handsome, honest and true, but he was from a poorer family and he was uneducated as so many villagers in China were. He had deft hands and would prove to be a talented amateur carpenter and a man with fingers that could coax flowers from reluctant buds and nurture vegetables to sprout with lush abandon.

But when he married my gran he was simply an uncertain teenager, like she was, and with the invasion of the Japanese a brutal reality after 1931 he increasingly became an insipid consolation for her.

In the first months of their married lives, they were made to work in the Japanese army barracks. They were put on shifts and when my grandmother got up to go to work, my grandfather was trying to squeeze in some sleep. When her long dreary shift finally ended, it was my grandfather's turn to work for the invaders.

Every day my gran lived in dread. She told me this when I had grown up enough to understand. The beautiful young bride was in fact still a virgin and was terrified that she would be raped by the Japanese or taken to be one of their comfort women. My grandparents were awkward teenagers exhausted from long shifts in the barracks of an enemy, and for many months their marriage was not consummated. My grandfather's distance from my grandmother's bed was the start of the slip of her respect for him.

It was not what either of them had expected of married life. Maybe when the match was made for them they let themselves believe that it would be a good match. Maybe they hoped they would come to love their chosen spouse and grow into the roles of husband and wife for each other. I read someone's personal account of arranged marriage once and she said it was like opening a present every day as the stranger presented a bit more of himself. But this was not the story for my grandparents. Their marriage turned out to be not just a disappointment, it brought about heartbreak and defeat – an experience a million times worse than that feeling you get when you know a glass is about to crash to the floor and you will not save it and in the next few seconds there will be fragments everywhere.

'I was scared every day that I was going to be raped by those bloody soldiers and I was a virgin,' she said, of course expecting that the first time she had sex with her husband had to be by his initiation and it was not a fear that she could express to him.

To add to her anxiety, my grandfather's family had been asking about grandchildren. A boy child, especially, was missing from the union and my grandmother was quickly being mocked as a failed wife as the months ticked by.

Maybe it was too much for my gran to share with me. Chinese people of my grandparents' generation preferred to take their pain with them to their graves. They would rather remain silent, with an unvoiced acceptance of their disappointments, because life was just what it was, the roll of a dice; surviving and raising the next generation was more important than dwelling too much on personal injury.

But I am happy she did and I am glad she did not think that I was too young to know. I was a teenager and I was old enough to understand the dread of rape and the weighty load of not being able to please the interfering aunties with their accusatory spite.

My grandmother told me about the consummation, too. When it did eventually happen, it was inelegant and clumsy. There was not the intimacy she must have hoped for or the release of her anxiety both in her body and her heart. The act should have removed some of her fear and it should have settled the couple into marital domesticity. But by the time she told her stories to me, my gran did not have any more patience for remembering the pleasant ordinariness of life as my grandfather's wife. The ordinariness that would have at least resembled a marriage that was tolerable.

The consummation and what must have followed were, however, enough for my gran to conceive. There must have been delight for her in those months as her belly grew with the promise of silencing the cruel aunties. She was maybe pampered a bit more, told to be off her feet, bought some or other specially prepared broth to balance her system and nurture the growing foetus.

The nine months went by and my gran gave birth. But it was not the desperately wanted boy child. This was a betrayal for my granny, because the pregnancy yielded a girl child who could not carry the family name. That girl child was my mother.

Later I would find out that there was also a boy child born to my grandmother a few years after my mother, but he survived only a few days. He did not even make it past his first full moon, the first month of life, which is the primary milestone of a newborn's life.

'He would have survived if only your grandfather had agreed to let him go to see the modern doctors, I know that, I know that ...' gran would say, pleading even after all those years. There were doctors who had started to move away from the remedy of old wives' tales and the hit-and-miss of homemade brews and potions. My granny probably trusted these remedies for most of her life, but when the child was lost, his death could be blamed on the one thing that was never tried – the one thing my grandfather never tried.

My grandfather must have had his own pain to bear when his son died. He never mentioned that child to us. My mom did not remember this brother who only had a fleeting presence in her toddler life. She remembered playing around the altar that my Por Por had erected for her dead son shortly after his death. And she remembered being scolded severely by my gran for fooling around the altar and disturbing the spirit of her dead brother. My granny was probably angrier than she should have been. But how could my mother understand that the anger was not for her but was directed at my grandfather? Anger also at the gods and the ancestors who had cursed her by taking her son away, and with him a part of her heart. For my mother, though, the incident was enough for her to hold on to her child's resentment for a brother she never knew.

My gran loved her only child and my mother was never like a consolation prize, but maybe my mother felt like that every time she clashed with my granny. My mother remembered the presence of the dead brother even years after he had died. The altar remained in the home, an eerie spectre stronger than the loss. Her dead brother took on a kind of phantom presence.

When my mom was in her late teens, she was struck by a period of illness and none of the healing concoctions my gran came up with made her better. My gran visited medicine men and women and followed their instructions for brews and poultices to the letter. She prayed to the gods, the ancestors and consulted with the elders as she always did when there was disquiet in her heart and her home. My mom did not get better. Then came a revelation, and one that made most sense. Her dead son was unhappy in the underworld and was causing ructions among his living relatives. He was lonely and in need of a bride.

I have heard of the macabre and spooky rituals of ghost brides, where a live person is said to be killed in a sacrificial murder so her spirit can be joined with the spirit of a dead man who cannot rest. In a spirit marriage, a man and a woman can be joined and the living relatives will be blessed for having fulfilled their obligations to the deceased. Fortunately, my gran opted for a symbolic ritual. Instead of sacrificing a live person, she consulted with her family and they made inquiries to the neighbouring villages. Eventually, they learnt of a young woman who had recently died and the two families arranged for a spirit marriage.

My mother only remembers her brother's seat in the altar was moved to a higher rung, symbolising that as a 'married man' he had taken on a higher position in the realm of the afterlife. My granny remembers that my mother started to feel much better and to emerge from her illness after that.

By the time I was old enough to talk freely to Ah Por, it seemed like much of her life had concertinaed into a few memories, so many of them painful and raw with every new mention of them. The misery and bitterness haunted her all her life. Towards the end of her life, they managed to chase her down, leaving her defeated and spent.

Even my Por Por's black mutt, the only dog she ever owned, fell into this bleak recollection. He had to be killed or her entire village would have had to forfeit their rations during the Japanese occupation. The villagers decided to slaughter and eat her dog. Chinese people do not eat dogs ordinarily, but meat in lean times was a delicacy and her dog's flesh could not go to waste.

'I could not eat my dog when they bought me back a piece of meat. But I cooked it for your mother, who was too little to really know the dog. That dog was so loyal. When we women went to help the neighbouring villages with their harvests, we would be gone for days and my dog would not eat until I came home. He would always come running to the edge of the village to greet me, when he finally saw us returning.'

I tried to separate those haunting memories from the images of the granny who would moan about our bad diets as teenagers but would then tell us where to find her stash of potato crisps, which she would have spent her pension money on to spoil us. My gran knew when there was a four or five rand increase in her telephone bill but she spent her pension money on these extras for us. She also saved up little pieces of meat for our two small dogs, Mozart and Snoopy, which we would bring along on our weekly visits to her retirement complex when we were older. She could not say the English names we had given them and she would shout that the dogs were not really allowed into the complex and that she could get into trouble, but then she would produce the neatly wrapped-up morsels she had saved during the week and let the dogs gobble them up on the small area partitioned as a kitchen in her cottage.

I tried to remember also the granny who told us stories as children with so much animation and vigour that we never tired of hearing the tales over and over again, and how we would gasp for air trying to breathe in between laughing so hard.

There were stories of old Chinese myths and legends. Like the two young lovers forbidden to love in life who in death would meet as two stars joined together only on one night a year, on the night of the mid-autumn festival. It is a full moon festival that falls on the 15th of the eighth month on the lunar calendar. On that one night a year, Ah Por would tell us we should gaze up at the celestial magnificence of the moon, and if we looked carefully we would be able to make out two stars that seemed to be moving closer to each other. They would appear to touch for a few magical moments, then separate as the night sky surrendered to day.

Another of my favourite stories was of an enchanted princess who washed up into a young man's life when he picked up a beautiful, odd-looking shell that was actually the princess's home. Bringing the shell home, he placed it on a table and went to sleep. The next day as he left to tend to the fields, he was unaware that the princess emerged from the shell while he was away. She cooked dinner and tidied up for the young man, then, satisfied with her task, she returned to her shell before he came back. The grateful but confused man decided one day to sneak back from the fields to find out who had been cooking him the delicious meals and he witnessed the magical princess climbing out of her shell. I do not remember the details of the ending well, but I am sure it led to a happy-ever-after as only magical tales can do.

There was also a less romantic tale about a man who was embarrassed by his farting and decided to carry a bottle with him every day into which he could let his fart escape safely. His idea, my granny said, was to store

31

up his farts so he would not be red-faced every time he let rip. The sound effects in my granny's story kept us breathless with laughter and we would ask her to repeat the story over and over again, especially the parts with the farts. Even now I remember the laughing better than the storyline.

Unlike Por Por, my grandfather, Ah Goung, never spoke too much to us about the past. Maybe he felt history was for those who had shared it or maybe we were always grandchildren in his eyes, even when we were old enough to drive him around in his battered, tomato-red Mazda or were the ones to sort out some official-looking bank letter. As his grandchildren, we did not need to be bothered with stories from a time before we were born. Maybe he simply chose quiet surrender to his rose bushes as the years rolled on.

Somewhere among the velvety blooms he could look beyond a failed marriage, failure to have a male heir, failure to amass the fortune that would have been the mark of success for a man who had swopped the land of mythical dragons for Johannesburg's streets of gold.

By the late 1940s, China was a tragic farce: it faced civil war, famine, the aftermath of the Second World War and the invasion by the Japanese that had started in 1931, the so-called September Eighteen incident. Mao Zedong's Great Leap Forward, his Cultural Revolution in the subsequent years to overturn the old orders, translated into more difficulties for villagers, people like my grandparents and my father's family. There would have been the risk of being shot or publicly denounced and shamed for being counter-revolutionary or being capitalist pigs. It was more paranoia than policy that guided the ideologies filtering down from Peking. For villagers and peasants across China, it translated into starvation and grinding poverty. Life was about survival only, struggling under harsh living conditions and subsisting on rations, food coupons and even a dismantling of many of the elaborate religious customs, rites and ceremonies that would have been a social glue and comfort.

Authors and researchers Melanie Yap and Dianne Leong Man, who write about the Chinese in South Africa, contextualise the exodus. In *Colour, Confusion and Concessions*, they write that by the mid-19th century the decline of the Chinese empire was in full swing. Natural disaster, famine, corruption and a general breakdown in social order were all made manifest in the wake of the two Opium Wars of 1839, and later between 1856 and 1860, and also with the Taiping Rebellion, which lasted fourteen years from 1850 to 1864. China was crippled economically and socially and more than 20 million people died.

When I read author and journalist Xinran Xue's *China Witness* I was simultaneously fascinated, saddened and buoyed by the oral histories and first-person accounts of the elderly 'forgotten generation' of Chinese – men and women who were a few years younger than my grandparents at the time they were interviewed in the mid-2000s. This book is filled with anecdotes and memories of a generation that lived under communist madness and also the euphoria of buying in to the propaganda while it was still good. But when things got bad, they went horribly wrong. One minute you were a party loyal, and the next you were being incriminated for the slightest thing that was suddenly deemed anti-party.

It turned neighbours into informants and it made friends turn a blind eye, just in case they were made guilty by association. Mistrust had an iron grip on the people living under Mao and toeing the party line was gospel, whether you truly believed or not.

They also worked hard on communal fields and even accepted that they had to be part of the government's hard-labour projects that needed the muscle of good men and women from the party.

Above all, I picked up the thread of a sense of pride. People were not defeated, even by the worst conditions. One woman separated from her children and family for ten years, whose husband had been labelled counter-revolutionary under the Cultural Revolution in the 1960s, said: 'I never cried. We had a mission as part of the national plan and not completing the mission was like committing a crime.'

I have often thought that this hardness, this rigidity was just about 'saving face', that obsession with not showing weakness or failure, even turning it into boastful conceit. After reading some of the accounts in Xinran's book, though, I saw something different. I saw that some of what swelled the pomposity was not just hubris but about holding on, a desperate grasp on to small hopes shadowed by bleak lives.

With so few choices available to them, it was to a place called Gum Saan, the Golden Mountain, that some Chinese turned. Most people who fled China from the late 1940s onwards came from the Cantonese-speaking southern regions. They would become the West's 'coolies', that offensive term that downgraded the people (mostly men) from China and India into a working class of illiterate, uneducated cheap labour as the world went into rebuilding mode after the Second World War. There was also the lure of being free men who could maybe strike it rich in the cities that had lapped up the gold rushes of the previous century.

Years later I found out that many early migrants to Johannesburg left the mainland not exactly certain of their final destinations. That is because the golden mountains of the world referred not only to Johannesburg but also to places such as Melbourne and San Francisco that for decades also had their own lure of the yellow metal.

I liked to ask migrants why they came to South Africa in the first place. Their answers were always about prosperity and pipe dreams of fortune, the belief that something better lay across the wide seas. There were also all the variables of chance and fate and an impossibly muddled view of a big wide world they could not know. They were cut off from the reality of geography and global politics. They were poor, unsophisticated villagers who did not have access to such information.

My grandfather knew, though, that he was heading to the supposed gilded mound in South Africa, not to one of the other golden mountains spread across the globe. My grandmother's older sister and her husband had left for South Africa some years earlier and had started a life that would bring them seven children, including a prosperous brood of six sons, and a small but sustainable spaza shop in Kliptown, Soweto. Over decades, it would grow into a provisions store that traded until recently when it was eventually sold. Competition had grown, markets had changed and the attrition of violent criminal fury against the comparatively wealthy, like this uncle with his business, meant a day of final trade had to come. And today their children have moved on from Africa, seeking their own prosperity and fortunes across new oceans.

Before all this would come to pass, the plan was for my grandfather to work for my grandmother's sister and her husband until he could set himself up, until he could send for my gran and mom. He left China in the late 1940s, when my mother was a small girl.

There is a black and white photo that I found in an old album that belonged to my Por Por. It is a family photo that was taken shortly before my grandfather set off on his journey south. My Ah Goung was in Western-style dress. He wore a pair of long shorts topped by a short-sleeved, collared shirt. His thick, ample hair was oiled and combed back neatly. It was a posed studio picture and my grandfather was propped up against the armrest of the sofa.

My Por Por was fresh-faced and beautiful. Her hair was pulled back and clipped on the side, showing her fine features. She was in a traditional Chinese outfit. It had a typical Mandarin-style collar and she was wearing a matching pair of trousers. Next to her was my mom, aged maybe two or three. She was in a little Western-style dress and her hair was neatly tied back; she looked like a shy cutie.

Por Por and Ah Goung looked impossibly young. When I gazed at the photo my heart went straight to this young family that had to make decisions that would put thousands of kilometres between them and shatter their innocence with it.

It would be eighteen years until they were reunited. I have no doubt about the years of separation, even though so many other timeframes and dates that I have about my family's history are estimates deduced from the overlap of stories. There was also the confusion of intersecting Chinese lunar calendars and Western calendars, illiteracy and foggy memories. The number of years here, though, are accurate because that number eighteen was the fulfilment of a terrible prophecy.

Around the time my grandfather set out, my Por Por approached a temple priest hoping for a prophecy of a prompt reunion with my grandfather. My grandmother was religious her whole life and had a connection with the spiritual realm that was like a completely innate sixth sense and was something I never questioned. She must have been emotionally torn by my grandfather's trip, but she would have had to hold on to some belief that it was the right move and that it would change their tough circumstances. Her unsettled heart would have sent her to the temple.

But that day the temple priest revealed a prophecy that would prove to be devastatingly accurate. This prophecy came in the form of *kau cim*. To *kau cim* is a traditional way to seek the wisdom and revelations from an ancient Chinese oracle. One hundred small flat sticks, each individually numbered and each with a corresponding parable, are shaken in a bamboo cup at a temple. Each stick has a symbolic meaning represented and can be interpreted by a priest.

As my granny held this container in both hands, she would have shaken the container gently, asking her one question over and over again in whispered prayer. As a single stick tumbled to the ground, she would have retrieved it and hurried off to consult with the temple priest.

'He said we would be separated for eight years or eighteen years and that is exactly what happened,' my granny told us years later. As she got older, my gran developed an agitated quiver in her head when she was worked up or when her nerves set her off. And though she had put emotional distance between her present and the many hurts that she had experienced as a young woman, that slight side-to-side quiver of her head betrayed her every time. It hinted at the eighteen years of not having a husband to speak to, a husband to take her side, no division of labour and no one to share a home with as a married woman. Eighteen years that would make her husband a stranger just like when they were first married.

I never fully appreciated my granny's strength, independence and the tenacity that was wrapped up in her tiny frame and her subtle, proper ways. She would survive, though, even if the prophecy must have come like a dark storm over her heart. She would survive to give her daughter a better life.

With the ghost of a boy child and an absent husband who had stowed away for Africa, my gran decided to find a life away from the Guangdong mainland. Many from her village had already left for the island of Hong Kong by the 1950s. They hoped this fragrant harbour, literally *Heung Gong* as it is called in Cantonese, would yield some of its perfume to them.

The British had resumed control of Hong Kong after its occupation by the Japanese during the Pacific War. As such, Hong Kong was a free port with greater political and economic autonomy, which offered the hope of breaking free from the unforgiving life on the mainland. By the 1950s and the 1960s, it was up to the mainland newcomers, these refugees, to revive the economy of the trading port. Their cheap labour would spark the era of manufacturing superiority that characterised Hong Kong. The time of the 'fong kong', as South Africans now say of everything made in the East, had dawned. It would be the start of fake flowers, knock-off textiles and plastic everything, and it was the sheer manufacturing output that was the way out for Hong Kong and a way out for my granny.

Life in Hong Kong meant an end to picking rice and working the fields in the villages. My gran also wanted my mom to be educated. Por Por took a job as a seamstress, working uninspired stitches in a hot factory of whirring sewing machines. The textile and manufacturing industries became the major employers for female labourers like my grandmother. For the first time my gran had an income and did not have to wait on the small remittances my grandfather sent along with the letters that someone helped him to write. But wait she did, for eighteen long years.

A Strange New Home

Ah Goung meanwhile had arrived in South Africa. Like most of the Chinese who entered the country, it was by illegal means. The National Party was in power by 1948, probably coinciding with the years of my grandfather's arrival. There was a strictly enforced quota system for 'free' Chinese, determining who was allowed to enter the country legally. The impossibly low quota numbers meant many people chose to try their luck via the unofficial route. Segregation and more quota systems at institutions like universities, schools and even churches would follow as the apartheid machinery cranked into action.

I have heard many stories of being smuggled into the country from my family members and other Chinese South Africans. They are stories of fear and terror of the unknown, dangerous journey; the helplessness of relying on strangers who were only mildly co-operative. Strangers such as the ship hands who took away night buckets and brought food and water with the irregularity and disdain that came with knowing the stowaways were left with little choice but to take what they got during the miserable long sea voyage.

My grandad made the trip anyway. After long weeks at sea, the ship curved around Mozambique. It was the end of the journey for those destined for the old Lourenço Marques. A number of Chinese migrants chose to be here instead of in South Africa.

Ah Goung went further south, until he reached the Durban docks. Maybe it was night time when the stowaways were smuggled off the ship. A contact was waiting for my grandfather so that he could be driven up to the then-Transvaal to be with his sister-in-law and her family.

Many years later I attended a lecture by a professor researching the emotional impact of emigration on families. It was the noughties and the exodus from a democratic South Africa had climbed to over the one-million mark in around fifteen years. To advertise her talk there was a photo of a family newly arrived, still on the deck of the ship that brought them to South Africa. The children had light-coloured hair. They were smiling, all neatly dressed and pushed up against the railings. Their parents stood a few steps behind them, also smiling. It was broad daylight and they all beamed with the promise of new opportunities that would meet them when they disembarked a few minutes after the shot was taken.

It was a beautiful photo of beginnings and possibilities for this family. But it saddened me, too, because I knew a similar ship would have docked for my family members, but they would not have stood on the deck smiling. There were no waving relatives anxious to scoop them up in their arms, no grainy black and white image to remember that moment that signals the start to a new life. It would only be in the darkness that the stowaways surfaced, taking in the starlit night briefly along with all the unfamiliar smells and sounds of the Durban docks, then they would be hurried off before they were seen, stopped and arrested.

Growing up, I attached TV images to my grandparents' and parents' journeys across the oceans. I imagined them hiding in false-bottomed trucks and disguising themselves with wigs and dark glasses. The reality was less dramatic, though no less frightening. As it turned out, the contact person would typically not only be the ride, but would also have arranged papers, illegal documents, for the stowaways. In South Africa, this transaction generally went quite smoothly. The community was tiny then, close-knit and loyal.

I had a conversation once with an old man who is over 90 today. By coincidence, we share the same surname, but we are not blood relatives. However, our shared clan name immediately establishes a kinship tie, binding us by the probable regional origins of our families. Old Uncle Ho summed up the closeness of the community back when he was a new arrival, even before the Second World War.

'You did not have to have the same surname, that did not even matter; everyone was your brother back then.'

So Ah Goung assumed a new identity and became this other person. Chinese migrants become 'paper sons', *jee jay*, a literal translation of the phrase used to refer to the people who bought or borrowed new identities from more established families who agreed to give their family names to the newcomers to avoid detection by the authorities.

I thought the term *jee jay* was very Chinese South African, a bastardised word that no one other than a Chinese South African would understand, a bit like how 'larney' for smart or 'robot' for traffic lights or 'now now' for soon confuses an English speaker who is not South African. Chinese South Africans say *mah dah* for police but the correct term is actually *geng tjuk*. But one day I did a quick Internet search and found the story of how paper sons came into being. It is a term believed to have originated in San Francisco when Chinese immigrants took advantage of a records building there being devastated in a fire in 1906. When the authorities were left with a gap in their records, the Chinese who re-registered themselves took advantage of the confusion and claimed to have sons who had migrated with them. No one could prove otherwise and so the paper sons were born. With these 'slots' or unfilled spaces, other new Chinese arriving in San Francisco could buy or borrow the slot and thereby become the paper son. It was a similar principle of borrowing and buying identities in South Africa.

My grandfather would also have had to take on an anglicised version of his name and he became Leon Hing Low. So many Chinese people have family names that do not match up with their brothers' or sisters' names. Apart from the confusion of the paper sons and paper daughters, there is also the fact that apartheid officials had no patience when trying to spell a name uniformly for a single family or to make corrections when they had erred, which clearly was often.

Now my Ah Goung did not have his birth name any more. He was alone and the streets were not paved with fortune as he may have been lulled into believing when he had made the long sea journey weeks before.

His new life journey started with helping his sister-in-law and her husband in their small Kliptown shop – selling mealie meal and half loaves of bread to the people of Soweto. Here, as Chinese traders, they were allowed to operate in the 1950s because they were not in a white suburb serving white people.

I thought this summed up the difficult but straightforward path of toil of my Ah Goung's early years in South Africa until he eventually managed to start up his own small butchery on the outskirts of Pretoria. But as a teenager I discover that this was not the case. I was shocked to learn that my grandfather was once in jail. It seemed so criminal, so wrong and bad to have a grandfather who had been a prisoner. I had grown up with a strict sense of following even the tiniest decree of government gospel.

Hearing that my ordinary, law-abiding grandfather, whom I loved so much, was once thrown in prison was one of the first realisations I had that things were not black and white and that authorities' laws and rules were not the same thing as justice.

How could Ah Goung be a criminal? Laws, I realised, were for people who fell into the tight inner circle of society. It became elastic at the edges and it was this edge that people like the Chinese and other non-whites bounced up against.

But the early Chinese in South Africa did not rock the boat, because they did not have rights like other citizens. The authorities' 'mighty word' kept them on a short leash. They may have gnawed at this leash but still it chafed around their necks. These migrants did not stray far from the law. You kept yourself safe by not drawing attention to yourself. You flew under the radar and hoped that you would be left alone, but this meant that you stayed on the periphery and remained outsiders.

How could these laws be universally accepted when there was no consensus in the experience of the law in the way it was applied? I still see this compliance in the fear my mother has sometimes; it was like the fear my granny had about getting into trouble because our dogs came along on our visits to her, this even though other pensioners kept dogs in the complex against official policy. My mom's TV licence is paid up; she panics if a parking meter may run out. Even though I am a grown-up now, she nagged me about a traffic cop's warning to replace a cracked number plate on my car. It took me weeks to get round to the plate makers, and every time my mother saw me she asked about the number plate.

By attracting little attention to themselves, the community closed in on itself but simultaneously left the door wide open for all the assumptions and stereotypes that go with the 'Ching Chong Chinaman'. Our 'Chineseness' meant we remained shifty and uncontained for some people. We were tied to rites and rituals that seemed weird and were therefore often perceived as frightening. We carry umbrellas over a bride's head as she leaves her

41

parents' home to join her groom. We bring home the spirit of the dead with smoking incense sticks and coaxed words spoken as if the spirit is a tangible entity that needs to be reminded of the path back home.

When I heard Ah Goung's story, I felt like he was busted and arrested because of this perceived strangeness. He was not a criminal but he was different and for that he was not wanted on these shores.

'I wonder who the bastard was who told on me,' he would say, still trying to screen the faces from decades before for the one who could have snitched on him. It could have been a customer at my great-aunt's store; maybe it was someone who held a grudge against him or the family. He did not close in on the suspect but he was still bitter about the time he had to spend in prison.

He was taken from my great-aunt's store and the magistrate sentenced him to prison and to be deported eventually. At the time Ah Goung was arrested, he had only been working for a few months at the store.

'Jail was a hell hole. The blankets were full of fleas and you would wake up scratching every night, but if you did not use the blankets you would sleep on the cold floor.

'The food was worse,' he would say. 'Tasteless slop with weevils that was not fit for feeding a stray dog.'

I wanted to know why no one had tried to get him out in the year he spent in prison; why did someone not help him? But there was not that luxury and the system of the time was not made for men like my grandfather to look for leniency or justice based on the context of his crime. My great-aunt and her husband would have tried to help, I am sure – they remained close and friendly until the end of their days – but they would also not have wanted to draw too much attention to themselves. It was part of the risk my grandfather took coming to South Africa and they all knew it.

The community was way too small, too yellow, too hidden to have any real power to ask for better treatment or to demand better representation.

I have often reined in my imagination about that year of prison in my grandfather's life. I did not really want to think of him suffering during that period. Now I do allow myself to see his isolation, his desperation and the futility of his longings and empty wishing. This yellow man was not able to speak any of the African languages with the men he was incarcerated with or with the warders who slapped the weevil-ridden food on to his plate. This 'Chinaman's' fitful sleep must have been filled with the anxious remembering of a daughter in a faraway place, a child he had made promises to. The days must have passed mostly in silence as he was so desperately isolated.

But then there was an astonishing twist of fate for my grandfather. He received a presidential pardon. A man he did not know, a man who represented a government he did not know, and a system that had landed him in prison in the first place, now gave him a get-out-of-jail-free card.

It was one more chance for Ah Goung to make this African destiny work, to not have to give more bad news to my grandmother in one of those letters penned by a community scribe. Maybe he could prove that he was not the loser he was sure she privately believed him to be.

I have one of my grandfather's first identity cards. It is dated 1959. This was years after he finally got out of jail and could stop hiding from the authorities. He was given the green laminated identity card issued by the Unie van Suid Afrika. It said 'vreemdeling' and 'alien'. My grandfather looked stern in the photo. His hair, which he was fussy about well into his old age, was brushed back Western-style. He looked the part maybe, but he was also strange, the alien, the unknown and the unusual, just like it said on the card.

It took many years for my grandfather to build up his own small butcher business, which he set up on a plot of land outside Silverton in Pretoria. There were a few other Chinese families in the area and his butchery serviced them and all the other non-whites in the surrounds. His home was a simple building, an old farmhouse with an outside, long-drop toilet and a shed containing a tin bath. My grandfather had made it as comfortable as possible, building up a wooden platform to support the bath and placing an old mirror on the wall, even though its edges seemed to give way to more rust each time you looked into it.

The shop adjoined the house, separated only by the fly-screen door of the butchery. The inside of the butchery was a pale turquoise colour with fading posters of cuts of meats and twisted curls of honey-coloured flypaper always spotted with dead insects. The L-shaped counters had old-fashioned fridges with slanting pieces of glass that sheltered slabs of meat, off-cuts, as well as blocks of butter and lard for sale. There were scales, weights and a humming fan endlessly fluttering the neat stack of brown paper that was always ready to receive slabs of meat to be wrapped up for a homebound journey.

Ah Goung merged his passion for carpentry and for farm living in this home of his. His garden became an Eden of Chinese vegetables that he would tend to before he opened up shop in the morning and maybe during a quiet dip in the day.

Inside his house he made wooden wardrobes, chairs and little steps on which to rest his feet or use to reach something stashed away above a wardrobe. He would later make little table and chair sets for us children and some of these survive to this day. He adjusted counters and put up simple shelves of planed and varnished planks of wood to make this space home. He spent much of his time in his own company, not being the kind of man who sought out drinking or gambling. Even if he had any romantic interests during those years on his own, they were never something he pursued, never something that reached my ears even long after his death and even in a community that feeds off gossip like fish need water.

My grandfather stayed close to a few friends, his neighbour and his sister-in-law and her family. One of my great-aunt's sons, my grandfather's nephew, was sent to Pretoria as a teenager to live with my Ah Goung during school holidays. My grandfather was a tough man at the time, it seemed; maybe he needed to be to make it on the plot and to make the small butchery work. He was impatient with weakness or prissiness and his sister-in-law felt that a school holiday or two on the plot would toughen up her fourth son, my Uncle Tommy, or as I call him my See Kou Foo.

See Kou Foo remembers that he did not look forward to those school holidays, even if they brought reprieve from the torment of his brothers who teased him for being a sissy-boy.

'There was that outside long-drop toilet that I had to use and I was sometimes scared to use it by myself at night. Your grandfather did not care that I was scared to walk out there alone. He was very strict back then,' my uncle told me years later. See Kou Foo was expected to work in the vegetable garden, serve customers in the butchery and help around the house, cooking the meals and cleaning up afterwards.

And my grandfather saw to it that there was no shirking or backing down from the daily chores that had to be completed. They were far from holidays.

As the years passed, their relationship mellowed into something more sensitive and understanding as the holiday routine became familiar schedules for both of them. The respect and affection they had for each other lasted until the end of my Ah Goung's days and my uncle laughs about those times now.

Meanwhile, those years in the butchery were part of the eighteen that my grandfather worked to meet his obligation to reunite his family. Sometimes I wonder whether it maybe did not take quite as long as eighteen full orbits of the earth moving around the sun. As each calendar month of struggle and saving passed with ordinary routine, it became more difficult to imagine reuniting with a woman who had become unfamiliar to him and a child who was a young woman and not the little girl of four or five he had left behind. But in the end, my grandad did what was expected of him and he sent for his wife and child.

Another Journey across the Indian Ocean

When my grandmother received the letter signalling that it was time for her to head for Africa, she must have realised that it was the final chapter of life in China and Hong Kong for her.

More than ten years of living in the bustling port city of Hong Kong had come to an end. From this place where she was making her own living, existing as a single mother against all odds and where her literacy was prized, she had to head to this Naam Fey, this 'Southern Darkness' as the direct translation goes, of her husband's letters and the few stories that had reached her ears. She knew that the seasons would change differently. There would be no snow like she knew with China's winters, and no typhoons like those that whipped the Hong Kong coastline, closed shops and sent people scurrying for cover. Even the sun would set at different times and the night skies would be unfamiliar, a random scatter of heavenly lights and not the constellations that she recognised. Her husband would be a part of this foreignness, too.

In Naam Fey she would be totally dependent on her husband and her prized literacy meant little because she could not speak the languages of this new place. She would be reduced to a mute – not able to speak her mind, not understood and without comprehension of what was being said by those around her.

When my grandmother gave my mother the news, my mother was elated. She would be reunited with her father finally. She could shrug off the moniker of 'abandoned' child. Her phantom father *did* exist and she was going to be rejoined with him in this exotic-sounding place of Africa, where some people had pale skins and others had pitch-black skins; some had hair that grew in tight small curls and others had a tumble of blonde locks, all unlike her dead-straight black shafts and the same dead-straight black shafts of everyone around her.

By then my mother was in her early twenties. She had finished middle school and had joined her mother in the textile factory among the steady buzz of sewing machines. She was a young working woman but she was finally going to have her daddy close by for the first time she could really remember.

In Hong Kong my mother had access to education that she would not have had in China. Even though it was quite basic, her schooling included English lessons in middle school. The teacher gave the girls English names – my mother's was 'Lima'. I am not sure how the teacher came up with the name; because my immediate association with Lima is Peru's capital I always imagine the names being given out to the girls as a teacher ran her finger across a spinning globe in a classroom.

The girls giggled and joked their way through English class as they tripped over the strange sounds and phonetic mystery of vowels and conversational phrases: 'Good Morning, Sir'; 'Good Morning, Madam'.

They figured they would not need to know English. Sure there were the odd *gwei los*, the white ghosts, that made up the white British ex-pats living on the island they had colonised since the cession of Hong Kong in 1842 with the Treaty of Nanking as the Opium Wars came to an end, but Hong Kong working-class people like my granny and mom would probably never have to 'Good Morning, Sir' anyone. And anyway, a violent shake of the head or a raised hand signalling an insistent 'no, no' was usually enough to dissuade any attempt at conversation – just the way they wanted it.

But my mother figured wrong. One day she would be heading for South Africa and there English would come in handy, even her schoolgirl phrases. And that day had arrived.

To this day her English is poor even though she manages in her own way. 'How was I to know that we would actually end up in South Africa for good?' she says.

My mother had met a young man in Hong Kong, too. She sometimes told us stories about him and how she fantasised about marrying this educated, handsome gentleman one day. Once or twice he walked her home and they occasionally swopped books. There was nothing serious about her crush, but it was filled with all the promise of romance.

My mother can remember knowing that their nascent romance would never go any further when she realised that in a matter of weeks she would have to say goodbye. It was also a farewell to the land of her birth and to the future she had imagined for herself.

She did end up writing a few letters to this young man once she had finally settled in Johannesburg, but their correspondence tapered off as they had less and less in common. It made me a little sad, as a child, that this was a love that never was. I could not make sense of all the maybes and what ifs and I could not know of my mom's backward glance of life when as a child I was still counting my years in halves.

For my mom, there were very few freedoms and even fewer extras as a child. There was certainly no room for boys even if it was as innocent as her friendship with this young man. As a child she recalls seldom being allowed to play as much as the children back in the village. While others stayed out late into the night, taking part in lantern festivals that marked the end of the fifteen-day new year celebrations, my mother would be called back home earlier than anyone else. Then at school in Hong Kong there was hardly a school trip she was allowed to be part of and she was not permitted to stay away from home overnight, and of course she never dated boys.

She grew to resent my gran hugely as she grew older. It was not because this romance was denied. But it seemed like all the times my gran said no finally made it easy for my mother to choose sides when the cold war waged between her father and mother went into full freeze many years later.

The pressure on my grandmother was immense. She had to raise this daughter, her only child, without fault or fingers being pointed at her and there was no one to share the blame with. She would not have known how to answer to my grandfather or his family if something had happened to my mother. And now she had to deliver her safely across the Indian Ocean and into the arms of an unknown land.

Still, this journey was for a better life, she had to imagine, and some of her friends must have congratulated her on her good fortune to be destined for a life in a city of gold. My gran must have let herself have that wish, too.

In a family album we have a black and white studio photograph of my grandmother and mom as a pre-teen girl. There is a studio backdrop of trees and deep cool pools and a serene, water-coloured world. It was probably a photograph taken to be sent to my grandfather. These studio backdrops were sentimental landscapes of sugar-coated denial. The truth was that Mao had set China on a path of disaster by the 1950s and into the 60s. And even though Hong Kong was in the hands of the imperialists in the form of the British, the spillover of the Cultural Revolution was evident on the island, too. Life was equally strained in Hong Kong where the majority of people were part of the working class, happy simply to hold on to low-paying jobs such as working in factories and on the docks.

It meant that my mother and grandmother would make the journey and put their faith in what my grandad had built up in the close-to-two decades of separation.

It was in the mid-1960s that my gran and mom paid their fees to be smuggled on to a ship. They packed the barest of their possessions, and they crossed the Indian Ocean in the same way my grandfather had eighteen years earlier. My mother remembers having to get rid of her Little Red Book, a standard issue from the Communists, and also a red scarf that she had been given somewhere along the line. She remembers ripping them both up and flushing them down a toilet. She handed over her identity card to her uncle, my grandfather's younger brother, who was working as a driver in Hong Kong at that time. Now, without an identity or a country, she could say she was a citizen of wherever she had to find somewhere new to belong.

My mother has vivid memories of the ocean crossing. She was stuck in a stifling, hidden area of the ship, which would be their home for the long weeks ahead. Still fresh in her mind would have been the goodbyes to her friends and the sad parting from the man she had started to fall in love with. She left many of her books with him as a parting gift. With each forward thrust of the ship, she would have felt life as she knew it slipping away.

My mom would tell us years later of the things she had to leave behind, not valuables and expensive possessions, but the small material things that web together a childhood – a book she read over and over, a dress she loved to wear or a pen with ink that flowed just right over a sheet of paper.

The windowless room where they were holed up would become like an airtight container of anxiety. To make matters worse, my mom had to share the space not only with my gran but also with another woman and her two young daughters.

'We were stuck in that little room sometimes for days on end before the ship hand would bring us some fresh food and water and let us sneak out to walk around a bit. Of course, we could not leave the room for long periods because we would be caught and thrown off the boat.

'There were these two girls with us who were such brats. I remember that in the beginning of the journey one of the girls had an apple. She took a few bites, decided she did not want it any more and threw it to the corner of the room. Then, a day or two later, when we had nothing to eat because the ship hand had still not arrived with food, the girl went to the corner of the room where she had discarded the apple. She picked up the now rotting fruit silently and ate.'

It was like a parable of the sin of wastefulness when my mother recounted that story.

I remember that story all these years later because it has metaphoric potency – how vulnerable the group of stowaways was on that ship; how circumstances change your attitude very quickly; and how humble pie or humble apple, in this case, always tastes like poison fruit.

This weeks-long journey was about the mercy of the seas and the mercy of some ship hand motivated by his fee rather than by kindness. But this hidden journey across the ocean was the only way for Chinese to get into South Africa and to circumvent the authorities' dislike for non-white foreigners and the quota system. My Ah Goung must have known the very real risks for his wife and daughter on that journey. He knew first-hand the brutal reality of imprisonment and the threat of deportation if they were caught.

Over the years I have found more literature about the indentured Chinese labourers who arrived in South Africa in 1904 to work on the reef's mines. There were newspaper articles, missionaries' accounts and distilled writings by historians and researchers for a modern audience. There were even postcards. In these graphic representations the labourers are exoticised, caricatured. 'Greetings from Chowburg', says one postcard in a book about early Joburg. It shows labourers with their long 'queues', the single, braided pigtail that was a sign of dignity and manhood for Chinese men, but often a symbol for derision and mockery in South Africa.

Historians believe that there were more than 60 000 Chinese migrant workers who arrived here between 1904 and 1911. The Employment Bureau of Africa (TEBA), the South African mines' recruiting agency during that period, even had an office in Shanghai because Chinese labour was so sought after. The men arrived from the northern parts of China as the dirt-cheap labour that would resurrect the ailing mines of South Africa's gold reefs after the Anglo-Boer War.

South African Chinese history scholars, such as Professor Karen Harris of the University of Pretoria, tell how the first piece of segregationist legislation in the country was in fact the Chinese Exclusion Act of 1904 in the Cape Colony. The indentured Chinese labourers who arrived around the same time to work on South Africa's mines had contracts that restricted their movements and freedom while in the country. Built into their contracts were strict conditions that all Chinese workers had to be repatriated at the end of their contract period. Their cheap labour was wanted, but they were not, and by 1911 they were put on ships and sent back to China.

They were the ubiquitous migrant bachelors and it is why today's Chinese community in South Africa knows that these mineworkers were not their forefathers. The men would not become 'free Chinese' after working off their contracts. They were not allowed to stay on in South Africa. They had to die here working on the mines or go back to China.

And die they did. Many of the men who arrived in South Africa never made it back to the northern provinces of that faraway mainland.

Researchers, such as Dr Yoon Park, have told me that probably those Chinese who had become so-called free Chinese by the dawn of the 20th century had written to their families in the south, warning them not to take up the contracts because the living and working conditions were appalling.

There is a graveyard in Germiston which I have visited a few times, a cemetery for Chinese migrant labourers. There are no tombstones, no flowers. You can only just make out the rows and rows of small humps flattened out over time. I spoke to two locals on one visit. They were brothers who had grown up in the area in the 1960s. They remembered riding their bikes there in between the rows of old graves and as they played they watched as a few people used the graveyard as a shortcut to get to the railway station that flanked part of the cemetery.

'Sometimes you would find a piece of rubber or something from a miner's boots. We were told that these were placed on top of the graves when the Chinese miners died. They never reused a dead man's shoes,' the one brother said.

They remembered that back then the graves were quite well taken care of, maybe because the land was still owned by the mines. They could make out the various graves and some sites were marked off with small metal barriers or lengths of chain-link that were meant to be decorative. The brothers also pointed out two slabs of stones believed to be the only two tombstones in the cemetery, tombstones of two priests who had worked among the mineworkers, converting these men to Christianity in the years they were far away from the deities and gods of their homes.

But nearly 40 years on from these brothers' childhoods and by the time I visited, the land was coming up for sale to be turned into townhouses. Heritage laws dictate preservation of all the valued things of memory, but there is also a property revival and there is no land to waste on memory, especially graves that belonged to a minority group of forgotten men.

It was a tough life for the miners and being forgotten is almost predictable. The invisibility of their lives was very conspicuous to me when I visited an old mine manager's house that has today been converted into a B&B. Back in the early 1900s, however, it was a house of secrets. Beneath the floor were hidden rooms and to get to these underground chambers there was a door disguised as an ordinary linen cupboard door. It led to the locked chambers of indentured labourers.

'I think the men never saw the sun because it is believed there were tunnels that led directly from these underground compounds straight to the mines,' the B&B owner told me. He also brought out a book he had which detailed the wages paid to the men on the mines. The Chinese were paid the least, less than both the South African white and black miners and that is why they were so sought after.

Eerily, there is a food cage that has been preserved in the old house. The B&B owner said it was via this descending cage that food and essentials were passed down to the men – discrete, never disturbing the civilities of the comfortable life above ground.

It was a haunting place to visit. The owner at the time I visited had put in red and green light bulbs in the basement chambers with their concrete bunkers. He had also put up a huge Chinese fan as decoration. He encouraged some guests to take their meals down in the bunkers as a way of reliving history.

I did not say anything when he told me this, but I thought the place held a creepy imprint of their lives, like the spirits had never been freed from these concrete cells. Ghosts seemed to slip in and out, passing by the gaudy, tacky decorations that looked like a film-set brothel.

The treatment of these men set the tone in so many ways for how the Chinese would be handled in South Africa. It was all part of the continuum of discrimination and it was also the start of the creation of an in-between space of half belonging and half being somewhere else for the Chinese. The Chinese labourers came to be charges of a Chinese consul general who was dispatched to meet the needs of these men. The diplomatic presence gave them some kind of loose protection from China, but not being citizens of the Union they also remained feared outsiders – the *geel gevaar*; the yellow peril that were not welcome in the first place.

By the time people like my grandfather and my father berthed in Durban harbour, more than half a century had passed since those men had helped to rebuild the mining sector on the reef and then vanished from the South African picture. The practice of racial discrimination and the idea of controlling people in oppressive compounds were, however, as fresh as ever. By 1956, the Group Areas Act would create the compounds of segregated townships and homelands and the grand apartheid plan drawn from the blueprints of years before were now in the statute books.

The waves of the Indian Ocean brought another ship to berth for a reunion. But for this family, it was not to be the scenes of running into each other's arms and falling back into love and into the closeness of people who never really leave each other even when continents and oceans divide them.

The unfamiliarity between my grandparents hardened. It never eroded, not even with the intimacy of shared spaces and their fusing into the roles that people accept as the marks of marriage. Instead, the reunion was like accelerant meeting resin and the start of a slow hardening.

Still, my grandparents stayed together, year after long year. Separation, divorce; these were words that tore at the inviolability of the most sacred of all unions and they were unheard of for Chinese people, especially for a small community like the isolated diaspora of the Chinese in South Africa. Pocketed communities, far from the motherland, are almost always the purveyors of the old traditions, the ones that attach a rigid inflexibility to tradition that they confuse as some kind of purity.

I remember a girl at school once, a new migrant from China, shaking her head and laughing when she heard me refer to my brother and sister in the old-fashioned way.

'You do not really call your brother Kaa Heng, right?' she giggled. I was confused and a little embarrassed. I thought maybe I was using a wrong term. After all, she was the first-language Chinese speaker, I was not.

'It is so formal, I call my brother Ah Gor or I call him by his name. Gosh, no one says "Kaa Heng",' she said.

It was a bit like that with divorce among Chinese South Africans. Divorce was unheard of, too bold, too un-Chinese. But eventually Ah Goung and Ah Por separated many years later and in a most bizarre way. They still lived in close physical proximity to each other, being next door, but never bothered to make the end of their married life official with court papers and lawyers.

I know as an adult that my grandparents were captives of the times and customs that they lived in and lived by. Sometimes I dreamt of different outcomes for my grandparents' story, hoping for other variables that would have made for an altered end result. But the story unfolded as it did the minute my Por Por and my mom stepped on the ship headed for South Africa. As they left the watery passage behind them, the machinery of illegal immigration fired into life for my family and turned the pages of my grandparents' doomed love story.

On their arrival in the old Transvaal, Por Por and my mom were given fake papers and new identities to claim; now they were paper daughters.

It meant more paper and incorrect dates and information that have left me confused about my mother's (and my father's) actual birth dates and their true ages.

Years later I heard the incredulity in a dentist receptionist's voice when she asked me for my mother's birthday so that she could retrieve her file. I said 'um' and then I asked her to hold the line while I looked for my mom's ID number. She held. I thought about trying to explain the confusion of paper sons and daughters and lunar calendar fickleness next to the steady Gregorian one. I imagined her tapping a pencil, twirling her hair and being sceptical of a daughter who did not know her own mother's birthday. I shut up and owned up to some of the shame with my silence. I could not explain myself out of that situation in two or three sentences.

My mother and gran took their new identities without question. For a long time my mother loved that the identity made her a few years younger than she actually was. Today it means more confusion for me and I am always doing mental sums when there is an official document that goes by the numbers in an ID book and not what we know as more accurate.

My mother's birth name was Fok Jouw Yee. Ah Yee is still what everyone calls her in Chinese, but her new identity in South Africa gave her the name Low Yee Wan, and eventually an anglicised version in later years meant my mother simply told people who did not speak Chinese that her name was Yvonne. It was an easy phonetic cousin to Yee Wan or now You Wan, as it is printed in her current ID book.

Along with new names and identities, they were given specific instructions for hiding, for staying out of the public eye and for being on the look out. For the first few months they lived like fugitives, shunted from location to location in a bid to evade authorities who might be looking for them; they could not be too careful. In reality, few people would have bothered to tell the authorities. On the outskirts of white suburbia, the authorities were despised with shared disdain and mostly the cops had bigger fish to fry. Still, my grandfather's arrest all those years ago was an ever-present reminder that one slip-up could be one too many.

'Those were really scary days; you would be afraid of every knock on the door or any stranger who arrived. I did not expect that it would be like that and I really did not know why we had to be in this horrible place in the first place,' my mother recalled.

Eventually, as the months worked themselves into a humdrum routine, with no cops coming around and no one asking any questions, my Por

Por and mom settled a bit more into life in landlocked Pretoria on my grandfather's small piece of land. Living here on the edge of the city and flanking the doleful townships must have felt so strange. Gone was the humidity of Hong Kong with its buzzing city streets congested with Chinese signage, even in the 1960s, vying for attention at every turn. Their room in the cramped flatlet in the heart of emerging Hong Kong high-rises was replaced with an old farmhouse without a single tall building nearby.

My granny started working behind the butchery counter, encountering black people for the first time, not understanding any of the languages the customers tried out on her, making mistakes and chiding herself for her errors. Then she cooked the evening meal for her husband and daughter as the sunset gave way to stars she did not recognise. And finally, she shared a bed with a man she called her husband but who was a stranger.

One of the things my grandparents always fought about was the way my Por Por cooked rice. She liked the grains softer, cooked for longer with more water in the pot. My Ah Goung preferred his rice firmer. They battled constantly over the difference made by a few splashes of water. These rice wars became daily skirmishes, a constant reminder of the distance between them, until eventually they stopped eating together.

There is a saying in Chinese about a man who eats 'soft rice', *sek yeun faan* or *tau hai faan*; it is meant to refer to a man who has to rely on his wife for a living. Maybe after my Ah Goung had to rely on his wife's family for work when he first arrived in South Africa he resented the reminder at every meal.

But my granny could also not give up what she wanted. It was almost as if she yearned for another body of water, the Indian Ocean, which would put a sure watery gulf between her and this life she had never wanted.

Another wedge that started to push into their relationship was the fact that my grandfather became a Christian. The story of his conversion sounds like the start to the Noah's Ark story, and it was close enough to make my grandfather a believer. The great flood in Pretoria happened when I was a small child, in the late 1970s. I remember only the aftermath of the natural disaster because I recall returning to Ah Goung's Silverton plot after the days of flooding and my parents measuring off the watermarks against the heights of us children. I remember the big rescue of things that could be salvaged, all limp with the imprint of having being soaked in water – and warped and wrinkled for life thereafter.

At the time of the flood, my gran lived with and worked for relatives of ours who had two shops in Denver. With the recent opening of their new shop they needed someone to help behind the counter. My gran took the job, grateful to escape the war between her and my grandfather, but also not having to separate officially and thereby keeping the peace in the family. My uncles' shops sold fish and chips, two-cent toffees and all the other odds and ends of corner cafés. Their house was adjoined to the one shop and my gran had a little room where she stayed – and thus missed the flood that hit the capital city.

Ah Goung, though, did not. The rains kept coming until it was clear that there was nowhere else for the water to go. On the day the flooding climaxed, my grandfather had started moving everything on to higher surfaces around the house and sandbagging the doors to keep the water from gushing in. Then he panicked about his old green station wagon, the Passat that took him everywhere. The car was in the most vulnerable spot on the open plot where the torrents were gaining momentum with every drop of rain that fell. Ah Goung could not simply watch his beloved car get washed away and his intention was to get to the car and drive it to higher ground until the water eventually subsided.

As he stepped over the sandbags, the polished veranda had vanished and the water had risen sharply in the few minutes since he had last checked. Still, he thought he could get to the Passat; he just had to be quick about it.

But he never made it to the car. The waters snared his feet and toppled him over, dragging him along with the current. No one was there to help my grandfather. His neighbours were also riding out the storm and they had no idea what was happening to Ah Goung.

He bobbed along in the water as it rushed towards an overflowing storm-water channel some distance from his property. Then he bumped against an old tree that had withstood the force of the water and he managed to clutch on to the branches. He felt his body come to a halt and when he opened his eyes the water was still moving but he was no longer being dragged with it. Ah Goung clung on and waited for help.

Night fell and still no one came. It was then that Ah Goung made a pact with God, the Western deity he had heard of but who did not fit in with the way he knew the world. His pact was to honour God as a Christian if he made it out alive. He held on to that tree the whole night, occasionally nodding off from exhaustion, but too cold and scared to fall asleep properly. At daybreak a rescue team found him. And when the rains gave way my grandad was a Christian.

Even though he kept many of the traditional Chinese observations that he said were his way to honour and remember his mother, he kept his pact with God until his very last breath.

My grandad did not have a church to belong to. He was a Chinaman who was not welcome in white churches. Instead, he worshipped with black people, with those whose churches were under trees, in quiet Sunday parking lots and anywhere else that suited their singing and dancing purposes.

My grandfather made the knitted plaits in red and green that he wore around his waist and around his wrists. He would make the same plaits to decorate a cross with Jesus Christ on it that he put up in his house. He stayed with these churches for years, not understanding the language much, but being welcomed anyway to say his prayers and to keep his promise from the time of the flood.

Years later, a Chinese Baptist church started up in the south of Johannesburg. It offered sermons in Chinese and Bibles and hymn books printed in Chinese. It became the religious home for my Ah Goung for many, many years.

My gran never understood this conversion to Christianity. A Christian God fell outside of her world view. Her spirituality was commanded by the deities and spirits of another realm, the patterns of the stars and seasonal dictates, the rhythm of prosperity and catastrophe and the merits that come with the loyalties to the ancestors and the gods that the ancients had worshipped along the continuum of Chinese custom.

My gran did have a kind of sixth sense for things of the heavens. It was a quiet piety and she never passed herself off as a devout person or dropped hints about 'supernatural powers' or mysterious and dramatic abilities.

It was not unusual for people to seek her out to ask for her interpretation of the Chinese calendars, the *tong seng*. The *tong seng* is an almanac not only of events and dates and the movement of the constellations of each new year, but also a book for clarity of all things in life. People trusted my grandmother to choose the best dates for marriages and funerals. She talked about *feng shui*: where to hang a curtain for a certain flow of energy, turning around the beds for a better night's rest. She also looked at hands and would make a comment about wearing a ring on a finger to stop money flowing away. She read the stories in the structure of a face and never dismissed a dream or the arrival of an omen that looked like coincidence. It was an inherent part of who she was and much of her simple ways and wisdom slipped into our everyday lives, too. Even my mother believed what Ah Por said about things of this other dimension.

But the gods and the ancestors gave Por Por no peace and no answers when it came to healing and mending her relationships with her husband and her daughter.

For my mother, her girlhood dream of being reunited with her father had come true, and she quickly fell in love with the idea of having a dad. 'I have not had my father around for so many years, why should I not stand up for him now?' was typical of what she would say, when one of us challenged her about her unfair siding with her father. My grandfather was always the hero and my grandmother was always in the wrong, as my mother saw it.

Details of the many arguments between my grandparents have become blurry over time. I know my mother grasped on to the discord, though, holding on to it hard enough to retell the stories often, as if constant retelling would make them real. I learnt to take the stories with a pinch of salt and to look for the context of the arguments because things were never as they first seemed.

My mother went from being in my grandfather's camp and having him as her favourite parent to waging all-out war with my grandmother. It was a war of snippy remarks, disparaging comments and of being dismissive of what was important to my grandmother, particularly of being reassured of requited love from her only child.

My mother would say my grandmother was plotting against her and was using us grandchildren as her devices of revenge. Whenever we stood up for our granny my mother would say: 'Yes, go ahead and plot against me, that is what your grandmother wants, yes, this is her revenge.'

We never knew what she meant about conspiring against her so my granny could score points of retribution.

My gran, though, forgave her daughter time and again. She even told us to tame our anger and she would chastise us for being disobedient to my mother as we became teenagers. When we moaned about my mother to her, she would simply say: 'Pretend what she says is just a bird singing.' Only very occasionally would she allow herself to agree with us and have a short rage at my mom. Then she would gather herself and make another excuse for her little girl's behaviour.

All of us Ho children had weekend and holiday jobs as we became teenagers. For a few days one holiday I was an extra for an American movie filmed in South Africa. They needed Chinese children to play Vietnamese villagers, chasing chickens and pushing bicycles before bombs went off to raze the props of thatch houses to the ground. They put cocoa powder on my face and we were given clothes to wear to make us look like poor, dirty village kids. In another job I got dressed up in a Chinese gown over my tracksuit and was issued a Chinese straw hat along with a group of other girls cooking up Chinese-themed dishes in a shopping centre. I was about fourteen and cooked badly, but fortunately I was paid to be part of the in-store promotion and not for any chef skills. I was Chinese, I looked the part and that was enough. But mostly we worked as waitrons at Chinese restaurants. Kelvin, Yolanda and I worked in Hillbrow's Litchee Inn, a restaurant that pioneered *yum cha* (literally, 'to drink tea'), a Sunday brunch menu of small portions of delicacies they called *dim sum* (literally, 'to touch your heart'), in the Transvaal of the late 1980s. We would serve up parcels of beautifully seasoned prawns inside rice-flour skins, so thinly rolled out they would steam up almost transparent, next to crispy fried taro-potato cakes filled with savoury fillings and delicate *char siu*, the sweet pork filling wrapped in flaky pastry. Sometimes we would buy some of the leftovers to take home and the owners would be kind enough to let us take a little extra because the restaurant only served its *yum cha* menu once a week and nothing was going to keep that long. We would take the treats to our grandparents whom we usually visited after our Sunday shifts.

Even as we put the delicious eats before my gran she would say: 'Have you put some of this aside for your mother?' or 'Take these home to your mother instead.' Even though the restaurant's food was delicious, my gran wanted my mother to have the treats. She put my mother first and she expected us to show respect towards our parents above all else.

No matter what my granny did, my mom's imagination, infected by her anger, became a virus of accusations. When my grandparents finally lived under separate roofs some years later, she accused my grandmother of being too friendly with another old man, a long-time widower, who was a mutual friend to both my Ah Goung and my Ah Por. 'She fixes his trousers but she would not even touch your grandfather's when they lived together,' my mother would rage.

I only knew this old man as a helpful Ah Buk, an old uncle, whose reasonable English proficiency meant he was the person many of the old people who lived in the same flats turned to for help, my grandparents among them. My grandfather, like us, never faulted this man's actions or intentions, but my mom persisted. She inflated my grandmother's small gestures of reciprocal kindness into betrayal of her place as my grandfather's wife, even though they were now living in two separate flats – ironically side by side, because they were the only units that were available for rent.

I remained friendly with this old man even after both my grandparents died. Sometimes I would take him canned foods – those tins of curried rice, stained yellow with too much turmeric or fake colouring, and chicken and vegetable curry, almost desiccated from the over-processing. But this Ah Buk loved them because he said he had not cooked properly for nearly 30 years since becoming a widower and the all-in-one meals were among his favourites.

He told me he liked to warm up a can of food, spread a bit of margarine on a few slices of bread and that would be dinner. When he did cook rice occasionally, he would freeze the leftovers so that he would not have to turn on the stove again for days. And yes, he did have fruit quite often, he would reassure me when I asked, concerned that there was a lack of fresh ingredients in his diet.

By then he had moved from the block of Lorentzville flats where he first met my grandparents to a small pensioner's cottage inside a retirement village, still in the east of Johannesburg. It was government subsidised and tiny but with a scrap of garden. It was much nicer than the unforgiving dark stairs and rentals of the Lorentzville flat.

It was this Ah Buk who was instrumental in helping my grandparents apply for and secure a cottage each in the same retirement village. I was always grateful for his efforts because even though the cottages were cramped, the retirement village life was more suited to old people and it gave both my grandparents comfort and enjoyment in the last few years of their lives.

In this Ah Buk's cottage there was large black and white photo of a smiling woman with a 1960s hairdo, fixed into perfection with hairspray. It was his wife. They had not had any children, but he never seemed short of friends or company or activities that kept him busy and he missed his wife dearly, that was clear.

He would tell me all of this as he served up a can of Chinese cooldrink, one of those drinks that are tea-coloured with jellied bits in it. I did not really like the hard chewy jellies but I knew he saved these cans of drinks for special occasions, like one of my visits. So I would munch on the jellies that never fully dissolved and let them slide down the back of my throat as I listened to some of his stories and we passed a few more minutes together.

Sometimes he would talk about my grandparents. Often he would say that it was a pity they never worked things out; often I would say I wished the same; then we would agree that it was simply never meant to be.

6

In the City of Gold

My father, Ah Kee, had already clocked up a few years in another part of the province by the time my gran and mom made their trip south to this mountain of gold, this Gum Saan. For my father there would be no gold, no promise of grand opportunity and also no turning back.

I never asked my father how he felt about coming out to South Africa. I wonder what went through his mind when the decision to leave Shun Tak for South Africa was made for him. How alone he must have felt, hiding on the ship, as the giant vessel separated from the dock and the only home he had known.

My Ah Ba had to make the journey to South Africa on his own. He had never even left his village before. He had no guardian, no parent. There was nobody to reassure him, to distract him from his fears with a joke or a story.

It might have been a small consolation to know that he was heading to a part of the world where two of his older brothers had moved in the last few years. He would have hoped for a reunion; maybe he daydreamt a little about what it might feel like to be the baby brother, to know the security and protection of having two big brothers when he landed.

But by the time my mother and father's separate worlds started to collide with my mom's arrival in South Africa, my father had already grown up very quickly. Gone was the timid teenager; gone, too, were his daydreams and holding on to old hopes. His China, like the fickle mists that wrap the verdant mountains of the mighty middle kingdom, was becoming more and more of an unsure memory.

When my dad left China, he was the village orphan and he was only a teenager, maybe seventeen, eighteen or nineteen. As with my mother, I cannot be sure of the exact dates or ages involved. Much was lost in the illiteracy of my dad's village life and it was only when I grew up that I understood how the superstitions and customs of a very different social structure could distort things like someone's age or birth date.

To begin with, there were very few written records from the villages that my family came from. There was that confusion between the lunar calendar and its Western counterpart. It meant important dates on the lunar calendar fell on a different day each year. Even oral histories conflicted and it just left more questions unanswered. In the villages people used to have many children because they knew several would die, and sometimes the young dead were ignored because there was no luxury in remembering for too long. Because of the high infant mortality in the rural villages, children were sometimes given nicknames such as 'dog' or 'pig'; it was a way to ward off evil spirits, my mother would tell us, when I laughed as a child about an Uncle Dog, as his nickname stuck even years later. Calling a child 'dog' would confuse the evil spirits that came in the shadows to claim infant souls. Another practice that was equally baffling for me to understand was the tradition of adding extra years to the age of someone once they died. It was an extra year for the death, then one for the heavens and one for the earth.

I was bewildered by these practices while growing up and even sometimes as an adult, but I have come to realise that superstition and seemingly bizarre practices are all completely logical, practical even. They make sense of life's cruelties by transcending the realm of plausible reasoning; here they cannot be questioned. They comfort bruised hearts when no healing will come.

For me, straddling two worlds of such difference makes me learn to lay down differences, side by side, letting them be separated but joined like a scar that knits together split flesh but leaves behind a dividing line that does not fade.

Still, it was like a sting to my heart that I had so many puzzle pieces of my dad's life and that so much was lost to the obscurity of superstition. I was frustrated with my father, too, for not having answers for me, even when I asked him. But my disappointment and sadness that the picture refused to take shape fully was nothing compared to the actual life my father lived in his village of Daai Dun in Shun Tak. Maybe much of it he did not want to remember, or more likely he did not want me to inherit the sadness by telling me too much.

My father was born the youngest of seven brothers, only three of whom survived into adulthood. There are stories of a younger sister who was sold to a rich family when my paternal grandparents could not afford to feed another mouth, especially as it was a girl child. My father had a few patchy memories of this sister he would have shared his first few years with. If she did exist, she could possibly still be alive today.

I wondered about this aunt sometimes. Was she real or was she a corruption of stories and memories grown murky over time? My father spoke of this sister occasionally and my mom also relayed the stories to us. But my father's cousin, my Aunty Peng, who was born about six years after my father, did not remember this girl child. I spoke to her at times about my dad, about her memories of the village she shared with my father. Sometimes, though, I was not sure if she was only trying to spare me the hurt of a sad reality for our family by telling me not to worry or to wonder about this aunt because she did not exist. I realised the economy of emotions among many older people in my community. Sadness and emotion were indulgent.

But if there was an aunt and she was sold off, it would have happened before my Aunty Peng was born or when she was only a baby. It was unlikely something so painful would have been discussed openly with her as she was growing up.

If this aunt is alive somewhere I hope her life turned out well and that her fate and destiny lived up to what her parents would have wished for her. It is not easy to think about a child being sold or given away but love in a time of survival does not look like anything I know now. Selling this child looked like a transaction, an exchange for a few sacks of rice maybe, but I think it was an act of mercy, desperation and of love. I know by the love my dad had for his parents, for his mom especially, that they could not have been parents who would have given up their child easily.

As I grew up, I realised that it was also not uncommon for villagers in China's rural villages to have many children – seven, eight or ten would not be unusual. Boys were favoured. A girl was a child you fed and clothed but who left your home; a son married, you gained a daughter-in-law and children followed.

Children in big numbers were an insurance policy, a hedging of bets that one or two of them would live to become adults, would have a measure of simple success in life and, in the Confucian tradition of filial piety, would be prepared to see their parents safely into their old age and ensure them a proper send-off into the afterlife. For my paternal grandparents, though, when their time came, the send-off was spare, like the lean, pared-down, hard lives they lived. Even simple final rituals should include funerary clothes, the incense and the paper money that secures prosperity and comfort in the afterlife, but I am not sure if my Ah Hea and Ah Mah got to tick off the whole checklist.

It was when my father was about eight or nine that my paternal grandad died. I do not know how the news would have arrived to the village and to my Ah Mah's ears. The day would have been ordinary enough as he and his two fishermen friends from the village took their small fishing boat out for the day, like every other day.

It was hard work and the men's efforts were more to feed their families than to build a business. They reserved rations for their families and then tried to sell and barter the rest of their catches of the day to the villagers. China was starving and it was also strangled by robbers and thugs who by the 1930s and 1940s had overrun the country.

That morning a group of bandits chose my Ah Hea and his friends as their target. I imagine that they had started back to shore with their boat. It was there that the criminals, like pirates, rushed aboard and ransacked their meagre possessions. There must have been a scuffle and my grandfather was thrown overboard. My Ah Hea was probably already injured as he fell into the water. He drowned in the briny depths.

His already poor widow was left even poorer and with a crushed heart as her husband and companion died. This country of hers, ravaged by famine, flooding, poverty and even the crime and violence of bandits, had now claimed her husband and left her children without their father.

The bleakness in Shun Tak county had already forced my father's older brothers to flee the village, to look for other opportunities. Leaving, however, also meant having to abandon their youngest brother and their mother. The hurt from this period of my father's life was forever tattooed into his heart. He did not speak too much about those days and I know that many specific recollections of his dad he had not taken with him to adulthood. Maybe it was a conscious choice to leave them in the past; it is one way to make room for looking ahead. From his few stories I did realise that what endured was his faithfulness and abundant love for his mother. Somehow it meant that as his child I would always fall short in my filial respects. His many sacrifices meant I would never have to be tested the way he was.

'We were so poor that sometimes your Ah Mah would boil smooth stones in a gravy so that we had something to suck on as we mixed the gravy into the little bit of rice we had,' my father would remind us as we tucked into a special meal or when we groaned about a dish on a dinner table that we did not really like. One I particularly hated was a dish of dried fish, steamed and cooked up with some vegetables. It was not that I hated fish but these fish were each no bigger than a pinky finger and they were eaten whole. They also had huge eyes and a streak of silver that seemed to take up most of their bodies. All the dish looked like to me was a plate of eyeballs with flashes of silver. But my father was not trying to mock our indulgence or ingratitude when he chided us; it was to remind us of the capriciousness of good fortune.

In the village my father often lied to his mother about the provisions they still had in the house. My Ah Mah had steadily grown weak and malnourished in the years after my Ah Hea's death, and many of the responsibilities, including cooking the meals, fell on my father, who by then I imagine was maybe thirteen or fourteen years old.

Even though the community would not have abandoned mother and son, everyone had their own demons to fight, the devils of hunger at their own desperate doors. My dad would often tell his mother he had eaten so that she would eventually agree to take from the small rations that the pair had. But even my father's efforts to get his mother to eat could not save my Ah Mah. Malnourishment and other illnesses of poverty worked their unhurried evil hand on her, squeezing out the life in her body steadily. Then, on a freezing night, mother and son made a small fire to try to warm up their tiny, poorly insulated house. By the morning my grandmother was dead. She suffocated in her sleep; her ruined body had no will to wake to another bleak day.

There were no photos of Ah Hea or my Ah Mah, this woman whom my dad loved so. With no photos, I conjure up pictures of this granny in my imagination. I try to see her smiling, a contented smile that wished patiently on possibilities and better days. Still, I sometimes close my eyes and I see images of a grey, shack-like homestead and a woman aged beyond her years inside a crumpled body, a woman with a son by her side whom she loved but could offer no future to. I wish I could free that image, release it with a happy ending.

For my father, the severance from his mother took a commanding hold on his young life. Sometimes it seemed like it never eased up its stranglehold, just reappeared in new wicked guises to add up to more pain.

I never got to meet my paternal grandfather or grandmother. I will never know if I have my granny's eyes, feet like grandad's, if something passed through that gene code to me. They were people who contributed to my DNA but were phantoms. For my father, though, those phantoms were like hauntings of love lost.

My father became the village orphan. Even though he had some extended family members who did not desert him, he was alone. He was not a small child any more but a teenager who could be every bit a frightened child. My Aunty Peng remembered spending time with my father in the small homestead almost every day. She was younger but he would plead with her sometimes to stay longer even when her own chores waited and her own parents called her home at sunset.

'I was much younger than your father, but I knew he was frightened to be there all by himself after your Ah Mah died. Of course he was scared, who would not be?' she told me years later, standing inside her provisions store in Brixton, shaking her head, remembering those grim days in the village. She helped my father to light a fire in the homestead, sometimes got some food cooking, or brought some from her family's own dinner and then ran off home before she was missed by her parents.

The misery of village life rolled on from baking summers to unforgiving winters for my father those first years after my Ah Mah's death. And it would lead to my dad's death. At least, that was what the villagers thought when they found my father's lifeless body one day. Maybe he had passed out, exhausted and hungry, maybe he had become unconscious from illness, I am not sure and neither was my father. But unable to revive him in the number of unsophisticated ways of the village, the family and the villagers declared my father dead. Without his own family present, his body was prepared for a simple, quick burial with hardly any of the important rituals of final rites and the small assurances that are meant to ease that passage into the afterlife. His limp body was laid on a makeshift stretcher and carried to the outskirts of the village, where it would be buried in a shallow ditch. But as they laid down the stretcher, ready to roll him into the dug-out trench that would make do for a grave, my father spluttered to life in an astonished gasp.

This strange resurrection earned him the lifelong nickname Gwei Kee (Ghost Kee) because he had literally come back to life from the realm of the dead.

Indeed, my father floated through those days like a ghost, not really present, with no rest and nowhere to feel grounded either. As he reached his late teens, it was decided by his uncles and other village elders that it would be best if my dad was sent to Africa. People from all over Southern China had for some time been leaving for destinations that had boomed out of gold rushes across the world. The village uncles knew that two of my dad's brothers had gone in the direction of the place called Naam Fey; that place south of Canton and across the Indian Ocean where there were rumours of prosperity and opportunity.

The villagers and extended family raised enough money for only one person to make the journey so my father travelled on his own. It required connections, organising papers and then paying for the passage across the ocean. Initially the elders thought that my father's older relative, a cousin, my See Buk (fourth uncle), would make the voyage first. But during the weeks that the decisions were being made he had shorn his hair unexpectedly. According to my mom and dad's stories it was because he had lost a wager and had shaved off his hair. The elders could not risk this shaven head. They figured that my See Buk would stand out like a sore thumb when he slipped into South African society. He would surely be caught and deported, which would be a waste of their resources and efforts to get someone from the village out to a possibly better life. So that Indian Ocean crossing would be made by my father.

Two battered suitcases with scuffed metal studs and thick leather buckles were all that my father arrived with in South Africa. I imagine that there were a few changes of clothes with something warm and something a little more 'decent', some basics of soap and a comb to tame an unruly strand of hair. That was all. There were no little mementos, no photographs and no extra bits of money hidden inside a sock.

'Somebody distracted me when we were smuggled off the docks and when I turned to look one of my suitcases was stolen.' It was my father's mocking welcome to South Africa. Sometimes he told us the story when he had reason to haul down the surviving suitcase from atop the wardrobe in my parents' bedroom.

It was used to store other things, like winter coats, by the time we were growing up. I would finger the thick straps on that leather case, soft on the underside where so long ago it had joined with a buckle to hold together all that my father brought from his old life. Occasionally then my father would talk a little about those first days after he arrived and when he had made the journey up to the old Transvaal.

One of the stories he told summed up perhaps the hardest part of my dad's early struggle in South Africa: other people's malice and viciousness where it was least expected. My father had started a small job somewhere, I think it was to help in a shop. It was unlikely that my father was expected to serve customers without an even basic knowledge of English or any of the local languages. His job was probably to be a general dogsbody, a coolie, cleaning the premises, doing some heavy lifting, packing and stacking and whatever else the owner might have needed from him.

Ah Ba remembered that one evening as the sun set he noticed that the shop became lit in the soft orange glow of an electric light. My dad did not have the luxury of electric lights back in his village and he was a little taken aback that even the small shop had the lavishness of electric lights. He carried on with the rest of his tasks, sweeping up the floors and tidying up for the next day's business. There was another employee, also a Chinese man, and my dad remembered that when he had finished up for the day he asked the man how to switch off the electric light in a storeroom. My father did not know that a switch on the wall would turn off the light.

'That old bastard told me that I would have to find a way to climb up and unscrew the light bulb and he warned me not to leave the light on before I left for the day. I spent what seemed like hours trying to stack up chairs high enough to reach the light fitting. And still it did not work. It was only after a long time had passed as I was moving things around trying to get higher and higher to reach the light bulb that I even thought about the switch on the wall. I switched it off and on again and off again, and then I realised what a cruel trick that man had played on me.'

It would not end with small cruelties and malice meted out by individuals, though. I am sure my parents expected hardship and discrimination even after their individual journeys here, but in Africa their skin colour would be the marker for their torment carried out by a system that was in statute books. It was suffering the humiliation of being ushered to the back of buses, denied entry into cinemas and restaurants, or in the last years of apartheid being able to work and live in whites-only suburbs but only with demeaning concessionary approvals, which was maybe the worst insult of all.

I have a document my father carried with him for years to keep him from being thrown off trains by the authorities. The A4 document is stamped by the Chinese consulate and is dated 1966. It declares my father a 'gentleman of good standing'. Someone else's arbitrary signature and a random stamp were a ruling on my father's character that was meant to protect him. My father folded that piece of paper into a neat rectangle and carried it in his breast pocket every day. The folds on that worn piece of paper were so deeply set they were like the mark left on a dog's neck when its too-tight collar is removed.

Two of my dad's brothers had headed south in the years before my dad made the same journey. The second-born brother, whom we called Yee Buk, Second Uncle, had come to South Africa. The sixth-born brother, Lok Buk (Sixth Brother), was in the old Lourenço Marques (now Maputo) in Mozambique. In Chinese you call elders by the place they have in the family hierarchy rather than by their names. So it is not Uncle Bob, but Second Uncle, Third Uncle, and so on. There is also no distinction in the term of address for uncles and aunts who are your parents' own brothers and sisters or their cousins. There are, however, different terms for uncles and aunts on the paternal or maternal sides of the family and also differences if they are older or younger than one's parents.

Fortunes for my Lok Buk were better than for Yee Buk. Lok Buk ended up spending almost a decade of his life in Lourenço Marques, setting up a small business. He had left behind a wife, a young son and a daughter back in China and the aim, as always, was to work and raise enough money to return to them. But the years wore on and he stayed in Mozambique.

There was a part of my uncle's life that he kept hidden from his family back in China. He had set up a second life with a Mozambican woman and it was believed he had two children, daughters, with this woman. It is still a part of our family history that is told in whispers.

Some years later my uncle did return to China and he had one more daughter. The anti-Portuguese and anti-colonial sentiment in the aftermath of the *coup d'état* was also the start of a civil war in Mozambique that would last nearly two decades. As that began my uncle knew that his time in Africa had run its course and the time to go back to his family in China had come.

As the story goes, my Lok Buk prepared a substantial amount of money for his Mozambican family and handed the chunky envelope to someone with strict instructions only to deliver it once he was well on his way back to China. He did not want the goodbyes, the tears, the explanations that would never be enough. He never set foot in Africa again.

My uncle ended up settling in Macau, once a Portuguese colony in China. He still lives there today, playing *mah juk* – the gambling game of marked tiles – on the streets with the other old Chinese men. He visits my aunt sometimes in a home for the frail and senile, where, since dementia finally knocked all recognition of the familiar from her, the family decided to have her admitted. He walks to the market to buy the ingredients for his evening meal, which can be Chinese sprouts and cabbage with a charred Portuguese *natas* egg tart for afters. Then he takes the many flights of narrow stairs back to the small flat that he has called home for decades.

When I visited Macau some years back, before it was returned to the Chinese officially, it was a place that had the unusual blend of being part-Portuguese, part-Chinese. It had European architecture of old cathedrals and the blue and white tiled mosaics reminiscent of a Portuguese coloniser, but at the same time it was thoroughly Chinese with the altars for deities taking prominent positions inside every store, signage in Chinese throughout the city and the meals cooked up with *bok choi* and the *natas* that have become Chinese-styled and are called simply *daan taarts* (egg tarts).

Macau is now my ageing uncle's life. But he was an African once and I wonder if he ever thinks back to the humid hot air of Maputo. Does he wonder about the children he fathered and the woman whose bed he shared a long time ago?

I could not read anything in the lined face that welcomed me into his home the first time I met this uncle. Even though we had photos of him I had to hold back tears the first time I met this man who looked so much like my father. We spent a short time together during my visit to Macau. Although I was immediately welcomed as family with none of the politeness reserved for outsiders, we never moved beyond the first conversations of getting to know each other. We never got to leapfrog to details about his life in Africa and to his memories of Africa, in a time before I was born.

My Yee Buk made a similar journey to Africa years before my father. Unlike my Lok Buk, he did not stop over in Mozambique but made the journey further south to reach South Africa. I imagine this was the brother my father maybe hoped to be reunited with during the long nights on the ship on which he was a stowaway. My dad would have known that it was the elder of his two brothers, my Yee Buk, who was in South Africa, while my Lok Buk was in Mozambique.

My Yee Buk's journey to South Africa happened close to ten years before my father's own journey, probably in the 1940s. But he was denied a South African dream by cruel fate. He contracted leprosy a few years after his arrival. Leprosy's unforgiving bacteria spreads where poor living conditions force people to live so close to each other that mucous and spit become weapons of tragedy. Weak immune systems make prime targets of men like my Yee Buk; his body was not strong enough to resist the onslaught. My uncle was not treated quickly enough, even though antibiotics were all it would have taken to cure him. Untreated, the disease fed on his nerves and his muscles, causing deformity and disfigurement. My Yee Buk was sent to a leprosy camp for non-whites somewhere outside Pretoria.

Years later, when I tried to find out more about the facility, I discovered that there were plans to change this long-abandoned site into a tourism destination that would boast a mall and a casino. If the plans ever got off the ground maybe the emptiness of malls and casinos would be a fitting epitaph for the leper colony.

I cannot fully make peace with the doomed destiny of Yee Buk's life. He arrived here as a poor migrant, with all its attendant difficulties of struggling to make a living as an outsider, then was afflicted by a disease that most people survive, and then he had to face being rejected by the community. In those days he would have been so scared and so alone. He was still a young man yet his body as he knew it was vanishing away painfully and he could no longer connect his mind and his body and he had no one to turn to for any help, support or comfort.

The authorities realised that he could not be deported in his state, so he was banished to the leper colony outside the capital city, an exile to a hell of the living dead.

I did get to meet this uncle when I was a child. I remember the simple room he was confined to in the leper colony. He was a shadow of a man by then. Leprosy had eroded his body, though he had not been contagious for many years. Initially I was afraid of his skeletal body and his hands that looked like they had been eaten away to only awkward, shaky knuckles. He could not speak properly any more, only mumble and groan, shaking his head sometimes and making noises. I supposed it was severe nerve damage. But I realised, too, that his speech would have been affected as he had no one to communicate with as the only Chinese leper. Like my grandfather thrown into prison, my Yee Buk was isolated by his skin colour and I sensed this even as a child. He was also detached from the community that should have been his own. The alienation from the community had destroyed him before the contagion had exhausted itself.

During visits my mother spoke gently to him as my dad stood by, running his thumb along his fingers, as he always did when he was agitated or thinking deeply about something, hurting that he could not engage with his brother. My mother's tone was empathetic but affected in that way you speak to someone when you can no longer have a two-way conversation. Yee Buk loved to draw and he loved to feed the ants in his room. As a child I imagined the ants were his friends; they were his most potent connection to all things alive in a world where living was a stutter.

I quickly stopped being frightened of this uncle. We took him stacks of paper and crayons so he could draw. He clutched the crayons that we brought to him with his distorted fingers and he drew the ants that were his only friends. He also sketched them on the walls of the stark room that was more like a prison cell than a home.

My father asked him questions as we spent a few more minutes in his room. He mumbled responses but they did not prompt any meaningful exchange. He always seemed happy to see us but I wished he could share more. In his muteness he faded into the space of phantom uncle for me, another person I shared DNA with but did not have a full picture of.

The staff were kind mostly, or at least when we visited. They left him to draw the ants on his wall. But it was clear that their care, like the facilities, was basic. There was a metal frame bed, a metal cupboard and a wooden table and desk.

My mom always set out food for him while we were there because she said she did not want staff to take the treats from him once we had left. Yee Buk was a good eater. He enjoyed the cakes or the *baos* and *siu mais* my father would have made sure to pick up from Chinatown before our trip to Pretoria. We watched quietly as he ate, the crumbs falling on his pyjamas. He was always in pyjamas even though we had bought ordinary clothes for him through the years. I guess it was too difficult for Yee Buk to work through buttons and zips with his weakened hands and staff were not too concerned about spending extra energy to get the residents dressed each day.

I remember my mother always being concerned that items we left for our uncle would be stolen. But there was nothing really valuable. The crayons, pens and sheets of papers held a treasure that was important only to my uncle.

One of my favourite artists today is Dumile Feni. Before I even realised he was famous I was drawn to the intensity of his works the very first time I saw his drawings as a student in Pretoria. There was a struggle in the images that he made on bedsheets and on walls. I understood the need to draw away from the convention of a piece of paper, a kind of impatience and urgency like a desperate way to break out. My Yee Buk's drawings were perhaps a way to break out of the imprisonment of a broken body and the imprisonment of long isolation from normal, loving human contact.

My real sadness was for my father. I remember driving back after one of those infrequent visits to the leper colony. We four children were packed into the back of the Cortina. As the journey home dragged on in the late afternoon, we would nod off. But I leaned forward to speak to my dad. Good Fridays were one of the public holidays on which we visited my uncle. I know because it was one of the few days a year that my fahfee dad did not work and therefore one of the few times we could make the trip out to see my uncle. I also remember that my father thought a trip to the Voortrekker monument, planted on the capital's horizon, was a good place to visit as a family, but because it was a Christian holy day the monument would always be closed.

My father talked about his brother as he drove and I inhaled all of my father's sadness, a heavy breath of melancholy that he could not do more for this brother and that their destinies had not turned out to be happier. By the time my father arrived in South Africa, the imagined reunion with his older brother had been dashed by fate. The leprosy ate at my father's heart, too, because it put up a wall between him and his brother, shutting them out from each other forever.

Years later, when it was estimated that my uncle was around 60 or 65, or old enough, some people in the Chinese community allowed him to be admitted into the Chinese old-age home in Malvern, recognising that contagion was no longer a concern. The home was not far from our house, also in the east of Johannesburg, and we were eager that he could be moved closer to us.

Payments and paperwork were needed, which were not things that my parents had readily for my Yee Buk. Because he had been state-managed for so many years, my father and mother had little to do with the official details of my Yee Buk's life.

A man from the old-age home arrived late one evening at our house. He pushed through our squeaky, short pedestrian gate. He was one of those talking heads in the community and one of the old-age home's trustees. We made him tea and he and my dad worked out the costs of admitting my uncle. We did not sit in on those discussions, of course, and at the time it was not anything we would really have wanted to understand anyway. We did know that it was serious adult talk and that it was a situation that father, too, did not wish he was in.

I imagine my father during the meeting, running his thumb over the tips of his fingers, tapping his foot. I know my father could not bear much more financial pressure and here was this man reminding my father about what he could not pay.

My father cut his fingernails close to the quick and he also bit them; they were always pink and raw as a result of his worrying. Eventually, when the man was convinced that he had flexed enough muscle, without being rude beyond the bounds of what Chinese custom allowed, he left. They had worked out a sum and agreed that the home's charity funds, collected from the community, would make up the shortfall along with a pension that they could now apply for on behalf of my Yee Buk.

The home was a better space for my uncle. There were other Chinese people there, all living under crocheted blankets in rooms that never quite got enough fresh air. Still, they gave him a sense of kinship and maybe a better level of attention than the perfunctory care at the leper home. We visited more often and it was comforting to see him surrounded by the ordinariness of homely things like pictures on the wall and plastic flowers gathering dust, and even the odd staff member or resident trying to engage with him as a human being. But it was clear that too many years had passed for him ever to be able to be integrated in a meaningful way.

Though I am sure he could understand a lot of what was going on around him, it was as if the gates of that place of quarantine had imprisoned his mind forever even after his body had been freed from that small cell-like space. My Yee Buk died in 1988 but I think his life had been shattered many, many years earlier.

The day that the news arrived about my uncle's death my father came home earlier than usual. The fahfee banks generally kept him away for many hours each day. His long work days were the norm we were used to. An unexpected early arrival was either on the rare occasion my father felt so ill he would head straight to bed, or because something horrible had happened. On this day it was sad news that brought him home.

We had already heard the news about our uncle's death from my mother who had taken the call from the old-age home's matron. My father arrived home already knowing the news, or knowing that something tragic had happened, even if my mother had not given him all the details over the phone. I remember him gripping the back of the sofa as he retreated behind a faraway gaze with the knowledge that his brother had died. He stood there, just holding on, not saying a word.

The same day my uncle died was also the night of Yolanda's graduation from a course at hotel school. My father's firstborn child had reached a milestone and was entering that portal where childhood dependence is set down and a child must pick up the mantle of adult responsibility. She would go on to study some more after that, but this was her first graduation and it was a night for parents to share in the achievement. This night was my father and mother's success, too; it marked the fruits of their hard work and sacrifice. My broken-hearted father smiled for his daughter, truly proud as she took her steps on to the graduation stage, as her name was read out and she received her diploma rolled up in the dollied-up toilet-roll inner. Yet his heart must have been aching for his brother who had died that same day.

Yolanda remembered: 'Dad was so excited that I was graduating but at the same time his brother had died. I remember that evening when we had the celebratory dinner at Litchee Inn. He tried to be happy, and I think he was. I also remember that dad wore white shoes with his blue suit that he had bought especially for my debutantes' ball when I was in matric, but the reason he wore those shoes was he had come back late from sorting out Yee Buk's things and he could not find his dark shoes and we were in a hurry to get to the graduation ceremony. I remember it like it was yesterday.'

I loved how my father looked in that suit my sister remembered. It was his only good suit – dark blue-grey with a slight shimmer to it. We children liked to match it up with a silky greyish-coloured tie that had a feather motif on it; my dad always obliged our childish fashion sense. There is even a photograph where he deliberately wore the tie on the outside of a V-neck jersey he had on under his jacket. He kept the tie we had chosen on display. I also still have a tie we bought our dad one Father's Day. It had three shades, offset with a goldish-coloured thread running through it along a diagonal. He loved it anyway even if it was probably impossible to match with anything.

The suit was posh; it was almost like a costume to me. It was so far from my everyday dad of casual rolled-up shirt sleeves and buttoned-down collars. The shirts he preferred were worn until the collars started to fray and fine ink trails from ballpoint pen marks congregated around the pockets. And they always had a breast pocket so that he could stab in a pen or two alongside his glasses case that clipped on securely.

He had bought that suit for Yolanda's debutantes' ball when she was a matric student a few years earlier. Yolanda always loved community events and activities and would throw herself into the commotion of things like cake sales and selling raffle tickets. By contrast, I was not interested and Unisda loathed the idea. Each year the young debutantes raised funds for charity and the primary beneficiary was the Hong Ning Old Age Home, the same home where my Yee Buk saw out his last days, so my parents had agreed to let her get involved.

Yolanda had also managed to cajole and beg my parents to buy two tickets to the crowning event of the debutantes' year, the glitzy ball. For my parents it was the most swanky thing that had happened since their own wedding and that was why the suit was bought and my mom had a dress made along with Yolanda's teenage glamorous gown. Yolanda's gown was an ice-white creation, an off-the-shoulder satin poof with diamant detail, topped off with a dubious perm.

My mother's dress was a long blue gown, simple and satiny with a little floral beaded detail at the décolleté. I think she loved its all-shiny frivolity.

I remember, though, that when my father got home early that night to get ready for the big ball at the Carlton Hotel he was in one of his bad moods. The fiery dragon's tail was twitching and we knew the irritability would burn and then ignite. Yolanda had been picked up by her date earlier but Kelvin, Unisda and I were trying to dodge the sparks.

I hid under the dark wooden table in the lounge. It was a mighty table in my child's mind. It was always covered in a plastic, hard-wearing tablecloth but its true magic showed when the tablecloth came off and it was pulled on either side to reveal a centre piece that flipped out to accommodate extra people. The table still dominates in my mother's home today and I am always delighted when it is unfolded to its maximum and its neat wooden bolts are pushed into place to create a perfect seam for the joined sections of wood.

Children know the comfort of small dark spaces like climbing on top of a stack of clothes in a wardrobe, listening to the world grow muffled and dark behind a closed door. In wardrobes the darkness would be taken over by the faint smell of mothballs from the small drawstring bags filled with the ice-white balls that my mom tied to the clothes rails.

The hiding place under the table, with its tucked-in chairs, was a forest full of forgiving dark places to creep away and not be found. On the night of the debutantes' ball, it was a perfect place to wait for my dad to cool off long enough to leave for their evening.

My parents must have felt a little out of place in that posh Carlton Hotel ballroom, but they did not care too much about airs and graces, even other people's. Once my father's irritation dissipated, it would have been a night for enjoying the food – a Chinese menu, of course, outsourced catering as always to a reputable Chinese restaurant to please the fussy palates of Chinese guests. Mom and dad would have caught up with a few friends and acquaintances who would have also been at the glitzy function and they would have taken some delight in my sister's moment to shine. Someone would have commented on my mom's dress and she would have said: 'Oh, it is just something simple; Yolanda insisted I have it made.' But she would have loved this bespoke creation, all silky and shimmery and garnering compliments.

Chinese families traditionally are not big on demonstrative shows of affection. There would be no hugs and kisses for my sister, no outwardly saying to her: 'We love you and we are proud of you.' The love would be shown by their presence, in their smiles for her as she showed off her practised waltz across the ballroom floor.

In some way this was a night for my parents to taste the city of gold at last. Here in the swish ballroom of one of the city's top hotels, with its bow-tied waiters, chandeliers and mirrored everything, they could almost believe that once there were gold coins scattered in the streets of the city.

Of Phoenixes and Dragons

Marriage is considered the most auspicious of events for Chinese families. It is rivalled only by the birth of a first-born boy child or maybe the 80th birthday of a man who has accumulated wealth, success and a brood of children and grandchildren he can be proud of.

Every parent's dream is to see their child succeed and that success is tied up with marriage and procreation. It was no different for my mother after she had been in South Africa for a year or two. She was nearing 25 when my grandparents felt she should find a husband who could take care of her and make a good life for her.

For my mother, like many women of her generation, the prospect of marriage came as the natural order of things and the validation of being a fully fledged grown-up. Marriage and a family is a guarantee of a new kind of social capital. It was like her dead brother moving up the rung of the family altar after joining with his own ghost bride. In my parents' day, many marriages were still unions set up by a *mooi yan bor*. This older woman was an unofficial matchmaker and go-between for families looking to be joined by marriage. Such busybody aunties would find prospective suitors and remind mothers that their daughters were not getting younger. This was how many introductions were made in those days. It was how many people found their birth charts drawn up by the stars and the seasons and elements of the Earth being scrutinised along with their family lineages so that a good match could be guaranteed.

My Ah Goung and Ah Por had heard from the small web of Chinese, including the odd nosey *mooi yan bors*, about my father. They would have heard that he had no family members in South Africa and was a fahfee man, a gambler, and that he was at least a decade older than my mother, by everyone's estimates. These were not particularly great attributes for a potential husband for your only child, but importantly for my grandparents, they heard that he was a good man, and enough people vouched that he would likely be a responsible husband and provider.

My father had a few loyal friends. Many were older community members who had come to know him in the years since he had arrived in Johannesburg. They became like older brothers and uncles to my dad. They spoke for him, recognised his loyalty and his reliability, his sense of responsibility and his respect for elders. Importantly their voices did matter.

So, my grandfather agreed to have my father around for tea on their small plot outside Silverton in Pretoria.

My granny and mother must have frantically cleaned up the little house and my grandfather would have been sent out that day to buy something special for tea. My grandfather would have taken his old green station wagon Passat to Chinatown in Johannesburg. The pastel green tank would have chugged into the city centre for my grandfather to pick up a cake along with the specialities of Chinese *dim sum*, maybe *bao*, the sweetish white buns filled with smooth, dark lotus seed paste or sweet roasted pieces of pork, *char siu*, and also small minced pork dumplings steamed piping hot in their paper-thin, doughy sheaves.

My dad arrived for tea with another man and his wife. The man's nickname was Daai Sak (Big Stone). I remember this man we called 'Uncle', even though he was not my dad's relative by blood. He had a booming voice that was matched by an equally big laugh. He had tufts of greyish hair that stood out around his ears that made him look a little like an owl as he greyed more and more. I liked this misbehaving hair; it suited this tanned, hard-working fahfee man who had grown into his role as a community elder, solid and unfussy.

The clincher of that meeting, though, was if my mother liked what she saw; she still had the final say.

'The first time I saw your dad he seemed quite tall to me and a bit on the thin side. He was fidgeting with his fingers a lot and he seemed quiet and shy. He did not say much when I brought out the tea from the kitchen to be introduced to him. But he seemed nice,' my mother recalled of that first encounter as she flipped aside the curtains that stood in for doors in my grandparents' simple home to have a look at this would-be husband.

I can imagine my mom and gran fussing over the tea in the kitchen and my gran reminding my mother to be polite and ladylike. My mom, in her typical way, pretended not to care too much, even though the butterflies in her stomach would have been fluttering up a storm.

And my father fiddled with his fingers rather than lighting up a cigarette, which he thought would not have made a good impression. His hair was probably impressive, oiled back but full and pitch black. The meeting was full of hopeful maybes, so it was a success.

There was at least one other suitor my mother remembers coming around for tea over those few weeks. But she says she did not like the look or manner of this other man and she agreed instead to be courted by my father when he also expressed interest. Being courted was the orderly, proper way to do things and that was what my mother and grandparents expected.

Theirs started out as a long-distance relationship because my father was running a few small fahfee banks in Johannesburg and my mother was in Pretoria helping her parents run the butchery.

When my father could make it out to Pretoria over weekends, he took my mom back to the haunts of Sophiatown and Ferreirasdorp, where there were cinema houses that Chinese people were allowed into. These were the areas where Indian and coloured communities lived and traded. The few photographs my dad had from that time all bear the shop stamps of small studios in Sophiatown. Around the corner was Chinatown and a little further west was the Newclare cemetery for coloureds, Chinese and Indians. It was also in these suburbs that a guy could take his gal out for a Sunday afternoon and not be harassed by the white cops.

In one of my mother's stories, she remembers being mad with my father for not pitching up one day for a long-awaited date when he said he would.

She said it was nearly a deal-breaker because she was not going to be stood up, even though this was, of course, not my father's intention and the life of a fahfee man did not have predictable regularity.

But there was no negotiation with my mother if she felt someone had stepped out of line with her. Throughout her life those lines of appropriate behaviour have been based on her idea of correct behaviour towards her, defined by her own ideas of social hierarchy. 'I am the older cousin', 'I am the mother-in-law' or 'I have no responsibility because I have married out,' are my mother's easy, but flawed (at least to me) reasoning.

My father took a far more relaxed attitude about matters of social order and correctness. He was less bound to the standards that my mother took as gospel. A particular barb in my mom's side while they were dating was a woman my dad was friends with from before he started dating my mother. This woman, a few years older than my father, had two small children but her husband had left her or something else that seemed scandalous when we asked about it as teenagers. My father would look in on the family from time to time and try to help out the single mom when he could but I know my mother disapproved of the friendship that she felt just was not proper. There is still a photo or two of a lanky woman and two small children that survived in the family albums. I remember my father chuckling at my mom's jealousy and her jibes that this woman was my dad's 'girlfriend'. I understood my mother's insecurity. My mom has always been a proud woman and as a young woman dating someone who could be her future husband she would not tolerate the intrusion into the social rules that she felt had to apply to her picture of perfect.

Perhaps my father was more easy-going because without family members in South Africa there were not so many busybodies to prop up conventions.

My parents did marry, within about a year of dating each other. For the longest time I could only picture their wedding day in black and white through the images printed on that special photographic paper with wavy edges and white borders, which proved that something extra special had taken place inside the frames. There are a few stiff photographs, all neatly posed on the steps of the University of the Witwatersrand.

My mother had a bob and dark eyeliner and a long-sleeved white wedding dress with a simple cascade of satin and lace detail. Around her neck was a gold chain, in heavy yellow Chinese gold, with a heart-shaped jade pendant. I recognised this later when as a girl I rummaged through my mother's jewellery.

My father was in a dark suit, with a thin tie and an attitude.

It was not like back in China where a wedding couple will, still today, wear traditional garments for at least part of the wedding day ceremonies. The bride's dress is also a central feature as it is in Western custom. It is an embroidered *cheung saam* in silk brocade with intricate beading and glittering thread offset on a mostly red background – red is the colour of all things lucky, happy and auspicious. The bride in China or Hong Kong will have a headdress or at least plastic flowers with dangling beads in her hair.

Back in South Africa, my mother's wedding dress was white in the Western custom of the time. White is a traditional colour of mourning in China, in fact, but the widespread adoption of Western-style outfits was a sign of the mingling of cultures and traditions under an African sun. My parents' wedding party was tiny compared to that of some other Chinese families. On my dad's side, the people who stood in for the family photographs were brothers of a different kind, men like Daai Sak, who had come to know my father in the years almost as a brother or a son. On my mom's side, there were my grandparents and my granny's older sister and her husband and children. Because my mom was an only child, there was also a group of made-up siblings lined up in pretty dresses, ironed shirts, topped with stiff, hair-sprayed dos and big smiles. In my parents' group photos, it is friends and extended family of cousins and their children that make up the sprouts of a family tree all standing on the steps of Wits University, the most common venue for wedding photographs at that time.

Years later, Kelvin and his own bride, both then Wits University alumni, would repeat that wedding ritual on the Great Hall steps; she in her cascade of satin and beads and Kelvin with a cravat under his chin and a carnation in his buttonhole.

I liked to look at those static posed images from my parents' wedding and search for clues of the emotions of that day. In some photos my father looked stern to me. I later found out it was because some of his cousins had made a fuss about being in photos because there had been a death in their extended family. My father would have felt that it was not disrespectful to the dead person for these cousins to choose to show him a bit of respect by being in the photo. It was one of those conventions that must have irked my father and his expression showed it. I could not tell much from my mother's sweet composure as the young bride. She would have been told how she should stand and place her feet. For years when we were growing up, we three girls have photographs in which our feet are placed at specific angles to create an impression my mother would say was pretty and ladylike. Mostly my expressions in these photos also showed how I felt about fussy rules and customs.

We did not get to see my mom's wedding dress ever. It was not bundled away with mothballs and memories in the back of a wardrobe. Instead, it was cut up by the time we children came along, reincarnated as something that outlived the expiry date of a single event. The veil, she told with thrifty contentment, was turned into a net to cover food from pesky flies. My sentimentalist heart sank, but I grew up to know better about what matters to my mother.

Decades later it was an aunt, Aunt Ah Peng, who offered to trawl through her old boxes to find the invitation to my parents' wedding close to 40 years ago. She said she knew she still had it somewhere.

I never even thought of asking my mom about the invitation. It never occurred to me that a sentimental memento like a piece of red cardboard, embossed with the double happiness – two identical Chinese characters written together to form a unity of happiness – as most traditional wedding invitations are designed, could be stashed somewhere in and among my mother's things. It still remains missing at this stage. How I would love to see my parents' names, written in gold or red, announcing their auspicious union. By contrast to my mother, I grew up as a hoarder of everything sentimental. I have held on to letters from teenage pen pals even though I have never re-read them, my soft toys all have names and when they were loved threadbare I sewed them up, patched them with sellotape and glued on new eyes. There are wedding invitations from friends and family members that I have never thrown out. Their gilded cards in bundled piles are packed in boxes alongside old birthday cards and teddy bears with chewed-up ears and scuffed eyes that I cannot say goodbye to.

One day, when I was about seven, I noticed an oddly shaped item on top of our pale blue, steel kitchen cupboards, a unit with tinny shelves and a simple counter covered with a thin waterproof sheeting that had a mock marble pattern. It was simply pushed up against the wall, leaving a small gap that collected dust and grease and little things you think you have lost forever.

Like everything else on the top of the cupboard, it was sheathed in a greasy plastic bag and rested on a bed of yellowed newspapers that lined the top of the cabinets. I nagged my mom until eventually she brought it down to show me. I settled on top of our blue Formica table so that I could have a bird's-eye view as the plastic sheath was pulled back. It revealed an oddly shaped straw basket that had a hinged lid and an intricate metal lock. I loved it immediately.

On the inside, the basket had a material lining that was bright red. It had moulded sections that were snug nests for a Chinese tea set. My mother handled the small cups with a tender relish. The cups were each painted with a phoenix and a dragon and rimmed with a gold trim. As my mom lifted up the teapot from the centre, it was more cylindrical than squat and its handle was not porcelain but a woven kind of straw. My mom told me it was the tea set she had used for her wedding ceremony, the one that my grandparents sipped from to give their blessing to the union.

A marriage tea ceremony has the bride and groom kneel in front of the older members of the families and offer a cup of tea. It is called *sun poh chai* (daughter-in-law tea). They offer up the tea and after the relative has sipped, they set aside the cup and congratulate the couple with a *lei see*, the double red packets of monetary gifts or a piece of jewellery that has been handed down through the family. The amounts given are linked to lucky numbers. There are no numbers with fours as that in Cantonese is *sei* and sounds similar to the word for dying. Instead, the numbers would be eights or threes, *baat* or *saam*, numbers that sound similar to the words for prosper and for being alive.

Memories of kneeling on the cool drapes of her white wedding dress to offer tea to her parents and her new family elders would have come back to my mother. Then she returned the cups and the pot to their crimson nests, hooked in the lock on the basket, refreshed the grimy plastic bag with a new one and returned her treasure to its spot on top of the yellowed newspaper.

Many years later we found something else that had survived. When Yolanda was at university, a friend's boyfriend told her that he thought he still had some old 8-mm footage from our parents' wedding. His father had long since passed away but he had given some work to my father and taken him on as a general farmhand when my dad first arrived in South Africa. Growing up on a smallholding this friend, Anthony, said he could remember my father as a cool young man that he wanted to hang out with; my father taught him how to tie his shoelaces, he had said with affection.

Anthony gave the cassette to us in a yellowed cardboard case and for years it was like a locked jewellery box that we could not look into because we did not have a projector.

It took some years still for the footage to be freed. Our dad had died by then. The man with the technological magic did not stay far from us and he accepted the coil of film from me with a nod of his head, assuring me that he was absolutely able to do something with it and told me to return in a week's time.

One week later he had a video tape for me. We gathered to watch the video the night I collected it. The video man had decided to dub on some sound because there was no audio track on the original. He had chosen a haunting instrumental rendition of 'Somewhere My Love'. For the first time I could see that my mother's bridesmaids had peach-coloured mini-dresses and my granny's neat two-piece outfit was a brocade of pale blue and silver. The static black and white photos came to life as the film footage betrayed the posed and poised silver halide images.

The film captured my parents walking towards the Wits Great Hall steps, the iconic facade of the central block of the university's buildings, my father strutting and puffing on a cigarette. He played up for the camera a bit with an exaggerated puff and a wave. My mom was coy, trying to keep from tripping over the clumsy froth of her wedding gown train.

We smiled and laughed in our living room that night. We saw our dad as a young man for the first time, not the workhorse that he became. My mother beamed as she watched and she kept talking over the dubbed songs and filling us in. The memories tumbled out of her and had her pointing out people at the wedding and remembering in full-colour detail. We asked about our dad – he seemed arrogant almost – and she smiled and said yes he was a bit of a 'ducktail' or at least a wannabe 'ducktail', sporting that greased-back, middle-parted at the back hairdo that was supposed to be a sign of the rebel and the Western-styled non-conformist in the 1950s and 60s. He swaggered more than he walked as the protagonist on that video.

Chinese weddings are big events traditionally and full of symbolism, colour and a display of customs and traditions. Even though my parents were legally married in a court, the real ceremony played out on their wedding day in front of friends and family and by following the time-held conventions that included the ancestors and the deities. My mother married out of her aunt's house. There is a small photo of her on a single bed dressed in her wedding gown as the activities buzzed around her in preparation for her big day.

The groom and his groomsmen arrived to fetch my mother but traditionally the men are stopped from collecting the bride until the groom pays a 'fee' to the sisters of the house; sisters here are all the unmarried women in the bride's circle. The young women block the entrance and demand a fee, usually starting with an outrageous amount featuring a lot of eights. Eight, which is pronounce *baat*, sounds similar to the Cantonese word for fortune, *faat*. When the men are not able to comply, the women come up with forfeits for the groom and his party to perform. Each fulfilled forfeit means they drop an eight from the fun until the amount is a fair sum that the groom can manage. The men will also arrive with a cardboard tray of flowers. It is a Western adaptation and includes a bouquet for the bride, corsages, buttonholes and other gifts that the bride's family accepts. More *lei see* is passed around throughout the day as family members pass on the monetary gift that is meant to bring luck and good fortune to mark the auspiciousness of the day.

My grandparents did not expect the traditional bride prices and the toing and froing of gifts, mainly because my father had been orphaned and was not represented by any of his own family's elders. But there were the traditions observed of gifts of dried delicacies of shiitake mushroom, shrimps, scampi and wolf berries and bolts of luxurious fabrics and linen. My mother also left her parents' home with a small trousseau that my Ah Goung and Ah Por had saved up for. There were heavily embroidered cushions and square cloths with four straps. They were actually handmade cloths to cradle babies on a mother's back. They were intended to be a lucky omen to rush on the welcome arrival of babies.

That night of their wedding my mother and father feasted like the happy young couple that they were. The tables were laden with eight courses plus dessert all with symbolic relevance and they sat under a sign of double happiness. There were images of dragons, the *loung*, and the *feung haung*, or phoenix, to represent the union of the man and the woman.

The reception was held at the Jack Eustice Hall, a small venue in the south of Johannesburg. When we were children my mother always pointed it out to us when we went down to Booysens Reserve. It was a venue that held a romance for me when I was little as I imagined my parents' wedding day. Even before the end of the 1980s, though, the building had crumpled, growing smaller and smaller as the grass seemed to creep higher up along its walls with bubbled and peeling paint. When I was last there, some years ago, the plot had been turned into a small-sized truck hire place.

But that night, the hall was splendid for this young couple. They were in a celebratory mood, ready to enter a new chapter of life as a married couple in the community. They moved from table to table being toasted by their guests. They were now Mr and Mrs Ho . . . just like it says on the small label my mother has written in English and affixed to a DVD cover of her wedding footage – the 8-mm film has made another technology transfer from video to DVD, even though my mother's Mr Ho did not get to see any of this.

Growing up with Mr and Mrs Ho

The newlyweds moved into a semi-detached Bertrams house before the dawn of the decade of the 1970s. They rented a room from an old Chinese widow, who also lived in the house. Mom pussyfooted around the old lady. She was not her mother-in-law, but some old aunties always watch for young brides to cook a dinner that does not get a nod from their husbands. Some old aunties also listen too closely at the bedroom door and ask too many questions about when a baby is going to be on the way.

It was a relief when some months later the old woman moved out, and arrangements were made for my mom and dad to rent the whole house.

It was a good thing, too, because my mother had not disappointed the old aunties. She was pregnant a few months after the wedding and soon Yolanda would make her entrance into the world.

Children make up the trinity of good fortune for Chinese. It is called *Fok*, *Lok*, *Sau* in Cantonese. Along with children, the other two pillars of fortune are wealth and abundance, and longevity. With children, the first prize is a boy child, the one who is able to pass on the family name, not a girl who marries out of the family.

That would come later for my mom and dad as my brother Kelvin followed quickly after my sister was born. There was a bigger gap before I came along, maybe because when the boy child was born the pressure was off a little. But in just under six years all four Ho siblings became the branches on the family tree that were born under a South African sun.

My parents never became rich, but it did not matter to us children. As the years passed we moved from a small rented semi-detached home to a bigger house, still in the east of Johannesburg. Our Millbourn Road house was not a mansion or anything fancy, but it was an achievement for my father. It was a step up from the semi-detached. Our new little gem that now came with a bond, had things we never had before: a garage, some built-in cupboards, wall-to-wall carpeting and the fantastic mystery to us of a bidet in the bathroom.

The previous owners, a Portuguese family, were amateur winemakers. They had caged in the backyard with a network of wire quadrangles to entice juicy red grapes to grow across every spot where the sun shone. We harvested some of the grapes and turned their plump, red bodies into juice. My parents also thought they would try their hand at making a bit of wine, Chinese-style, of course. They enlisted the help of a family friend who had a 'recipe' for wine. The old uncle arrived one weekend for the big brew. The kitchen table was ready with sugar, yeast, buckets of collected grapes and the mess to come. First came the bleeding of the grapes, strangled in a homemade muslin bag. Mom recycled the cloth from the imported long-grain rice we ate, washed the old bags, cut them up and sewed them into the more manageable sizes she could always find uses for.

The grapes splattered patterns of juice on the tiles and the unprotected kettle and kitchen cabinets. Mom carried on squeezing as the old uncle looked on, putting on his glasses every now and again to scrutinise his notes.

Long weeks passed and then came the 'wine' tasting among the adults. We children were grateful we were not supposed to taste the strong-smelling yeasty stuff.

The Ho-made wine was deemed not bad, though my mom and dad and probably this old uncle had never in their lives drunk wine before. And so the wine was to be shared. Over the next few weeks friends and family who visited walked out of our door with samples of the wine and the grape juice all bottled in the plentiful stash of dark green glass bottles that the previous owners had left behind.

Then came the stories – the wine clearly had some kick and friends would tell how they mixed up the juice with the wine by accident. Mom took the calls giggling, covering her mouth with her hand, then laughing some more.

The days of the grapes came to an end. Eventually we got rid of the vines. They were too dark and gloomy, my mom and dad agreed. The old concrete wine press was used to store junk, piled higher and higher each year we lived in the house, and the mini-cellar was transformed into another storeroom for more things that my mother could not let go of – tea sets never used, lunchboxes without lids and all the bargain bulk purchases that helped my mother make her budgets.

Meanwhile, the wires that remained after the vines were cleared made great stepladders to get up the old peach tree that had found a gap of soil in the concrete backyard. I sought out the view from the roof sometimes to see the sunset's orange arch over the city.

The furrowed bumps of the roof's zinc sheeting pushed into my bum; you could not stay very long, just long enough to listen to the dogs claim the coming night with volleys of howls and barks. I watched neighbours slip into their backyards to bring in the laundry, slip-slopping their sandalled feet as they shifted along the washing lines undoing pegs, putting the pegs back into a peg bag and stashing a growing pile of fresh laundry into a waiting bucket. Others were in the kitchen, standing over stoves, moving plates around, getting ready for the evening like the rest of suburbia.

The Judith's Paarl home was perfect with its knobbly peach tree trunk to climb, a backyard level enough to bounce a ball on and later also to set up a fold-away ping-pong table that my mother and brother created, sawing, drilling and painting it into green and white reality. They even attached wheels to make it easier to move around; Kelvin's technical orientation classes were paying off. My dad bought a plastic pool, too, for the backyard and the hot December holidays saw us begging mom to add more and more water. She refused, shushing us with talk of how it would rack up the water bill. We kept trying to edge up the water level when she was not looking. One time Kelvin deliberately left the tap running overnight.

My mom screamed us awake the next morning. We were clumsy and forgetful, she shouted. We nodded in agreement, not owning up that it was a deliberate 'accident', then waited for the heat of the day to splash in the pool that finally looked like the one in the TV advert.

Even dad would come home on a Saturday or Sunday afternoon and decide to go for a swim. Mom would have to go and find a pair of swimming trunks far back in a wardrobe so that dad could have a dip. We have a set of photos that still makes me laugh. In the first picture dad is in his swimming trunks, barely containing a belly of middle-aged spread. In the second photo, mom is with him; she is laughing and dad now has a shirt on, Hawaiian-style with bright motifs. I remember what happened. It was a novelty to see dad in his swimming shorts so we took a picture of that. Then mom said it was terrible that he was posing without a shirt on so he put on the shirt, but it only made him look more comical because it looked like he had no bottoms on at all in the second photo.

As the days wore on, our feet started to squelch along the film of algae that formed at the bottom of the pool. It was the first sign that school was just days away. Soon we would drain the pool into the vegetable patch, no wasting of course, and it would be dried out and folded away.

We spent eighteen years in this house. Again Yolanda, Unisda and I shared the biggest room. It was painted blue and had a flower-painted lampshade that was a wonderful upgrade from the naked bulb in the Bertrams semi.

In our room we brought our dolls to life with the stories we made up for them. Ours were not fantastic Barbies but we loved our plastic wonders with their arched feet ready for small plastic heels, their impossibly tiny waists, their green or blue eyes and the hair we ran toy brushes through. I dressed my doll up, with dresses my mother sewed or scrap pieces of material I could tie into my own designs, to go to a ball like Cinderella and to meet a prince, even though we did not have a Ken doll.

The bedroom also saw me suffering from long bouts of coughing. As a child and into my pre-teen years I woke the household with my coughing fits from something like bronchitis that kept me from my sleep. First Yolanda would come to my bed to try the trick my parents would use by adding an extra pillow or two under my head. I knew I was keeping them up but my lungs would not co-operate. Then eventually mom or dad would come into the room with the Vicks. Two types; the first was sweet menthol that would cool my angry throat and chest. Then there was the Vicks they rubbed on to my back and chest to soothe me and get me back to sleep.

Along with the Vicks, mom and dad had other potions and remedies of healing that were from far away. If I had a cough, the next morning there probably would not be the ordinary Joko tea, our standard morning fare. Instead, inside my mother's little stainless steel teapot would be heads of dried chrysanthemum flowers infused in hot water. I hated this 'clarifying' tea as a child. Bits of petal and pollen always made it past the strainer and I would be gagging and sticking my fingers into my mouth to retrieve the endless little bits of desiccated flower. It had a clean, strong smell that I could not bear. Mom tried to make it more palatable with a bit of sugar or with a sweet to chase the tea.

'Drink up then you can have a sweet,' my mom would say to us as we walked into the kitchen and groaned as we were greeted by all the mugs lined up with a sweet next to each. We would eye out the cups, seeing which one had the least of the icky tea, then try to make a grab for it.

We would hesitate and mom would start to get cross. 'Don't start your nonsense, drink up quickly, it is all cooled down already.'

My mother also made another brew, a bitter, truly medicinal tea, the *leung cha*, also a hot brew for cooling the system and bringing back the body's balance. I much preferred this bitter tea to the floating bits of petals and pollen from the flower brew. Mostly I just thought about the sweet we were getting afterwards as we all pulled a face and gulped down the tea.

There were also a few made-up remedies, concoctions from old wives' tales, common sense and creativity. For bee stings my mother said a paste of sugar and water could draw out the poison from the sting. There was butter on my knee the time I collided with a big rose bush in a relative's garden. For a tummy ache my mother took a peeled hard-boiled egg along with a silver coin (my mother used some of the special R1 coins that she reserved and which she said were genuinely silver just because they apparently sounded different when they were tapped) and wrapped the combo in cloth so she could roll it over our abdomens. It was probably the heat that calmed our cramping tummies but as the coin became discoloured with a dark grey stain my mother was convinced that the toxins had passed through the coin and were contained in that boiled egg that was now the egg of sickness and had to be thrown away.

The years passed and we became teens. The remedies felt increasingly foolish and backwards. I turned more to my diaries and journals and spent hours dreaming into the pressed ceiling of our bedroom of all the possibilities of when I would be older.

I kept a diary for many years as a girl. On the front I scribbled 'strictly private' and I also included a death threat for my prying brother and sisters. I found hiding places for my journals, shoving them under my mattress or under stacks of other things I was hoarding. My stash of Christmas cards grew with letters from the pen pals I picked up in Botswana and the United Kingdom, a girl in Cape Town and a dear, dear friend who left our school in Standard Three. Candy was the only white child in our school where her mom was the English teacher for the seniors. But when her mom left her teaching post at the Chinese school, Candy left, too. It was the end of Standard Three, we were nine years old and in our group of four, with my friends Pamela and Christmas, we gave ourselves code names – Small Mouse, Medium Mouse, Tall Mouse and Big Mouse. Candy was Big Mouse, not because she was big, but even with Pamela as Tall Mouse, Candy still towered over us, her short-by-comparison Chinese friends. When Candy left the school, she ended up being a pen pal even though she lived in the same city we did.

In my diary I would write about the one or two boys I thought I was in love with. I would muse over their passing comments or some other fantasy I could nurture in my head, and in my diary.

On the lined pages I raged against my mother for not understanding me. I wished her dead, then I would beg for forgiveness, then wish that I were dead. My parents were just not cool enough, they did not understand, they were old-fashioned and so strict about everything.

In our garage there was an array of second-hand cars over the years. There was a tank of a BMW, so old it still had a speedometer with a needle that ran from west to east and headlights the size of footballs. I was embarrassed by the monster, especially when it had to be fired up to chase down the school bus. On days that we missed the school bus my mom, and sometimes my dad, would drive from stop to stop to try to catch up with it as it left the eastern suburbs along Louis Botha Avenue to Bramley where the Chinese school was. It was teenage humiliation personified for us. Dad would manoeuvre to cut off the bus, hooting and waving. When the driver saw him, or maybe his pyjamas with their fleur-de-lys patterns or some other repeated logo across the cotton two-piece, he would stop. Of course, by then everyone would be peering out the window and the old BMW would be heaving as it came to an exhausted idle and we made our shuffled exits.

For many years there was also our much-loved blue Mini that my father bought for my mother a few years after she finally learnt to drive. The little car had two doors and back windows that only pushed open a few centimetres. It was the car we would rush to, knowing it meant my mom had arrived to fetch us from the bus stop when it rained. Highveld storms saved us from the weekday uphill walk home. From the school bus we would make a dash for the tiny car, pull its passenger seat up and over and tumble into the car that is called 'mini' for a reason. Unisda, Kelvin and I took the back seat, Yolanda as the eldest got the front seat. The Mini only had one windscreen wiper, the windscreen was so small. I loved that little car that took us everywhere while we were growing up.

The Mini also took us to a roadhouse at the edge of Hillbrow or to the local Wimpy when we were due a treat, or when my mom decided to splash out. Mom was a dedicated mother, cooking up noodles on birthdays and turning slabs of pork into slow-roasted crackling and glories of fat and flesh. She also simmered clear soups for clarifying some or other ailment and seeped bitter teas to lower our fire or breath, to *har hei*, when we were ill, like those chrysanthemum teas. It was all about tweaking the balance and equilibrium for a healthy body. But my mom also liked treats sometimes, even the Western ones.

So every now and again we had the enchantment of something like the roadhouse's banana split. A strange little bowl, like a glass nest, would hold scoops of ice cream wedged between the fruit as chocolate sauce made marbled swirls across the glass. Toasted sandwiches with cheese turned into dripping goo would also be on our roadhouse menu of Western food.

In our house we also acquired a quintessentially Western invention – a plastic Christmas tree. We anointed the green spikes each year with tinsel, miniature reindeer and smiling snowmen. Every year my mother would buy each of us a new decoration. One of my favourites was a little white mouse with big eyes, a red cape and a plastic violin. Even as an adult I look for the little mouse each Christmas and place him on his bit of fake evergreen among the tinsel that has survived from when we were children. We learnt to sing Christmas carols and strung Christmas cards across our mantelpiece.

But we were a home that also prepared for Chinese new year with a spring clean; the pantry was restocked, the incense at the altars was relit and dishes were cooked that had lucky-sounding names. Dishes like *faat choi*, the fine, black strands of seaweed whose name is meant to bring good luck. Some of the dishes included prawns fried in chilli and garlic. Prawns were cooked because they are called *har* in Chinese, for joy and laughter, as in ha ha, hee hee.

There was also the celebration of the moon festival and of the mid-autumn harvest that dominates the lunar calendar, edged into second place only by new year's. We ate the rich, sweet moon cakes heavy with their crumbling dense pastry, embossed with writing and their lotus-paste fillings with a preserved, slightly salted egg yolk at its centre to represent the celestial orb as it grew heavy and full, a reminder to give thanks for the autumnal bounty. Even though we were so far flung south, we stayed linked to these festivals and commemorations of another hemisphere's seasons and calendars. Our remembrances were made with dumplings wrapped in banana leaves for a sacrificed sage, a hero drawn from a distant history of emperors and dynasties. We also had a Confucius Day at school, meant to show respect for the wise teacher and those who followed in his footsteps. It was Confucius's teachings that were hallowed, but the day was also supposed to be about showing respect for elders, teachers and life's lessons.

On this day, which we celebrated at the end of every September, some rich man on the PTA would pass out *lei see*, the red lucky packets, to all the schoolchildren. We all got R1 each from this man to splurge on Fizzy Bites sweets that went for 10 cents a roll or a packet of crisps for 40 cents.

We loved the *lei see* but as the saying goes 'there's no free lunch'. Our Confucius Day *lei see* came with the price of having to sit through a special assembly that included the PTA honcho making a very long speech.

As he walked to the podium to deliver his speech in Chinese, followed by a few words in shaky English, the older children would set their stopwatches. Peep-peep, peep-peep the watches would fire off in synchronicity, setting off snickers in the lofty school hall that was overseen by a picture of Chiang Kai-shek in the front and Sun Yat Sen in the back. First came the muffled laughs, then the vicious glares from the teachers who could not pinpoint the culprits among the cross-legged mass seated on the floor.

These worlds blended easily for us as children – moon cakes next to the custard slices with French names and spongy cakes representing a tower in

Portugal next to steamed Chinese *baos*. The Portuguese cakes came from a bakery that my father liked to shop at in Bertrams where there was a big Portuguese community. It was also the merging of the world of the *lei see* packets in bright red with gold writing along with Rudolph the red-nosed reindeer at Christmas and chocolate Easter bunnies. We were told these were hollow to remember the empty tomb of a resurrected Jesus Christ; we thought it was rude that the manufacturers had cheated us out of all the chocolate that could have been in the middle.

To be one of four siblings was a good number as we grew up. We were like a readymade cricket team, Ho-style. We made up our own rules; if you hit the ball on to the roof it was a four, if you hit it into the veggie patch it was a six. Six because by the time you had lifted the spinach plants searching for the tennis ball or crunched through the vines that spread out with winter melon buds, the batsman would have run up a victory.

There were enough of us to play hide-and-seek or whatever made-up games we concocted. We played our version of fun Olympics; we scooped water from one section of the yard with a lunchbox or old tea tin and carried it to the other end and then we saw who had managed to spill the least. Kelvin built makeshift ramps for us to fly our bikes over. We had two bikes between the four of us. And we balanced across beams that we would set up between two chairs to get crowned the Ho champion of whatever school holiday.

Before we had the backyard of the Millbourn Road house, we used the *stoep* of the Bertrams house to play games of balancing on the rounded edge that marked the end of the front passage and the start of the tiny split garden. We would distract each other to see who would topple first. We also dangled yo-yos here and Unisda and I tried to mimic Kelvin's tricks like 'walking the dog' or 'around the world', and we sent tops spinning across the fine cracks that lined the red floor. The *stoep* was polished a shiny red after years and years of Cobra polish filled up old cracks that pooled with water when it rained.

This *stoep* was also where my mother's love for plants flourished in a mish-mash of old cans, faded biscuit tins and plastic pots balanced on chipped teacup saucers and lids of old lunchboxes. This place was home to flowers sprouted from shared clippings, nicked nodes from neighbours' gardens and the feisty propagation of spring onions that needed little more than a bit of soil to grow. Many Chinese also believe that a good dousing of human urine collected in night buckets makes the spring onions grow thicker and stronger. We were not children of the village, and even though my mom persists with the practice to this day, it grossed us out and we always pulled up our faces in the determined, dramatic way that children do so well.

The urine sprinkled on the ground around the spring onions, like the miscellany of mismatched pots used for her plants, was characteristic of my mother – practical and intuitive rather than scientific and determined. She was sensible and frugal and her unsentimentality was hard-boiled, impenetrable.

My school pinafore dangled way below my knees as I started Grade One as a five-year-old with the 1970s coming to an end. Mom said it was so I could grow into the pinafore and be spared the unsightly telltale signs of a released hem that would divide the faded fabric from the released hems of virgin pinafore. I remained convinced that I looked like a geek kid with no knees and it did not help that my school blazer was Yolanda's hand-me-down or that my home-done haircut left me with an uneven fringe. In primary school I was teased by a few girls who told me only boys wore trousers when mom decided it was ridiculous to keep replacing ripped stockings for a child over the entire winter season. She said I would wear trousers – they were warmer anyway, she would say with brisk dismissal as I began to protest.

I also survived hand-knitted jumpers, when everyone else has the finely machine-knitted ones bought in the uniform Mecca of Burgers Brothers in Mayfair. This was where all schoolchildren in the province went to buy their school uniforms. When we did have to buy something that my mom could not make, we undertook an annual trip to the store in the days before the new school term. We children would run through the racks and racks of school uniforms, poking fun at some schools' regulation hats and coveting the pink-tasselled sashes of others.

The shop attendant folded the blazers and uniforms in brown paper before slipping them into plastic bags. Mom or dad counted a wad of notes and left with not much change. I knew how much it dented my parents' budget, but there was also delight knowing that I had my own new blazer.

I even made it through the carefully Tippexed-out mistakes on my book labels as my mother wrapped our books and put labels on the top right-hand corners at the beginning of each new year. Even as I begged her to replace the labels, she said something like: 'It is a waste of a label and no one will notice.' I would sulk and be cross that she had made the mistake in the first place. But how could her neat, clear script of the English language make allowances for what was little more than her making outlines of long and odd words – like 'Comprehension' or 'Science'.

My mother was the hands-on parent. She attended PTA meetings and my father went to work. My parents did not care too much about getting involved at school the way some parents did, like 'Mr Red Lucky Packet', who was out to impress others and smooth the way for his children. But my mother always did her bit. She made us cakes for fund-raising and she came to the library days when parents were asked to buy extra books to bolster the shelves of books and encyclopaedias.

After one of these events the media centre teacher told me she was truly pleased my mother had bought a set of educational finger puppets. Parents overlooked the sewn-up felt faces, choosing something with spines and small print over and over again. At first I was a little embarrassed that everybody else's parents went for the safe option of no-nonsense educational literature. But as it sank in, I realised my mother, in her own way, always knew there were more ways to learn than just through books.

It was my mom who woke us up in time for school and packed our lunches. She cooked dinner and ate our meals with us in the hours before my father finally returned home. She was the one who ticked off the list of erasers, coloured pens and crayons that we needed to be educated in this Western world.

Polishing everyone's school shoes was my task each week and I sometimes had to be nagged to get around to it. But I developed my own method of just how much polish to apply, how long to wait for the waxy goodness to work its magic as it baked in the sun and how to work the polishing strokes quickly enough to get a sparkly shine afterwards.

Mom shouted at us when we forgot to offload our lunchboxes in the kitchen sink on a Friday afternoon. Left in our schoolbags until Sunday night, the lunchboxes would grow wild and stinky, full of strange moulds and furry spores that she would have to clean out.

We lost our lunchboxes often and it forced mom to go to the extreme of etching our names into the boxes, in Chinese and English, with a sharp knife. While other children had printed labels on their jerseys and gym shorts, my mother painstakingly sewed our names on to the tags with her neat stitching.

We attended the Chinese school in Johannesburg. It started off in End Street in Doornfontein, with the motorway arching overhead like a constant concrete cloud. It was a spooky, grey building without a blade of grass anywhere. I started nursery school and Grade One at this school, until the community secured better premises in Bramley.

The community was so small that when I started Grade One I had just seven classmates. We learnt the English alphabet with its vowels, consonants and capital letters, as well as that each has a baby letter, too. We also tested out our sharpened HB pencils on the sequenced strokes that made up our Chinese names. Chinese names start with the surnames first, followed usually by two other characters that complete most Chinese names. Interestingly, the first thing I ever published was written in Chinese and submitted to the local Chinese newspaper. It was a simple piece I wrote in high school that started with 'My name is . . .' and included who my parents were, my hobbies and the pets I loved.

The school had moved to its Bramley Park location by the time I started Grade Two. I found out a few years later that the school that used to be at the site was actually only a primary school, but our entire school, primary, high and two kindergarten classes, all fitted into the new premises. There was even room for a school cat and years later a hostel was built on the same site.

There were only Chinese South Africans in our school but by the time I reached high school there were a few Taiwanese children who had joined us. They and their parents were part of the new wave of Chinese migrants to South Africa in the late 1970s and 80s. The Taiwanese were welcomed by the National Party government. Unlike my parents and that generation of stowaway Chinese, these new migrants had something to offer: trade. Sanctions had hit the country and the breakaway island of Taiwan was still willing to do business and to bring in its investment dollars.

Even with a few Taiwanese students, by the time I finished school in the early 1990s, we were a class of only fifteen matriculants. Small classes meant that we did not have the benefit of a wide subject choice for our senior pupils and we were not part of any major school sports leagues that had dedicated coaches and expensive kit for their top teams. Our sports field was a grass patch for everything from potato-sack races for the juniors, to playing makeshift baseball and every other unstructured sport that PT teachers could concoct.

But small classes did have an unexpected benefit. Even in this tiny Transvaal Education Department school we got more individual attention and teachers could actually teach instead of worrying too much about unruly behaviour. The majority of teachers were state-paid, white teachers. They took up their posts here because they could expect well-behaved, courteous and hard-working students, which was the behaviour drilled into us from when we were little. Growing up I did not realise there was something like a Chinese work ethic.

When I started work, a white colleague of mine who had gone to a Catholic school with a few Chinese children, ribbed me when I was fussing over some small detail: 'What is up with you Chinese kids? If you are not top of the class, then you must be second in class. Why don't you just relax a bit?'

I rolled my eyes, threw a pen at him from across the room and ignored the stupid stereotype. When I went back to study as the only Chinese student in the class at varsity, the anthropological data again showed up the same thing: Asian students scored better. I was proving them right, too, with my marks but I put it down to being an older student. But good anthropology always points to context and of course it has nothing to do with genes but with socialisation and following the worn path of what those within a grouping conform to.

On some level, I fitted that picture as a child because growing up was about discipline, respect for elders and a determination to excel or die trying. It was not for personal achievement but for your family's honour, sparing your parents shame.

At school we jumped at bells, lined up touching the shoulders of the child in front of us, to be perfectly spaced. Detention and visits to the principal were dreaded punishments and for the most 'wayward' children. What constituted wayward was pretty regular really, from wearing non-regulation hairbands to backchatting a teacher.

We did our homework, jumped up to greet teachers and there was even a class monitor who screamed 'chi lee', in mandarin, the command that got us scooting our chairs back and standing to attention. 'Cheeng lee' the

103

monitor would continue, and we would say '*lau shu how*', the mandarin for good morning teacher. If it was one of the white teachers the singsong greeting was 'Good morning Mrs So-and-so and welcome'. The teacher nodded, greeted and we got back to work.

I suppose it was the expectation our parents had of us. In our family, mom reminded us frequently that the Chinese school had been set up by the sweat, toil and even blood of the early Chinese. The community had fought to establish a Chinese school in Johannesburg, even though they knew they had no rights and no bargaining chips as second-class citizens.

One of the key negotiators, who travelled between Johannesburg and Pretoria to meet with authorities regarding the Chinese school, was killed in a car crash returning from one of these meetings. At the old Chinese cemetery in Newclare, this man's monolithic tombstone stands proud. When we visited the cemetery, we were always encouraged to pay our respects and to place a flower or two to honour his efforts.

My parents, like so many other Chinese parents, thought that the Chinese school was the best educational option for their children. The small school did not have the money for extras like swimming pools, a proper science laboratory or student exchange programmes. But the extras did not matter too much because Chinese parents placed a higher premium on retaining some of our 'Chineseness' at a school that would promote Chinese culture, language and with it the ethic and discipline that they expected from us. We ended up with school mottos like a 'sense of shame', not a more child-friendly 'humility' or 'modesty'. It was hardcore, and it was the way it was meant to be, a little like the shame my mother called up when she said, 'Have you forgotten the name of your father's village?' They wanted us to grow up knowing other Chinese children and in that way to have some hope that we would marry within the race.

Even without the extras, I was well aware that our school was not the worst. Only a few kilometres away from our school in Bramley were schools in Alexandra township that did not even have the luxury of enough school desks for everyone or glass in some of their windows.

I did not stop to question why the children were worse off than we were and I did not ask why we did not all go to school together. Sadly, I simply trusted that this was the way things should be.

Most of the children in the Chinese school came from families where fathers and mothers were shopkeepers or fahfee men and women, or both. But nobody spoke about fahfee; it remained an open secret. Many years after school I interviewed some friends and acquaintances for an anthropology research essay. Many of the people I interviewed were my peers and they said it was the first time they had ever spoken openly about fahfee, even to other Chinese people who were not in their families. Friends said they kept to the code of silence because it was what was expected and it was what would protect their families from the police and the authorities. Unlike my dad, most of them had a front that they could use: a shop, a video business, a butchery. But they all knew that fahfee was how food was put on the table.

I also asked them how they navigated the questions as they got older and entered into broader society, a mixed society. How did they answer that ordinary question, 'What does your father do?'

Many said they invented something, some said they changed the subject, but they still kept to the code of silence and they still bore the weight of the stigma even if it was internally.

Stigma and silence came to be so much a part of our lives because we existed outside of the law essentially. So we got these dual identities – one we owned up to in our inner circle of community and family and another that we claimed or managed when we were in the company of 'others'.

But even if our parents were seen essentially as lawbreakers by the government, our school was run with unquestionable discipline; mostly the children toed the line and stayed within the boundaries of what was expected. Even the so-called naughty children were nothing like the teenage nightmares that we heard about.

We went along with the way of the world, we did not question, we followed a state-approved curriculum and we accepted the picture of life as the apartheid government presented it in its textbooks. We did not register that it was a history that did not include the context and reality of our lives.

The bus drivers, garden staff and kitchen staff at our school were all black or coloured. We called the coloured man Mr Abrahams and we treated the black staff with the respect that was expected of us but we still called them only by their first names. No one bothered to tell us their surnames.

As the years went by, there were a few teachers who shook things up a bit and their lessons pulled back the blinkers a little for me. I am grateful because we were painstakingly protected from the outside world and I did not realise how much until long after I matriculated.

105

In my early high school years an English teacher, Mrs Southey, pushed the boundaries. Years later I realised that her covert way of teaching us to challenge the world as it was presented to us in apartheid South Africa must have made her hugely unpopular among those in the Chinese school establishment who would have stuck to the model of not rocking the boat, of keeping us insulated from the evils of the outside world for our own good.

Still, this teacher made her point. When we were meant to follow the government syllabus to commemorate the Great Trek anniversary, she asked us not for an historical essay but to write a typical propaganda speech that the Voortrekker leaders would have used to stir up the would-be trekkers to pack up and go. When she chose a book to read it was *To Sir With Love* about a black teacher in an all-white school and the lessons of prejudice and stereotype and ultimately of humanity that came from those pages. When we were new teenagers, all infatuated and filled with raging hormones, she once commented: 'The children in the schools in the townships have the same issues that you do; they are also fighting with their parents and worrying about their pimples and the boy that they have a crush on.'

It was a light-bulb moment, though years later most of my classmates from that time just shrugged about these lessons; they could barely place this teacher, who predictably only lasted two years in the regimented rigour of a school that could not tolerate such out-of-the-box thinking.

Mrs Southey, though she may never know it, was one of my 'extras'; I preferred her lessons about the wide world I knew nothing about over a school pool or a computer centre.

Johnny Depp, Segregation and Sequins

School was our job as children. My father went to work, my mother looked after the home and we had to go to school. That was all. I never knew the concept of being rewarded for doing well at school. I still cannot understand the negotiations of parents with their children about good behaviour or about doing well. The promises of gold stars lined up on a chart or a car for a matric pass did not feature in our family.

We were expected to work hard, do better than we thought we could. We did not slack off or squirm out of things that we were not particularly fond of. We never missed school unless we were so sick that it even scared my mom.

At best I was average at school. There were a few subjects I did better in than others. Languages proved to be a strength; anything involving fractions and equations terrified me, as did the prospect of playing netball for weekly PT sessions on the grassy sportsfield. I was so bad at team sports that even some of my own friends chose me last when they got to choose players for their sides. Then again, I could not blame them as I ducked the flying volleyball I was supposed to lift up over the net and my aim for a netball or basketball hoop almost always was a miss.

Education was a priority, though, and I knew I had to keep at it. Each term we brought home our report cards. My mom looked at them first. The first term was usually a breeze. My mom looked at the symbols that we had got and she might ask us about a subject where she could see we had strayed from the first few letters of the alphabet. It was the second and third terms that presented more problems. Now there was something to compare with and if we had slipped through the year, then we were grilled about our not being able to keep up our grades.

Each time we came home with our reports we also left them on the table for our father to see when he got home. By the time he saw them, they had already been signed by my mother. He called us over and gave us the same pep talk as my mother had and also told us to keep working harder.

We were all expected to make a showing at the school prize-giving awards every year without even a word being said about it. My brother swept the board clean a lot of the time. Kelvin achieved in the classroom, and in almost everything else from ping-pong to debating, tennis and maths Olympiads. He went on to be head boy and, unfathomably to us, he even had girls interested in him. We girls did okay; Yolanda, the motor-mouth, did well in speeches and debating but mostly we brought home certificates and book vouchers for things like bagging the odd distinction or two, or good progress or some other pat-on-the-back-type award. But we scraped by and mom lined us up for pictures after these prize-giving ceremonies with our blazers neatly cleaned especially for the awards. She took a few frames on our Kodak camera that flipped open to make a wonky 'L' shape that doubled as a handgrip as you framed your shot. Then she lined up my brother's trophies on the mantelpiece and put our certificates into albums. She would say, 'Good, well done, now you must keep it up for next year.' Apart from Kelvin's fancy trophies that were part of the floating silverware for the school, we girls sometimes came home with a baby trophy, the kind that is smaller than an egg cup, and the school was happy for us to keep those forever. Over the years, they filled up with the odd paper clips, a few coins, lost screws that used to fit somewhere and a host of small things without a home.

Even the floating trophies had to survive their year in the Ho household. Most times my mother bought some Brasso and Kelvin polished them up to return them for the next year's prize-giving. One year, though, one of the trophies dropped on the floor and one of its 'ears' broke off.

'Just tell the teacher that it broke,' we urged Kelvin to own up as the day for returning the cup crept up.

But he had a better idea. Inside our mess of a hardware cupboard was one of Ah Goung's old soldering irons and the pliable wire that is melted to form little droplets of metal. This was Kelvin's plan to rescue the cup.

We gathered around him under the kitchen's fluorescent light, like there was an operation that was going to take place, remembering a little how he had 'operated' on Unisda's and my talking bears years earlier only to leave them mute forever. He tried to keep the metal patch as neat as possible but the soldering iron was angry against the silver-plated cup and flared up with a grey burn stain. The droplet of melted metal had also turned out to be more blob than delicate droplet and oozed out untidily.

Kelvin found sandpaper, more Brasso and went to work, but it was not going to escape notice. All we said again was, 'Just tell the teacher,' grateful that we were not going to have to do it.

These pieces of embossed paper and engraved silver cups did make my parents quietly proud. They kept working precisely for these. And if we kept working hard and achieving, they knew that they would have given us the best chance when we became adults.

School was also the sum of our social lives. If a social activity was linked to school or being organised by the school then we could convince our parents to let us go along. They said no most of the times to things like sleepovers, parties and weekends away, although as I got to high school my parents let up a little on keeping us from all the freedoms that we thought other children had. Yolanda and Kelvin had navigated the strange seas of teenage life with relative calm. They did come home from the movies, they did not make phone calls from jail or end up being in rehab, and this paved the way for Unisda and me. But we still grew up not really asking to go out much. We knew our parents did not approve and we took it mostly as just the way things were done in our house.

Birthdays were not about invites, jumping castles and party packs. Our birthdays were spent with our family as Ah Goung and Por Por came by either on the weekend before or after our birthday. Sometimes we got to take a cake or two to class to share with our homeroom teacher and our classmates on our actual birthday.

To celebrate, my mother bought a cake and set it up with candles and then she fried up a tray or two of noodles. She finally sliced cabbage and carrots with strips of chicken or pork cooked quickly in a hot wok fragranced with a knob of ginger and crushed cloves of garlic. These became the accompaniment to the noodles. Sometimes it was a simpler version of the noodles with spring onions, ginger and garlic, just as good to eat. Noodles at birthdays are a must; they signify long life in Chinese symbolism. Sometimes as a treat she hauled out the mini-rotisserie oven that my dad had given her. She skewered in a chicken dunked in her own marinade and set the bird into the TV-like oven to cook slowly. The chicken completed each revolution with a plonk and wobble on the uncertain rotisserie rods until it crisped up into golden deliciousness.

Before eating, the food and cake were arranged on a tray and taken to the various altars in the house. One for my ancestors, the *joe sien*, and the other for the gods of the home, placed at the entrance of the house. My mother lit candles and incense at the altars to invite the ancestors to the celebrations. She whispered a few words over the food, a blessing and a prayer, and then clasped her hands together. Then she lifted the tray to offer the food and poured a bit of the tea and sometimes whisky on to the floor or the side of the tray. This symbolised sharing with the ancestors. The birthday girl or boy did the same and we would mimic the ritual and think a little about our granny and grandad whom we never got to meet.

Only then would we sing happy birthday, in English, around our feast, bringing out the old Kodak to snap a few shots and then cut the cake and make a wish in the Western way of blowing out candles to make a secret dream come true.

If we were not celebrating over a weekend, it would likely be something after school. We would save a slice of cake and some noodles for my dad, who arrived home much later. If it was a weekend he would try to come home early, or at least take a few hours to be home to cut the cake with us. But if he came home after the cake cutting we would flood him with the stories of our family party as he sat down at the dinner table. I would take him my gift of a teddy bear or doll or dress to show him my newest object of delight and to thank him, even though I knew my mother chose and bought our presents. He would put a forkful or two of cake in his mouth and indulge my excited stories. Like my mom, he was not big on sweet stuff, but he ate some of my birthday cake and fussed a little over my present as I twisted the doll's leg to show him what it could do or kissed my new teddy, showering it with the love that is set aside especially for new toys.

The last day of school was always a highlight. To begin with, it was a civvies day. For weeks we would plan what we were going to wear on that last day when we could leave our school uniforms on their hangers at home. That top with that skirt, what chunky earrings we could team up with our shoes or what cardigans would be fashionably stylish enough to drape over our shoulders. My mother hated us tying jerseys around our waists, she said it looked tacky and cheap.

The last day of school was also about sanding off the graffiti from our tables, giving our classrooms the big once-over, doing the windows, dusting shelves and polishing them up for the new year and cleaning the school grounds completely. We came to school with dust rags and Mr Min wood polish and went aerosol wild. We lined up for a final assembly and then we were off with screaming and clapping as the last bell of the year sounded and we went to have the big outing of the year.

Just about everybody in the school went to the movies in the old Ster Kinekor cinema in the centre of town. I went with my group of friends and we wandered through the Carlton Centre a little, looked around a shop or two before having a burger and milkshake at a Wimpy and then crowning off our day with a movie. The other favourite was to go ice skating at the Carlton ice rink. We would re-familiarise ourselves with being on the ice after a year's absence, then we would go round and round as lights flashed across the frozen arena and songs by Aha and Depeche Mode filled the cooled space.

By the late 1980s, Chinese children were allowed access to these public places so the world seemed fine to me. There were Slush Puppies to slurp and songs from Erasure and OMD to hum along to. The world of apartheid seemed far away. We knew that the world was split between black and white. We Chinese were the small wedge that fitted somewhere in-between, but even this striated racial madness seemed to be the ordinary order of things. I did not know that we were considered second-class citizens, or more accurately, that we were in no-man's-land for the apartheid government – too white to be black, but too black to be white.

I trusted completely that the adults knew what they were doing. It was my job to bring home a good improvement certificate at the very least and not to smoke or get pregnant before I could drive. Their job as the grown-ups was to keep the world in the serene balance of my childhood fantasy.

Our Afrikaans teacher, a wise, no-nonsense woman whom you respected and feared simultaneously, had been with the school for decades. One of her earlier memories with the school was being asked to leave a theatre when as a white woman she had taken a group of senior pupils from our Chinese school to watch a play.

When she told the story I was scared that it could happen to us, even though the 1990s were already on the horizon. My teenage self was mortified at the idea of how embarrassing it would be if we had to be humiliated by being turned away from a play or festival event. I imagined the white children who would be lined up with their tickets, pointing and snickering at us as we had to make our way back to a bus.

That never happened to us but racial cleavages were still keeping the country apart and the 1980s were nervous days. At school, the safety drills of the mid-1980s were part of the anxious everyday. Every few months the siren went off and a crackling message came through the school intercom telling us to observe the siren as a drill. During these drills we were supposed to discern whether it was for a fire, for stones and bombs being thrown through the windows, or if it was a hurricane about to hit us. We were to leave the windows open or closed, depending on the drill. Then we had to push our desks against the walls and take cover under them. We were also supposed to have taken careful notice of posters of mines and bombs that were put up on noticeboards throughout the school. If we were good children we would have examined carefully the 3-D posters of limpet mines and other explosives and been on the lookout for these strange objects throughout the school. They looked frightening enough, but I did not appreciate their capacity for evil. I was too young to understand apartheid and all its devices of destruction. I was more concerned about the possibility of a hurricane in Bramley Park.

Still, we all did the drills; we took them seriously and naively anticipated the day we would get to see if pushing our desks against the walls and crawling under them did stop flying Molotov cocktails.

At the same time, our parents made us cautious of dustbins in town; it was about the only inkling I had that things were not exactly as they should be. The Zibi bins, named after a no-litter campaign mascot at the time, were dangerous, we were warned. Each dustbin was a possible receptacle for a bomb, my mother reminded us, as we returned a Nancy Drew or Tintin book to the central library that we visited on many Saturday mornings.

'Do not stand anywhere near the dustbins. Stay inside the library and get to the bus stop just in time so you are not waiting there for too long,' my mom told us.

The world may have been a dangerous place but I did not connect it with politics or the leaders that we saw on TV. My world remained carefully insulated at school and at home.

Government schools were not allowed to talk politics and politics was not part of our home either. High school came with other crises for me. There were pimples to zap, hair to perm, or not, boys to talk about and the weekly *Pop Shop* videos to watch. On our bedroom doors and walls were the pictures of the dream boys of the 1980s: Johnny Depp, hot from his *21 Jump Street* days, River Phoenix, before he dropped dead from a drug overdose, and George Michael, before we knew what being gay meant.

I hated my teeth more than politics or racial segregation and uprisings. My teens came with the catastrophe of bone and enamel gone wild in my mouth. I never showed my teeth in photos or my hand was always cupped over my mouth. My lips remained steadfast guards against the skew and crowded teeth. I dreamt of braces, the miracle wires that could straighten my teeth, like some children had. But we could not afford braces and I never asked for them.

But there was a stroke of luck. As we were in a government school we had annual medical check-ups. A nurse arrived and she set up her makeshift rooms in the science laboratory. She weighed us, measured our height, checked our eyesight and told us to say hello to 'the mouse' in her special box every time we heard it squeak softer and softer. She also checked our teeth, gave us pink fluoride tablets and sometimes there would be a dreaded injection for some or other inoculation.

It was at one of these annual check-ups that she must have felt sorry for me or been horrified by my unruly teeth. She put in the paperwork so that my teeth would be looked at by an orthodontist at the University of the Witwatersrand dental school.

Essentially, her signed documents meant I got to be a guinea pig with ugly teeth for postgraduates at the dental school to sort out. I was probed and examined as doctors selected their cases. The weirder the better, I guess, and my teeth made the grade. My doctor was an Indian man whose friendly eyes seemed extra-large as they peered out above his surgical mask for the years I said aaaaah in front of him. He was the only non-white doctor in the department and I realised that sometimes he was treated a little differently from his white colleagues. I picked up small things, like him coming in only at the tail end of a joke and being greeted as an afterthought as someone sailed past the room with its four or five dentists' chairs. I could not know for sure what went on, but there was something uneasy and a deliberate distance that even I as a teenager could pick up on.

As my doctor he did all the right things. He tut-tutted at me for not wearing the painful elastics that bound my teeth like unforgiving harnesses. And he felt sorry for my near-raw gums, scraped by the wires that sometimes worked themselves loose in between my visits.

It was on one of these many visits that I realised that being Chinese also meant people treated you differently, a little like how my doctor was treated. Every few months I took a few hours off school for an orthodontist visit. My mother drove me to the dental school first thing in the morning, waited for me and dropped me off back at school.

On one of our first visits to the university, we were shunted from administrative person to administrative person. We eventually ended up at the receptionist who was supposed to attend to us and all other patients. The woman saw us enter the room but ignored us. We patiently took some seats near her and waited for her to be ready for us. Eventually my mother got irritated, but not wanting to upset this white woman she simply cleared her throat in an exaggerated way.

Suddenly the receptionist sparked to life. Not to finally give us some assistance but instead she turned to a colleague and said loudly, 'Oh, this woman has something stuck in her throat.'

I was about fourteen at the time and I was shocked that my mother, trying to be unobtrusive even after a really long wait, was being dealt with so rudely. I understood the sarcasm right away and was sad that my mother still had to do the whole 'Excuse me, please lady' routine to this ineffectual and rude receptionist.

Chinese were officially classified as coloured under apartheid. We were never honorary whites as some people believed, confusing Chinese racial status with that of Japanese in South Africa. In Yap and Leong Man's book *Colour, Confusion and Concessions,* the authors included an anecdote that brings into clear focus the insanely degrading and even oxymoronic business of being 'honorary white'.

They write about how a bus driver refused to pick up a Japanese man he thought was Chinese. The man turned out to be a Japanese consul staff member and the incident erupted into a diplomatic furore. The Japanese consulate demanded an apology, the bus driver and the city transport had to say sorry, but still the drivers could not tell the difference between a Chinese person and a Japanese person.

The authors went on to quote the *Rand Daily Mail* of February 1962, which reported at the time:

So once again we have this queer logic: the Japanese must be allowed to swim with Whites because they are important commercial allies. The Chinese must be admitted because it is hard to tell the difference between them. And apartheid, they say, is a matter of principle.

But the Chinese did get more concessions than other non-white groups. By the late 1970s and 80s, Chinese were allowed into white Catholic schools, Chinese were for some time allowed into universities under a quota for coloureds and they could even stay in whites-only suburbs if their neighbours did not object.

My Uncle Johnny, my mother's cousin, who I call Mmm Kou Foo, for the fifth uncle, was the first and only one of his six brothers and sister to go to university and graduate. He still has the documents and letters from the neighbours who had to give their consent to allow his family to live in their home that was not in a so-called grey area. He had to ask ten would-be neighbours to the left of him, ten to the right and those in front and behind him if they minded that he, my aunt and their three young sons would live there. I have heard similar stories from other Chinese families who had to go through the same exercise in humiliation.

In primary school I did not appreciate the complexity of this situation; I simply thought Mmm Kou Foo's house was big and fancy when he hosted family parties. The thatch roof was a novelty with the grass all tightly bunched up under the wooden rafters. There was also a perfect green lawn and the pool was like the icing on a cake.

Even when I had left school I thought the Chinese were lucky to have a concession like being able to live in a nice white suburb, as Mmm Kou Foo did, and I thought we should not complain too much. I also thought we did not have the vote because no Chinese boys had to go off to do their military service, which was a fair enough exchange, I figured. I knew others suffered more severely than the Chinese.

It took an outsider, the American researcher Dr Yoon Park, who worked extensively interviewing and writing about the Chinese community in South Africa, to set me straight some years later.

'No, Ufrieda. How demeaning do you think it must have been for people like your uncle to have to go cap in hand to speak to his neighbours, just ordinary citizens, to ask if he could have their permission to live among them?'

She was right, and she went on to put all her insights and findings into the book *A Matter of Honour*, which gave voice to the Chinese South Africans in ways I think they did not even believe they were entitled to. Dr Park's book finally validated so much of the Chinese experience, including mine.

But in my child's world it was a long time before I even understood the bizarrely complex layers of apartheid and of oppression; of what was acceptable and what we came to think was acceptable.

I still believed everything was as it should be. We were made to believe that being in a Chinese school was a privilege. Discipline and morality set us apart, we were also told. Heritage and culture made us strong and the ethos of working harder and being ever humble was all we needed to succeed, even if we were being prepared to become part of a divided society where we would be given the scraps.

The formula saw us learn a few Chinese songs, we practised the dances that had us clicking chopsticks to folk songs and we took sharp blades to paper in the old art of paper cutting. I even tried my hand at Chinese calligraphy but I never mastered the balance of flow, stroke and proportion. We had a few Chinese teachers who took us for our Chinese classes. They were not paid for by the state but by the community and the school itself. They shored up our cultural education.

We also had funding from the Taiwanese government. It was a peculiar set-up. The majority of the children were South African born, and came from Cantonese-speaking families who had a mainland Chinese history. The Taiwanese government represented the Chinese who broke away to the island under Chiang Kai-shek. Even though people from the island and those from the mainland were all Chinese, the historical disconnection could not have been greater. There was the barrier of language and the divide of the independent island with the lifestyle of Westernised South Africa.

But the Taiwanese had by the late 1970s, as a pariah state in the eyes of the Chinese, found diplomatic and trading common ground with the pariah apartheid state. This relationship meant the Taiwanese involvement was tolerated by the South African government. As for the Taiwanese who arrived in South Africa, their government knew that immigrant children needed a familiar place to be educated and so it donated books, helped out with funding and implemented a policy to teach Mandarin. Even though Mandarin was the official language of Taiwan and Beijing, it was useless in the 1980s and 90s for those of us who spoke Cantonese, at home anyway. We were taught the phonetic alphabet, the 37 *zhuyin* characters commonly called *bopomofo* (a term made up of the first four phonetic characters) that in different combinations make up the basics of Mandarin pronunciation, especially as it is taught in Taiwan. Then we went home and unlearnt them with our mother tongue, Cantonese, and the increasing encroachment of English in our homes.

Language is always central to a culture, and being Chinese somehow seems to survive even beyond the language connection. Being Chinese is almost like an essence you carry in your blood, even when you can only just muster a greeting in the vernacular. You cannot escape what shade of skin you are born with.

As I grew up, I saw many young Chinese people rebel against their Chineseness. Teenage heaven was the Western model of blue eyes, blonde hair; the perceived freedom of sex, drugs and rock 'n roll; and Johnny Depp. It was a seductive picture, so tantalisingly dissimilar to having to obey your parents' old-fashioned rules and spend weekends helping out at the family shop or recording fahfee numbers as another of the expected chores that everyone in a typical Chinese family is assigned.

Then, in 1989, we could not ignore that we were Chinese after all. From across the oceans, students who were not blue-eyed or had coffee-coloured complexions were doing something completely radical and teaching me about democracy and the fight for freedom.

Tiananmen Square was burning and the mighty public plaza in view of Peking's Forbidden City was the scene of a bloodbath for freedom.

We saw it all on TV – students, academics and protestors standing defiant for those things called democracy and reform, while tanks mowed them down and gun shots made them fall to the ground bleeding.

Yolanda and Kelvin were both students at Wits University by then and they were all swept up with this fight so far away. I was in high school, unsure of these new words but I joined them anyway and built a papier mâché replica of the goddess of democracy and hummed along to the cassette tapes Kelvin and Yolanda brought home, full of Mandarin freedom songs that played over and over again.

We identified more with this struggle far away without even knowing that there was a man called Nelson Mandela fighting for freedom. As we pasted more newspaper over the statue in solidarity with a cause in another world, we did not know what was happening in our own backyard. It was our socialised norm; we could see China burning and the Berlin Wall falling but we were still bricked in by the lies and secrets of apartheid.

After 1994, and especially after 1998 when the ANC-led South Africa opted for diplomatic ties with China over Taiwan, many more Chinese nationals ended up on our shores and continue to arrive. The people I meet these days come from the far-flung expanse of the Asian landmass. Some of them are from close to Siberia in the north and others nod with regional familiarity when I tell them about where my family villages were situated. They connect me with the motherland. You can take on the nationalities of other countries, you can align yourself with whatever current political ideology is in vogue but you are always overseas Chinese in their eyes; you are still the sons and daughters of the Yellow Emperor, you are Tang Yun, they say. It is the same thinking I hear from so many Chinese nationals when they speak to me about Taiwan or Tibet. There is almost stubborn disregard for complexities or realities about people's identities, their culture. They and I hold that essence of being Chinese, and that is all.

By high school we felt that Chinese classes were a waste of time. We attended class, went through the motions, but we also knew that we never had to write an exam in Chinese; it was not part of the syllabus as stipulated by the Transvaal Education Department and Chinese was not what we thought would be part of the world that we would inherit in our future.

One of the Chinese teachers had the most beautifully made-up classroom. He transformed his one bookshelf into a cabinet of Chinese culture. He painted it, put up beautiful ornaments of fans and traditional old ink wells and covered the whole cupboard with plastic sheeting.

But we were naughty and rubbed the sheeting until the static drew all the tassels of the fans and all other frilly bits to stick to the plastic.

We all took part in altering strokes on the calligraphy that he painstakingly wrote on the board. We rubbed out strokes, added a few extra ones and giggled at each other when Mr Wu tried to figure out what had happened.

Then one day a group of girls decided it would be funny to add a few of the eucalyptus leaves that spread across the school yard to Mr Wu's big beer mug of Chinese tea. That was going too far, I thought, but still I was complicit for saying nothing and for having less respect for this teacher who taught a 'less valued' subject.

I wish I had taken those Chinese classes more seriously. The gaze of the 21st-century world looks to China as the rising economic dragon, breathing its fire all over the globe and especially in Africa. Knowing this now, I really wish I had not used the Chinese classes to finish off maths homework or to cram for a test later in the day. I also cannot help feeling a bit like my mother, who, as a schoolgirl, did not pay too much attention to her English classes because she thought she would never have to say to anyone: 'Good morning, how do you do.'

Maybe it is the fate of the Chinese diaspora wherever they end up and especially as time erodes memory. Sometimes I look at online discussion groups and Facebook postings made by overseas Chinese communities in places such as San Francisco. There is that same feeling of ambiguity and puzzlement about being Chinese but only having a phantom umbilical cord to the motherland. I can almost hear myself in the questions on these Internet sites. There is uncertainty and doubts of origins and belonging. There is confusion over history blended with stories that are handed down generation after generation. There is what is lost in translation and the mystery of context one simply cannot know.

'I am just one mixed-up Chinese girl'; 'Pity all the books we are reading are written in English by people who are not Cantonese'; or 'Please can someone give us the Cantonese Class 101' are some of the messages. I smile a little and feel sad a little, because I know there are no simple answers.

But even as mixed up as I felt straddling the two worlds, especially as a teenager, my parents expected us to take school seriously, especially the Chinese classes.

Our school introduced a holiday winter school when I started high school. It was a week-long programme open to all Chinese children, not only those who attended the Chinese school, and it was meant to bring together the community's Chinese children to ensure a cultural infusion with cooking, karate classes, dancing and Chinese lessons. My mom and dad approved and my mom was excited when we came home with recipes from a guest chef.

She was a Taiwanese lady who did not speak much English; she waved her arms about a lot and exaggerated the techniques so we could get what she meant as we gathered in the home economics laboratory. We were supposed to make a Chinese savoury pancake. The chef started to divide out little bits of dough to each of us. We took our floury blobs and fiddled with them as she carried on cutting up smaller and smaller pieces. Then she realised she did not have enough for everyone.

She shouted at us but we did not know what she was saying; her arms went again and eventually we realised that we had to hand back our blobs of dough. To our horror, as each blob returned, we could see that some people had washed their hands and others had not, making for spring onion pancakes that very few people chose to eat.

The winter school made my mom particularly happy. When we came home and told her about another song we had learnt it was sometimes one she could remember from her own school days and she broke into song, testing her memory and her voice box.

Winter school was also a way to widen our circle of Chinese friends, even though the only people we knew growing up were other Chinese children anyway.

Kelvin and Yolanda, who were right royal teens, made and took phone calls from their new friends. Unwinding the telephone cord to its maximum, they pulled it around the side of the passage and cradled the receiver until their necks and arms got tired or until mom screamed for them to get off the phone.

Mom and dad supported most of the decisions taken by the school because they were about the enforcement of rules and the inviolability of discipline, Chinese-style. They might not have understood the intricacies of the breeding cycle of frogs as it was taught to us in our biology classes. And they did not particularly appreciate why we put on nativity plays in primary school, but they did understand that school was about rules and about the gospel of the teachers' words.

It was why my mother paid for scientific calculators and geometry sets when I was in high school, and it was why when I was little, she sewed cloths to drape over my head as I played another primary school shepherd herding a few cotton-wool and cardboard sheep across the desert of the dusty school hall stage.

My mother would take up her seat in the audience of the darkened school hall. She watched me sing 'Away in a Manger', not understanding too much about this story of the Christ child born in a stable to a virgin mother and the winged mystery of the angels, but she would be there anyway.

And as always at these school functions she duly prepared a plate or two of eats as each parent was expected to do.

I cannot remember my father ever attending more than one or two of these concert nights, prize-giving events or arriving at school for a parent-teachers' evening during my entire school career. He was always working. We did not sulk about it or get angry with him for not being there. His absence was almost like a contract with us; he worked hard and we had to work hard at school. A sealed deal.

By high school, despite my best efforts, science had become a completely foreign concept to me. Chemistry bombed and physics and I were like two vectors going in opposite directions. In maths, equations and theorems terrorised me and even accounting confused me with its reconciliations, its double entries and all the columns that needed to be filled in. I disappointed my parents as I failed science and only scraped by in maths. I had to rethink my subject choices completely by Standard Seven. Even the principal, who was our maths teacher in high school, said: 'You know, Ufrieda, Chinese people are supposed to be very good at maths.' I had no answer to her comment. She made me sound and feel like a genetic dud, someone who had failed her 'Chineseness' because I could not tell my parabolas from parallelograms.

I was able to help friends decipher a soliloquy or do '*met ander woorde*' in Afrikaans but I remember a friend nearly throwing herself and me down the stairs when, despite her best efforts, I simply could not understand calculus.

I had to fumble through maths as a compulsory subject but eventually I saw the light with science and chose to change to business economics. I spent every Thursday afternoon doing extra sessions to catch up on the lessons I had missed. At stake was the all-important university exemption I had to get in my matric year.

Failure to get a full university exemption would be the ultimate disappointment for my parents. I remembered them beaming as Yolanda passed and went to university and likewise with Kelvin. I remembered the happy congratulations my parents received and their smiles and pride they could barely contain. I needed to get that same reaction when my name appeared in the national newspapers in my matric year.

For my parents, a university exemption meant they had given us a key to the door out of the life they did not want for us. It was the fulfilment of the contract of their working and my working at school. To miss out was to be sentenced to the burden of the uneducated, to the world of shopkeepers and fahfee men, men like my dad.

Paradoxically, though, education also put more and more distance between us and our parents. As the world opened for us through books and new knowledge framed with a Western world-view, it pushed us further and further from our parents' outlook on life.

A news bulletin in English started to make more sense to us than it did for my parents, especially my mom, whose English was even more basic than my dad's. His work outside the house exposed him to more English and the languages outside our home. Yolanda and Kelvin started to take up positions leaning over my dad or mom's shoulder when they had to open up a letter from the bank or when some other official correspondence needed deciphering. 'Well, I am not an educated person like some people,' my mom would snipe at us as we got older and used increasingly rational arguments when we butted heads.

The West had also won over our walls. Johnny Depp's and River Phoenix's pictures with brooding eyes and flicked-back hair stared out over our beds – the white boys my parents feared. They never made us take down the posters but they did not like the idea that we hero-worshipped pop idols of the blond, blue-eyed brigade.

My parents also had to contend with the Western phenomenon of a matric dance, that symbolic graduation from childhood into the adult world of things formal and proper like high-heeled shoes and bow ties. The matric dance meant trips to dressmakers, shoe shops and the Oriental Plaza, the fabric and haberdashery hub in Fordsburg where they stocked fabrics with names like lamé that were as glittery as their names sounded.

Fortunately for me, Yolanda and Kelvin had also eased this path for me with their share of sequins, dressmaking, cummerbunds, corsages and, of course, dates. Yolanda's poor dates and dance partners were subjected to all the embarrassing jokes and jibes that we as the younger siblings could muster, peering through curtains, howling and giggling into our T-shirts as they rang the doorbell.

My parents were supposed to be a little more at ease with this farewell dinner when it was my turn to dance through the schoolyard rite of passage.

'So have you found a partner yet for the matric dance?' mom asked me one afternoon after I had got home from school.

I was not thinking about it too much at that moment and jokingly I told her I was sorted out.

'I am taking a boy called Donatello to the matric dance,' I chirped.

'What kind of a name is Donatello?' my mother asked, and I joked that he was a hot Italian.

My mother did not get the joke and she started to get tetchy. She did not believe me when I told her I had come up with the name because it was a character from the Teenage Mutant Ninja Turtles, the four green reptiles turned mutant heroes who saved the world from their gutter hideout, which I watched on TV most afternoons after school. I took her tongue-lashing and put it down to something being lost in translation and left it at that. But a few nights later when my dad was home a bit earlier than usual, he called me to him before I went to bed.

'Mom tells me you are thinking of asking a white boy to your matric dance.' The lecture was coming, so I rolled my eyes and tried to tell him my Ninja Turtle defence.

He listened but it still did not save me from a lecture. My dad said that white men were not a good choice for Chinese girls. He said they did not understand or have respect for the traditions and customs. I had only to look at some of the people we knew, he continued. My father angled the story to an old family friend. She had had a failed marriage with a Chinese man and became involved with a white man who started treating her abusively. My father was called in often to intervene, calm things down or to take her and the children away when her boyfriend acted up and could not be reasoned with. I nodded, silently cursing the turtles and my silly joke.

With my sequined dress and my hair done up, I went to the dance with a Chinese boy whom I did not know, but who thankfully was not too much of a reptile.

My Father, the Fahfee Man

Townships and locations, those *kasis* where black people were forced to live in divided South Africa, and all the shadow places in the oblivious white suburbs, were my father's office. He clocked in every day for a boss who controlled numerous fahfee banks around Johannesburg. As midday approached, my father, the *ju fah goung*, got behind the wheel of one of his boss's cars and drove off to 'pull' fahfee.

I am not sure where 'pull' comes from but it sticks as an English term that people use for fahfee. Maybe it has something to do with the arm action of gamblers at one-armed bandit machines; maybe it is because the ma-china literally pulls out a small piece of paper at each round of play that bears a number between 1 and 36. Betters who match the number the fahfee man has chosen in that round of play are the winners.

A fahfee man's betters are arranged in groups called *choangs* or 'banks'; it is another word that sticks when Chinese people refer to it in English. The fahfee man comes to his betters wherever they usually gather, outside their factory gates or on the dusty streets where they live, or on the street

125

corners of white suburbia. At each bank, the betters' bets are ready and waiting inside numbered and labelled purses, wallets and bank bags. To bet, the player writes the number of his or her purse or money bag on to a corresponding betting slip. Mostly, these are printed on cheap newsprint-type paper and cut into sheets that are slightly smaller than an A5 size. The fahfee man supplies these.

I am not sure where they are printed because, of course, fahfee is technically illegal and they cannot be confused for any other use. You could and still can get fahfee betting slips in shops all over Chinatown, even though they are not displayed in shop windows like stacks of dried Chinese egg noodles or clingfilm-wrapped bow ties and bottles of imported soya sauce. Instead, the shopkeepers disappear to a back room and return with something that looks like a weighty rectangular parcel wrapped and sellotaped inside plain newsprint or brown paper.

The printed fahfee betting slip is not compulsory, though. A corner torn from a cigarette carton will do; a scrap of paper saved from a half-empty page of a notebook or the back of a flyer are all acceptable. The fahfee man may moan and groan about the tacky, untidy note every now and again, especially if it is a piece of cigarette packet with scribbling on that holds a winning bet. He will pay all the same. The better selects the number or numbers he thinks will be played and also writes down how much money he wants to bet on each of his lucky numbers. Then he has to make sure that the exact amount that matches his bets is placed in the purse.

Fahfee numbers are conjured up from the fantastic possibility of dreams, symbols and the personal interpretations of life's uncanny coincidences.

When I started my first reporting job on a community newspaper, the receptionist would call me to her around lunchtime on most days.

'Give me your arm, my darling, I have to rub you for some luck.'

In the beginning I would look at dear Phyllis with questions all over my face. She would laugh a bit and grab my arm. 'I am betting with the Chinaman today so you have to bring me some luck.'

I laughed as she explained and let her have my arm.

When the better has done deciding on her numbers, she hands her purse to a runner whose job is to collect all the purses, wallets and money bags that will make up the bets for each round of play. The runner mostly checks that purses are numbered properly and are sealed so no money falls out because 'being short' of the exact betting amount is usually how pay-out disputes occur.

The runner is the betters' man; they choose him, but he has to be accepted by the ma-china as a suitable go-between. He is the one who hands over the bets and simultaneously receives the all-important slip of paper on which the fahfee man's chosen number is written at each round. He announces to the gathered betters what the number is and he sometimes stands by when pay-out disputes get heated. For his role, the runner receives a small stipend from the fahfee man.

In return, the runner is expected to collect the purses on time for the fahfee man's arrival and to encourage new betters to join the bank. And he initiates new betters into the peculiarities of the fahfee man and their fellow betters. They talk about the fahfee man. Is he a decent person who may occasionally allow a few credits for regular players or the occasional small loan, or is he difficult and grumpy? Maybe he is argumentative and aggressive when there are pay-out disputes.

The runner will also fill in newcomers about what numbers the fahfee man seems to favour, numbers that have been played recently, the 'can't comes', numbers that cannot be played during specific rounds, and the usual size of bets, even though there is no limit, and what times the fahfee man arrives each day.

And the fahfee man always arrives twice a day, every day, except on Sundays when he may only make one trip. When he arrives, it is in full view of all the betters, children and whoever else hangs around. Everything is done in full sight of the betters and especially the runners. This way there are fewer arguments later. The fahfee man hands over that day's number to the runner once he has passed his collected purses through the car window. The runner takes the number, unfolds the small rectangle of paper and the word passes around the gathered betters what number is being played. Some betters may show their happiness outright, whooping and clapping their hands. Others prefer staying quiet but confident as they wait for their purses to return bulging. Others kick the ground or shake their heads as the announcement of the number means they have lost the few rand they shoved into the betting purse just minutes before.

Sometimes I joined my dad on his fahfee rounds during school holidays. One of us children often tagged along with my dad when he was in the mood for some company during the more laid-back shifts. He did fewer banks, missed out the factories that would have closed for the holidays, or made only morning rounds to others over the height of the Christmas holidays. It was an opportunity to have him to ourselves on those trips, mostly because he could not have all of us children with him on his route; it was work after all. Once or twice I went out with Kelvin and my dad; I probably nagged long enough for my dad to give in and let me tag along, even though Kelvin, who would have been more helpful, was already in for the ride.

My dad's boss was a man we called Gou Sok. Dad worked for him from the time I was about eight years old. My father was hard-working and loyal and was respected and generally well treated by this man and also by his colleagues. Even some of my dad's older friends and compatriots called him Kee Gor. Gor is a word for an older brother and many people called him by this informal but respectful title.

One of my dad's biggest responsibilities was to *num ju*, to 'think up' the numbers that would be played each day to the betters at the various banks, even those run by his colleagues. My father was particularly good at this peculiar skill that involved working out numbers in a mix of statistics, superstition and a little bit of his own luck. The statistics came from the information carefully recorded in the square-lined books. Recording data was called *cheow ju*, literally scribbling down the numbers, and creating recorded data that each player in each bank has played for as long as they have been part of the bank.

There are casual players, regulars and even once-off players who may try their luck. By looking at the playing tendencies of the betters and reading the mood of each bank there was some kind of a process of elimination that would point to a best option of the 1 to 36 numbers that my father could choose. But it was not a process of science because it could not count for the whimsy of superstition and for the mystery of sheer luck.

Gou Sok would officially close down the banks over the December holidays but he would allow his employees to run them as their own for a week or two a year and my dad almost always decided to work in the extra time, as did the other men who worked for the boss. My father could pocket whatever winnings there were, but he would also shoulder the losses; it was a gamble.

That was when we got to go out on the fahfee route with my dad. I enjoyed those work trips. I got to sit up front with him and set off in the late morning knowing we would only be back home well after dinner time. My mom would remind me to take along a jersey, just in case.

In the hours before we left the house for the fahfee routes, my dad would sit down at our dining room table. He was absorbed, focused on the neat script that filled the stack of squared A5 notebooks that made up the record books. Somewhere in between sitting, examining and making notes, my dad would work out or *num ju* what seemed like a magical formula for winning. It is a formula that is mockingly capricious, but when it obliges, it guarantees a bounty, like it did on the day Pinky came home with us.

This was how my dad's work day began and it was a quiet time in our house; we were told not to disturb him. 'Go play outside', 'make the radio softer', were always the start of the sacrament of *num ju* in our house.

The only time we would disrupt his ritual of 'thinking up the numbers' was to bring him a cup of tea. Sometimes we would spill a little of the tea as we walked from the kitchen to the dining room table. Sometimes dad would moan that we were being careless, but mostly he would simply pour the tea back into the cup that hardly ever matched the saucer, slurp, let out the aaah of a satisfying swallow and let his gaze fall again, as it had done countless times before, on to the pages of the well-thumbed record books.

Occasionally my dad could not settle on the number he wanted to play and then he would call on Lady Luck with everything from throwing a few dice to folding up pieces of paper with possible good numbers and then selecting a random number from the small origami of folded squares. But even when he did this, it was not all random; it was as if chance and luck had to be part of the perfect recipe to guide him to the right number to play. Sometimes we were asked about our dreams and my mother also told what she had dreamt about. Those dreams were meant to spark something meaningful for my father as he sat and tapped his feet, sucked hard on a cigarette and worked through the record books again; sometimes there was just no way to connect a pattern of coincidence.

But as the clock ticked on, my father finally had to make a decision. From a ready-cut stack of matchbox-sized slips of paper, he would eventually write a number on one and the corresponding bank. Then he rounded up the record books, took the last few drags on his cigarette and stubbed it out in that determined grinding way that smokers extinguish their cigarette butts. Ready to go, he put everything into two or three fabric bags that would hopefully come home swollen with money. My mom had made those bags for the fahfee men. They were made from a soft, denim-type fabric and she had sewn on reinforced handles to carry the heavy coins.

Then we were on the road, heading away from all the places I knew and ending up far from the suburbs of traffic lights and walled-in gardens, these places where people decorated with garden gnomes and house numbers next to a caricatured snoozing Mexican under an oversized sombrero.

The suburbs gave way to patches of undeveloped *veld*, then came the start of the townships and locations. Homes pieced together with sheets of zinc and roofs held down with rocks vied for a few centimetres of space with a neighbour's house or a perimeter marker of a patchwork of chicken wire and odd bits of salvaged wood and scrap metal long ago succumbed to rust. Apollo lights, the towering street lights, sometimes split into three extended arms, sometimes a solitary one, stood in for trees, and there was hardly a blade of grass anywhere.

We made a few turns, around streets with no names and no pavements, and arrived at a bank. Dad's regular betters greeted him as the car slowed down next to them. They called him 'Jackie', the 'kie' derived from Ah Kee, I assumed, and they smiled and asked about me and why I was there, how old I was and all the nice exchanges and encouragement that people reserve for small children. They waved at me from outside the car and then it was back to business.

Hopeful fahfee purses, wallets and bank bags were fished out from sweaty bras, some of them wrapped in lucky strips of animal skin or tightly bound by an elastic band and they tumbled into the cardboard beer crate that my father used to collect the purses and wallets.

The cardboard box echoed back the soft clunks of the purses and money bags hitting the firm corrugated bottom. At that moment I pleaded with ridiculous repetition in my mind for a win for my dad from this bank. I hated the disappointment of a loss for my father, because I knew for him that even when so much was a gamble in what he did, it was not a random, careless act that brought him to these townships.

My dad would tell me the number he was playing that round and I was given the job of opening up zips and seals to save him the task. It was really just something for me to do without getting in his way. I always went for the pink purses and the yellow ones first, or occasionally there would be something unusual like a glossy plastic purse with big flowers printed on it or, one of my favourites, a purse made to look like a panda's head with big black-bordered eyes and a flash of fake red leather for a happy tongue. It had a click-lock mechanism. I would pull out clammy notes that showed up the bodily intimacy people have with money and I would watch as my fingertips turned more and more grey throughout the day as the long journey of the exchanged coins from the purses seemed to rub off on my fingers.

As I got older, I was allowed to be helpful with more grown-up tasks. My job then was to open up each bag, remove the betting slip carefully and then check for the number that was being played. On the printed betting slips it was easy to see if someone had a winning bet. But on the handwritten notes I would check over and over again to make sure I had not missed anything that could lead to a quarrel between the better and my father later. When I was sure, I would upturn the purse and throw the money into the cardboard crate and put the betting slip aside. At the end of each bank's round, my father would gather together the betting slips, roll them up and snap an elastic band around them. On to the column of paper he would write the bank's name and stash it into the money bags my mother had made. These would be brought out later in the night and entered into my dad's record books so that he could keep an up-to-date record of play for the rest of the week.

If the number did come up, I had to stack the purse on top of the betting slip and wedge them between the dashboard and the windscreen, waiting there for my father to count the pay-out once he had finished going through all the purses. I would get more and more worried as two then three then more purses would find their way up on to the dashboard. I started feeling like I had bad luck and that somehow my hands were making them win against my father.

I did not understand the pay-out system that well and I did not really comprehend the actual value of money. I only knew that when my father had to return money back to a purse it was not good. And my child's calculations measured out winning bets as setbacks for my father. Later, I found out that bets were paid out at a one-to-28 ratio and there was a one in 36 chance of choosing a winning number. I am not sure how those figures came about but they have more or less stuck. A winning 10-cent bet earned the better R2.80. The better lost the money on any other bets that were made.

My father had quick hands. He tugged at zips and plucked apart the plastic bank-bag seals, and all other carefully sealed purses and bags doubling up as pouches for a bet. He scanned betting slips, quickly checked that the money corresponded to the bet and as he did the maths in his head, his hands were already picking through the coins and notes and pushing pay-outs back into purses.

When my father beat his betters, wins came in the jingle-jangle of coins and some notes emptied into the beer box. But his hand also dipped back frequently into the cardboard box stash and some purses were returned with a bulge that showed that the one-to-28 pay-out had smiled on the better that day.

When my father was losing, especially on the days when it was his own money on the line, the agitation and frustration sometimes commanded his body like a possession. His jawbone became pronounced, his tone grew sharp and he barked at runners for no reason. He took it out on his cigarettes, Dunhills from a maroon box in his breast pocket. He dragged on them deeply then tapped the ash out of the car window with his right arm that was tanned distinctly darker than his left arm all his life.

A fahfee man is not your polite local butcher or the plumber who calls his clients 'ma'am'. Sometimes I thought my father was harder than he should have been with his betters, but as an adult I realised that even the attitude was part of the fahfee man's life; it was not a business for pushovers.

On most occasions, my father's anger dissipated even though his frustration was not easy to shake because it played out in a tally of losses in his head. I am sure I made mistakes, allowing some coins to slip out, missing a better's win and with it causing unnecessary disputes, wasting time and giving him more headaches than he needed. But he never shouted at me or stopped me from coming out with him those few days each holiday.

We went from bank to bank and then we re-did the whole routine again as generally there were two trips to a bank each day. These coincided with the betters' lunch breaks and with when they headed home or when they were already home from work.

Sometimes we went to a smallholding and stopped a distance away from some beehives. The plot owner farmed bees and sold honey. My father bought a few jars that the runner was dispatched to buy for him. The yellow-topped lids held back dark viscous sweetness that dad liked to dissolve in his tea. There were also jars jammed full of perfectly formed hexagons, repeating themselves over and over, forming the honeycombs, the raw honey, that my dad also enjoyed and said was a healthier alternative to sugar.

Among the smallholdings in the Eikenhof area south of the city that made up some of my dad's banks, we would make trips to the poultry farms. My dad's order, made via the runner again, was for eggs in bulk, trays stacked neatly on top of each other and carefully deposited into our car boot. It was the same with some vegetables and fruit that came straight from the farms, not pre-packaged.

With the shopping done, we would head back out to most of the banks we had been to earlier in the day. Now, though, everything was in darkness. I remember the dim, gloomy glow of the location lights high above the ramshackle township houses. We waited for runners in this orange haze of the lights, the Apollos, outside someone's small home, or parked inside the range of some fluorescent lights outside a spaza shop that had electricity. My father switched on the car's interior lights and we went through the routine once again as the township came to life with people who had returned home from the city.

Betters congregated, waiting for my father to arrive – he was their hope for something extra for that night's dinner table, or when they lost, it meant going without a new pair of shoes for longer than planned. I guess, though, he always represented hope, because gamblers are eternal optimists.

On those days with my dad, I did not have to share him, neither with my mom nor my siblings. I saw how money was made in our family and I saw dad in this other role, not as husband and father, but navigating relationships with people who were not friends or colleagues and not even customers really.

There was a competition and a game that made the fahfee man and the betters more like opponents. But they could not be too far apart either. They needed each other. Dad needed them to bet; the bigger the pool the greater the odds for him to make a profit. The betters needed dad as an opportunity, even in the form of a gamble, to add meat to that week's menu. And fahfee needed apartheid, too.

Fahfee needed two groups on the edges of society, separate but bound together, to connect momentarily in the collusion of circumventing the ways of the economic mainstream. The end goal for both groups was to walk away with a few extra rand in their pockets even if it meant they were taking from each other.

Theirs was a pact forged from their mutual conspiracy against the apartheid system. The ma-china and the poor black man of the townships were pushed towards the periphery; neither was part of what whirled in the tight inner circle: white wealth.

There was infighting, too, as dad and his betters were drawn into the vortex of dispute – it was part of the game. Dad would stand his ground;

the betters, with their heads leaned into the car window, would disagree with gesticulations or shaking their heads, also standing their ground. None was ready to back down. And then my father would just drive off, incensed and frustrated and maybe also adding a bit of dramatic effect. He would return for the evening round to fight again or be ready to give in, whichever move he decided to make in the hours he had to cool off and to refocus.

Drama and dispute aside, there had to be a shared respect so both sides could take the steps to engage in fahfee's dance of superstition, suspense and survival. It was what they did day in and day out.

And fahfee also showed up the humanness of connection and the ordinariness of transaction, both parties understanding how harsh things were when you existed on the edges of opportunity. I remember my father occasionally grabbed a few notes from the beer crate and gave them to the runner sitting nearby.

'Go buy cooldrinks for everyone,' he said.

The runner disappeared with people shouting their orders and instructions after him and he turned his back, telling them to shush. We would be in the car emptying the purses and wallets when the runner arrived back. Dad would wave his hand telling him to keep the change. Then Cokes and Fantas in their cold glass bottles were passed around. Someone would produce an opener and that was also passed around. We all drank in the fizzy, sweet coldness like it was not a day of work after all.

Dad was an outsider here, but he was also tied to this world of hard-working men and women. He understood what it took to make a bet, to gamble not for fun but for the hope of changing the day's fortune. In the townships, I saw for the first time how the dusty streets turned the barefooted children's feet a chalky grey, how houses were not lit with electric bulbs but with gas stoves and candles and that rough hand-painted numbers distinguished one house from another. There were no snoozing Mexican wall-hangings of the suburbs, no garden gnomes or dogs back from the parlour with ribbons in their hair.

One time, as we left the township, we saw a man with no legs trying to push his awkward, broken body across a road. His clothes were dirty and torn. The slow-motion scene played out in front of us as the man lugged his body across the ocean of tar. My father rolled down the window and handed the man a few of the large R1 coins with their leaping springboks.

Dad shook his head and a soft 'Shame, shame' dropped from his mouth as the man writhed determinedly to complete his task. We drove off.

I never asked my father why black people lived in townships and why there were no white people there, or Chinese people for that matter. Why was life so hard for some people? My father never offered any context of the world created by the hand of apartheid, the world that we lived in and the world we slipped in and out of as the *ju fah goung* and his daughter. All I could feel was the same useless pity of a few coins tossed to someone in need and knowing that tomorrow my father would be back, and the man with the broken body would still be dragging himself across the road.

The world of the townships seemed so far away from my other world of textbooks with punctuated sentences, learning about capital cities or how to do long division – the things my dad and mom felt were what we should be concerned with. The world was full of nuance, full of all these other lives and different ways to make a life. In my child's mind, everything fitted in as I was told it should, but I also saw that people slipped in and out of where they were not supposed to be under apartheid's dictates.

One holiday shift, Kelvin, dad and I drove past a young woman standing at the side of the road with her hand extended, waving down a lift. It was not unusual to see young women in this position, it happened often, but this time we stopped. Something was different – she was white. I did not understand why we had stopped for this woman when there were so many others we passed on a daily basis.

Years later it became clear to me. Dad knew better than we did who fitted in where and when, and a young white woman on the outskirts of a township at dusk was the wrong fit.

To Kelvin and me it seemed simply a friendly gesture to stop. Kelvin got out of the front seat to join me in the back. We assumed all adults got the front seat by default. I could not remember ever having a white person in our car, and certainly not a pretty girl with long blonde hair. Kelvin, who had kicked off his shoes in the course of the day, used his toes to push forward the seatbelt clip, trying to be discreet. But the young woman noticed and when she smiled at him we both giggled into the back seat of the car.

We knew the fahfee day ended when the dusty road and orange gloom of the Apollos led back to the tarred roads. Here, working traffic lights commanded order, houses were hemmed by neat lawns and house numbers on walls were not hand-painted scrawls but shiny and polished brass cut-outs or glazed ceramic plaques.

We arrived home and as the car idled in front of our gate we jumped out to undo with a noisy clank the metal chain-link we kept on our garage gate. Pulling each side open, we waited for the car to pull in; the brake light illuminated our legs as we re-wound the chain and anticipated the sure clip of the padlock my mother kept hooked on the diamond mesh fence she had erected to coax creeping flowers to bloom.

'Have you locked the gate?' my dad asked, as he almost always did. He probably checked it again before we went to bed, but for now our yes was enough.

We carried the bags of money that were also stuffed with the fahfee record books and the fahfee slips from the day's play. As we walked through the door we dragged our feet a bit, exaggerating our movements. We had been out to work after all, and we wanted to mimic our dad a little; we wanted to feel like the man who had put in a hard day's work with tiredness as the badge to prove it.

Whatever real tiredness we felt was a truncated version of what dad went through every day, and this was a holiday shift for him. Mom shooed us off to wash up quickly as she put the final touches to the evening meal. One of my siblings brought my father a cup of tea and he sat back to relax a little bit before dinner.

Holiday time brought the unusual pattern of eating our evening meal together as a family. With dad home, we would swop and shuffle to fit all six of us around the rectangle of our blue Formica kitchen table. Dad sat at the head of the table – and invariably it was now him, not my mom, telling us to lock the dogs out of the kitchen so we could eat or mumbling something about us holding our chopsticks properly. Once the meal was done, we settled down to TV. But the day's fahfee takings had to be counted and the players' betting trends recorded and made ready for the next day's rounds.

A newspaper was spread down its broadsheet centre. The homemade fabric bags, heavy with coins, were emptied out like a roar of thunder to count the money. Once the notes were scooped up, it was down to the coins. We felt out the sameness of the coppers and silvers, then stacked the springboks, proteas and blue cranes into columns and zipped the coins into plastic money bags.

If everyone was in a good mood then I knew my dad had had a good day. If my mom or dad passed us a few coins or maybe even a R5 note each, then I knew it had been a really good day.

My grandfather, Fok Yat Gou
(who became Leon Hing Low),
with slicked-back hair and wearing
a Western-style suit poses for a
photo some years before leaving
China for South Africa.

My grandparents and my
mother pose on a studio couch
for a photo.

My grandfather becomes an alien, a 'vreemdeling' of the Union of South Africa on this identity card.

My mother, Fok Jouw Yee, as a young woman in the years before she became a stowaway destined for South Africa.

My father, Ho Sing Kee, young and handsome, hoping for the City of Gold to offer up some of its fortune.

My mother and my grandmother, Low Wan Yuk, pose for a studio shot. They sent this photo to my grandfather who was a world away trying to make a life in South Africa.

My parents in their dating days in the veggie patch on my grandfather's plot outside Pretoria.

Mom and dad's wedding day.

Dad as a young fahfee man in the room he worked in before heading out for the banks.

My father and others in the community are wowed by a fancy Rolls-Royce that's worth posing next to.

Me on a park lawn.

The Ho siblings at a park in Johannesburg. As always, Unisda and I have something that matches, in this case it's our handbags with cats embroidered on them.

My parents as tourists at Chiang Kai Shek Memorial Hall.

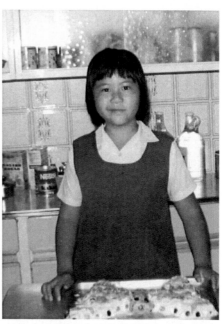

I show off my butterfly cake, baked and decorated by my mom and Yolanda.

On holiday in Durban. Dad wades in to cool off his feet, but the beach is really a treat for us kids.

Mom and dad attend a swanky ball at the Carlton Hotel in Johannesburg.

My green-fingered grandfather shows off a mighty winter melon, a Chinese favourite, grown in his retirement village garden.

SOUTH AFRICAN RAILWAYS.
SUID-AFRIKAANSE SPOORWEË.

General Manager's Office,
Hoofbestuurder se kantoor,

JOHANNESBURG.

Ref/Verw: G.33/6. *NO 60/141.*

To all concerned.
Aan alle betrokkenes.

The bearer of this letter Mr./~~Mrs.~~/~~Miss~~ *Ah King Ho* ....
Die toonder van hierdie brief, mnr./mev./mej.

is a Chinese gentleman/~~lady~~ of social standing, and when jour-
is 'n Sjinese heer/dame van stand en is nie verplig om in die

neying by rail is exempted from travelling in the reserved saloon.
gereserveerde wa te ry wanneer hy/sy per trein reis nie.

Reservation officers, ticket examiners and
Plekbesprekingsbeamptes, kaartjiesondersoekers

others concerned will, however, require to exercise their
en ander betrokkenes moet egter by die aanwysing van sitplekke

discretion when allocating accommodation. This letter must be
hul diskresie gebruik. Hierdie brief moet getoon word wanneer

produced at the time accommodation is being reserved.
sitplekke bespreek word.

If, at his/~~her~~ specific request, a coupé is
Indien hy/sy spesifiek versoek dat 'n koepee vir

allocated for his/~~her~~ exclusive use, the surcharge provided for
sy/haar uitsluitlike gebruik aangewys word, moet die ekstra koste

in Clause 79 of the Official Railway Tariff Book must be levied.
waarvoor in klousule 79 van die Offisiële Spoorwegtariefboek
voorsiening gemaak is, gehef word.

This authority is valid until 31st December, 1966.
Hierdie magtiging is geldig tot 31 Desember 1966.

for/namens GENERAL MANAGER.
HOOFBESTUURDER.

for CONSUL GENERAL OF CHINA
JOHANNESBURG, SOUTH AFRICA

12 MAY 1966

My dad is called a 'gentleman of social standing' in this document that was needed
to keep him from being tossed off trains during the apartheid years.

Weekend Dad

All too soon, the school holidays came to an end. Cheery and upbeat adverts on TV signalled the coming dread: 'Back to School is Cool'. We groaned each time the adverts started. Who needed reminding that soon the 6.30 a.m. alarm would be piercing through our dreams and our days would be ruled by more bells at school?

The adverts were a signal for my mom to start making notes about sales and special offers. Her bargain-hunting skills were unsurpassed and what she bought she placed in a locked stationery cupboard that we were not allowed to go near without her supervising the distribution of erasers and pencils, paint sets and boxes of chalk, crayons and rulers that kept snapping. By the time I was in matric my mom still had a few exam pads that she had bought for only 99 cents many years earlier.

January seemed to have an in-built accelerator, like the month was an autobahn for time. Before we knew it, the early morning alarm was beep-beeping us back to school.

We went back to seeing dad very little during the school week. While he was getting in his last few hours of sleep, we were walking to the school bus past dogs that rushed up to the fences and cars that started to crowd at traffic lights in anticipation of the coming rush hour.

At night we would be packing away our homework or brushing our teeth before bed when dad made it through the door; sometimes we would be in bed already.

Weekends gave us a bit of dad time, especially if he got home a little earlier on a Saturday afternoon. We never expected to go anywhere and we never nagged to be taken out or for treats. It was not that we were extraordinary, good children; it was simply that it was never expected.

Watching *Magnum PI* together, and maybe the night-time movie if we managed to stay awake, was a good-enough Saturday night. Sometimes mom made one of her triple-layered jellies we could eat in front of the TV. Our happy anticipation rose with each layer she added throughout the day. We loved choosing the mould, too. We had a rabbit with almond-shaped eyes and a bump for a tail and a racing car, which was Kelvin's favourite. There was also custard, the instant powdered kind that cooked up in a yellow volcano in minutes. By the time it was ready to serve, it was cool enough not to burn our tongues but hot enough to make our robot-coloured jellies ooze and pool, returning to their liquid origins.

Strict as my parents were, they were not austere. They wanted us to have treats and, when the budget allowed, there were also outings and holidays. The drive-in was a favourite, especially when we were all small enough to be bundled into the back of the Cortina. Our haunt was the Top Star. Built on top of a mine dump, it stood as a landmark to the south of the city until 2010. Depending on where you were in the city, you could sometimes see the giant screen turn the night sky into a silent movie of flickering scenes, joined together by your imagination for dialogue.

When dad and mom made the announcement that we were going to go to the drive-in, we knew we were finally going to connect the movie with the scripted dialogue. Our Cortina wound its way to the top of the old mine dump, flattened on the top to make room for this starlit park-and-view. You paid per car, not per passenger, and our car was always full of passengers, not to mention armfuls of blankets, pillows and teddies.

You were meant to tune in the car radio to the frequency at the drive-in but it would often crackle with static. You could also use the piped-in audio from a speaker that was affixed to poles that cars could park next to.

We chose our spot and drove up to the speaker. Dad immediately started fiddling to get everything working. When the signal went dead, dad was never convinced it was the speaker that was faulty. So he would keep fiddling. Eventually, he gave up and we drove to another spot. In this new spot, we all adjusted ourselves to maximise the altered view of the screen and dad started all over again to tame the crackle.

With the audio finally in synch, we could connect the picture and the sound and the silent movies of the night sky we knew so well from afar took on a whole new audio delight.

For whatever reason, we always seemed to watch double bills with horrors as the second feature. It was why we were ready with our teddies and blankets. As the terror reached out from the screen and headed for our car, we wanted to have a furry friend to squeeze. We girls often had more than one teddy each because tough-guy Kelvin would eventually also grab for a teddy once the baddie made his move or the lurking supernatural evil force emerged. This was before PG ratings and the idea that young children could absorb too much of the plot of scary movies. Mom would say, 'Just close your eyes and try to sleep', but this did not block out the scary music, the heavy breathing and the screams that worked into a perfect crescendo of Hollywood fear.

The final credits rolled and we had not slept a wink, even with our eyes closed most of the time. Worse still, there remained a ride back home in the dark, dark night. Places like the secluded mine dumps were perfect hideouts for a psycho with a chainsaw, a werewolf scavenging among the moonlit trees or a vampire in need of an anti-anaemic fix. We closed our eyes as we wound down the dark circular track of the Top Star drive-in until we felt the road straighten out under the car's tyres and we knew soon we would be safely home.

Another treat for us was our roadhouse outings. Piled into the car, we drove north of the city to the Doll's House, which was on Louis Botha Avenue. As a child, it seemed to be at the far end of the world, making the trip a real adventure. Dad ordered chicken and mayonnaise toasted sandwiches, burgers and chips and soda floats. His window was rolled down halfway and we held our breath as the waiter carefully set the specially made tray to hang over the glass, leaving our food floating in mid-air. It was all part of the roadhouse adventure we loved so much, sitting in the back seat and drinking tall glasses of cooldrink or maybe a cream soda float, deliciously sweet and fizzy and topped with soft-serve ice cream adrift in a sea of green. These foods were fantastically foreign to our daily menu, making them all the more yummy to us.

One time, after one of our meals, dad flicked the car lights for the waiter. He asked for 'puppies' for us children. The waiter nodded and scribbled something on his small notepad. Devastated at what we thought was about to be served to us, we started pleading: 'No, Ba, we do not want puppies; please, Ah Ba, we do not want any of that.' My father just told us to shush.

Our waiter emerged from the food pick-up spot a few minutes later. He carried a tray with a spectacle of strawberry, ice cream and cream all swirled up inside sundae glasses. Maybe he was going to another car? No, he was heading straight for us. They were 'parfaits', in my dad's imperfect French, but we ate our 'puppies' happily as our parents laughed.

My dad also did 'posh' from time to time. Posh for us was a trip to Mike's Kitchen in Market Street in the centre of town. The restaurant had red and white decor, proper tablecloths with tiny red and white squares, booths with cushy seats and even tables for two where diners could peer out of the windows of the old building with its thick stone walls.

My dad usually ordered ribs for us, but what we loved most was the salad bar. It was a fascinating and completely foreign idea to us that you could fill your plate from the deep bowls of vegetables displayed under lights and you could daub the vegetables with oils and dressings or pile up your plate with vegetables and other bitty things all slathered in a creamy pink sauce. Later I would learn the names for these things – from the thousand island dressing to the croutons – and we also demystified the phenomenon of the finger bowl.

Joburg's inner city was an outing in itself. Its tallest building, the Carlton Centre, offered a bird's-eye view of the city. The elevator raced up so fast we had to clear our ears by exaggeratedly faking yawns. Once at the top, we walked up to the windows that surrounded the whole floor and we peered down to the matchbox cars on the ground. We dared each other to stand closer to the window panes. Mom or dad kept telling us to be careful, then they dropped 20 cents into the timed binoculars so we could look over to the pale yellow of mine dumps to the south and at the lights of the city all around. I did not think about what lay beyond the mine dumps, which was the sprawl of Soweto where there were no neat green and red roofs, trees or regular streetlights, where the townships of the fahfee betters were.

Instead, we trained the binoculars to the east. 'Can you see our house?' dad always asked and he pretended to make out a landmark that we should be seeing, maybe the round cylinder building of Ponte, and we peered more intently into the binoculars as if the harder we looked the more certain it would be that our house would come into focus.

Our main annual family outing came at Easter when dad took a few extra days' break as the religious holidays freed up his calendar. As Good Friday arrived, we knew what was coming: the Rand Easter Show. We headed out after an early dinner. The cars' lights were already turned on and so were all the lights inside the showgrounds. We joined the human snakes making their way to the cashiers and the turnstiles.

Once through the gate, people dispersed as they headed to the halls they wanted to see first. We hurried, too, dragging our parents, urging them to walk faster. Then we saw it – jar upon jar of honey making the light around the display golden. The best of the best of the viscous goo was marked with a ribbon rosette. The honey display was a staple of the Rand Show, as was the icing-sugar sculptures. Some women's guild members created dolls' houses and scenes with Easter bunnies, hens and decorated eggs. We walked in circles around the displays, calling each other to look at some little detail we had just seen.

The Rand Show was a highlight, but it held a shadow of terror, too, for us children. One year Yolanda got lost in the crowds, sending us into a panic. She remembered that a man with a cigarette popped her balloon. She was distracted as she looked up at where the balloon had been and then down to the fallen piece of string dangling around her feet. When she looked up again, we had disappeared into the thick of the crowds. She burst into tears. Kindly strangers took her to a designated pick-up point, but minutes of panic ticked by when we could not find her anywhere. Then an announcement came on the public address system and thankfully we knew where she could be found.

She remembered: 'I was so scared not just because I was lost but because I knew when I was found I would be shouted at for running around or not listening to mom and dad. But when dad came he was glad to see me, and in fact he bought me a rabbit-shaped balloon, one of the more expensive ones. I guess he was just glad to have found me.'

It meant we received an extra lecture every time we arrived at the Rand Show. We were reminded to hold hands as we drifted from hall to hall where faux leather sausage dog doorstops and the latest vegetable slicers competed for attention. Even dad succumbed to the special prices and we ended up with a sausage dog with its plastic eyes and two flaps for ears. That was the Rand Easter Show of 1981 and the dog survived into the new millennium; I know because my mom marked his ears with the date he came home with us.

Of course, there were the rides, all lit up with people screaming on the roller coasters, gripping on to guard rails as their heads were thrown back. As the rides ran out of steam and people got off with smiles plastered on their faces, talking fast and gesturing wildly, we begged to be allowed to have a taste of the rush, too. 'When you are bigger; it is too dangerous,' mom would say. Then she distracted us with the carousel ponies with their mechanical prancing and their slow orbit around a mirrored centre as tinny music played.

We chose our horses carefully as we waited behind a closed gate. Then as soon as the attendant opened the gate, we raced to beat other children who had eyed out their favourites, too. Dad and mom waited for us as we went round and round and up and down, holding all the extra jerseys and jackets and with a few ride tokens still fluttering from dad's hand. He invariably suggested the Ferris wheel, the family ride we could all do. We swayed a little in our capsule as we were shifted up one by one until the whole Ferris wheel was filled. Then the man with the lever and button brought the metal ring to life. We rose higher and higher until the people with balloons and glow-in-the-dark bracelets grew tiny and we could see out over the lights, across the parking lots and towards the darkness of Soweto, whose people we did not even realise were barred from the Rand Show gates.

Christmas was the big exhale for our family. Finally dad got to slow down for more than only an afternoon or the night or a long weekend.

The city was infected with the spirit of the season and came to life in lights. We went downtown on slow drives to see the fairytale lights strung along the lattice of the main routes in and out of the city. We stopped off at the old Library Gardens fountains and walked around the fountains lit with lollipop-coloured lights at the bottom of the pools. The water sprayed up in jets at their own synchronised pace. We stepped on to the short walls of the pools and let the spray of water wet our shoes; then we rushed over to the next fountain, shaking off the droplets.

Sometimes we did some window-shopping, strolling along the shopfronts of the old OK Bazaars in Eloff Street and peering at the appliances for sale and the mannequins and curly-haired dolls with their stony eyes and magnificent fake eyelashes. They were displaying children's clothing and the windows were edged with a border of fake snow made with spray-on white mist. Sometimes my parents even held hands; it was so not the Chinese way and it made us children giggle.

Christmas in Johannesburg was also about the dioramas that were put on display at Joubert Park, in the city's green lung. By the 1980s, Chinese people were permitted to enter these public areas or, at least, our family was never turned away. I did not know then that these were restricted places for everyone who was non-white, including the Chinese.

There were some black people at public events like this, but there were no children or families, only black men ringing a bell, selling ice creams or assisting their bosses who had stalls selling food, trinkets and balloons.

As a child, I had no perception that this was odd. Those warm Johannesburg December nights were for my own selfish enjoyment. The park was turned into a fantasia of coloured light, floats and displays. Goldilocks and the Three Bears, Red Riding Hood, Jack and the Beanstalk and all the creatures of fiction's wonderland moved and sang on their fixed platforms among the candyfloss sellers, the ice cream vendors and the man with the helium balloons.

Dad usually treated us to the pastel shades of candyfloss and we tore off the airy sugar that came inside the puffed-up plastic bags. We stuck out our tongues, showing each other the magic of the wispy pastels turning dark and syrupy as the candyfloss melted. Sometimes we also got a balloon each. We never pleaded or nagged for these things; either we got them or we did not. When we did not, we were disappointed but we did not stamp our feet, sulk or cry because we knew they were extras and nice-to-haves that my parents had to dig deeper into their pockets for.

When we did get balloons it was pure helium heaven. We chose one from the box the balloon seller showed to us. He took our choice, stretched it a bit and wrapped its rubber lip snugly over a gas cylinder. Unisda and I especially liked the balloons that were shaped like a long-faced bear with two protruding ears and a smiley face printed on the expanding rubber. Yolanda and Kelvin sometimes chose those, too, or they picked the oversized balloons that had something that rattled inside them.

Mom tied the balloons in an elaborate knot around each of our wrists and we watched and waited for our balloons to follow our steps as we ran in between adults' legs, to and from the diorama displays.

When we got home, we tied our balloons to the ends of our beds and went to sleep with them bobbing. In the morning, we found them still smiling but sunken halfway as the night had stolen their helium breaths. We rushed outside to the *stoep* with them, whirling around and around to try to get them back up into the air. But they drooped further and further until they touched our feet and shrank into spent rubber.

The Easter and Christmas festivals of the West had a parallel significance with the traditional Chinese gatherings of *haang ching* and *ching ming*, the so-called grave-sweeping festivals. These sound morbid, but a gathering of the clans with extended families all sharing one space always sparked a festive mood. A clan is all those who share a surname and the kinship tie draws them together during these two annual festivals when they remember the ancestors and the threads that bind over generations and across the oceans that separate Africa from the East. Money was raised from donations and this would be used for charitable initiatives in the community and sent back to the villages in China to be used for projects there.

Dad was also part of a kind of community *stokvel*. We called it *gung wui*, the communal pot of money to which members contributed every month and drew from when they needed a lump sum. Of course, there were rules in terms of when and who got to draw from the pot. There had to be checks and balances and equitable distribution. More than the money, the community pot, like the dinners for *haang ching* and *ching ming*, was about gathering, restoring old connections and sustaining a financial net for the community that did not have to rely on things outside the community circle, things like banks or anything else that had a whiff of authority and institution.

Each *haang ching* and *ching ming*, individual families would go to the cemeteries to clean the graves of their family members and to lay down flowers for the dead. They also performed the rituals of lighting incense and candles and burning paper money, each sheer sheet embellished with a wash of silver or gold and folded to resemble ingots from a time before paper money. And they offered up food to the ancestors by placing a tray of eats at the foot of the grave, or at an altar in their homes. The tray, filled with bowls of rice and a few prepared dishes with chopsticks laid out, would be lifted three times – once for heaven, once for the earth and once for the deceased, like we did when we celebrated our birthdays. There would also be little glasses of whisky and teacups with tea on the tray. A little from each would be poured out on to the ground to resemble the offering and invitation to the people who had died to join in the meal. After the ceremony, the food could be eaten, but only after the incense had burnt out, only after the ancestors had eaten.

The candles, incense and offerings made up the ritual that creates a portal to the ancestors. Years later, I watched a Chinese comedy about two friends. One dies and enters the afterlife. He appears to his friend first in a dream and then they start to communicate. As they chat the dead friend always reminds his mate to pour a little beer on the floor, saying he is getting thirsty in the afterlife. The scene flashes to the dead friend holding an empty glass. The glass starts to fill up as his friend in the land of the living tips his glass to the ground. They drink together like they were never separated.

In the old days, the clans would have gathered for these remembrance feasts at their villages, I imagine, each village taking a turn to play host. In South Africa, though, the feasts and the remembrances are held at a different gathering point: a Chinese restaurant. Included on the menu for *haang ching* and *ching ming* is always something vegetarian, mushrooms maybe, and sheets of dried bean curd and crunchy wood ear fungus. The meat-free dish is in honour of the dead and the old Buddhist and Taoist ways of doing no harm to sentient beings.

It was not the religious philosophy that mattered but the traditions and the customs, the ritualised actions that gave shape and form. In fact, Buddhism and even Taoism, as I came to understand it as an adult, are very different from what I encountered growing up. Religiosity then was about respect and remembrance for ancestors, for gods and heavenly protectors, all done with smoky incense and fast-burning red votive candles, superstition-inspired bows and prostrations, and little jade amulets and trinkets worn around a wrist or a neck for warding off evil and misfortune. Some people even tied these around babies' tummies. At best, the ritualised effort and the conformity pleased the gods; at worst, it could do no harm and all the while it bound the clan with memories of ancestral union.

Once the *haang ching* and *ching ming* meal was completed, usually with pots of Chinese tea and fruit, the bill was paid for by donations. Each Ho family that had arrived for the meal was expected to cover its portion and also to put in a few rand extra. The collections were placed in a brown paper bag; nobody checked who gave what, but there was always a bit of gossip about the big eaters, the inconsiderate eaters, those who took the good pieces of the chicken or who ate up all the pork crackling before anyone else could start on the shared food. There were also those who were stingy with their money, underpaying a little, not leaving a tip or a donation. Even the brown paper bag could not hide some sins.

The dinners were always held on Sunday nights to accommodate the fahfee men and shopkeepers who would ordinarily only take a Sunday or Sunday afternoon off from work. It was the same with weddings and funerals. I used to think that there was something religious or superstitious about Chinese funerals being on Sundays. Only years later did I realise that it had no significance other than the fact that Saturdays were still working days. Celebration and final respects would have to wait until the cash registers rested and the fahfee rounds were done.

Not all Ho families attended these dinners but many of them did and still do. There were several other Hos in my school so it was a treat to see each other over the weekend at these dinners. After the meal, we children ran around playing hide-and-seek in all the new spaces of the restaurant. One of the most popular venues for the dinners was Litchee Inn in Pretoria Street, Hillbrow. I also ended up working there on weekends as a teenager. This suburb hummed with its seedy but throbbing nightlife, a cult cinema, a massive shop dedicated to selling books and even a Wimpy where the odd black person sat next to a white person as beggars, drunks, police vans and old women shuffled along to buy a litre of milk from the local Checkers, even in the segregated 1980s.

To get to the restaurant you had to enter an arcade which was always someone's urinal or ashtray. But then you would round the corner and get to the restaurant escalators. The walls, papered over with designs of bamboo stretching from the floor to the ceiling, showed you were about to enter somewhere quite different.

We loved to race up and down the escalators, running up the downward escalator, sitting on the rails for a seated decline. We would play until we were scolded by someone for making a nuisance of ourselves or until the restaurant receptionist turned off the escalators in frustration. Then we returned to our moms' sides, a little exhausted and a little defeated for being caught out for misbehaving and we would wait to go home.

For the adults, the after-dinner interaction was about networking a little, sharing some community news or snippets from the villages back home. It was informal but all-important; for my father these were like his cousins, even though they were not cousins by blood, only by name. Sharing a clan name meant you were connected and for a man with no brothers around him, these connections mattered.

Another Day, Another Dollar

Dad's boss, Gou Sok, was a newer migrant to South Africa, arriving in the 1980s. His son had been in the country for some years already and spoke English fluently, used an English name and had married a woman who was also South African born. When Gou Sok came to South Africa, he stepped into a more properly structured life. He had more capital and more business savvy than those who entered as stowaways in the 1950s and 60s. Arriving in the 1980s meant he was able to leapfrog some of the stifling restrictions that had been in place for the Chinese – he did not have to contend with fake papers, being a paper son or living in grey suburbs and staying on the periphery in the same way as the men and women who arrived in South Africa in earlier decades. With his son already in the country, his wife and daughters would follow.

Gou Sok and his wife initially lived in a flat in Doornfontein. This became my dad's base for work where he clocked in each morning on the ninth floor to run through the numbers he would play before he and his colleagues drove out just before midday to the various banks.

Unlike the holiday shifts we accompanied my dad on, now the day was longer, with more banks and probably more betters with everyone back at work. My dad and his colleagues would only get back to the flat at around eight in the evening.

The fahfee men ate their evening meal together because the work day was not quite over even as dinner time came around. Dishes would be cleared and then it was down to counting the day's takings. The money had to be accounted for and then the banking happened in the next few days. As in our home, an old newspaper would be split along its spine and the bags of money tumbled out on to the newsprint for counting.

The records for the day were put into the small, square-lined notebooks; only then, as the ashtrays filled up and the unfinished sips of tea grew cold, did the fahfee men go home.

Even though Gou Sok was a decent boss, my father and his colleagues went through the grind of making someone else rich. But dad stayed with Gou Sok for many years because he knew he was appreciated and Gou Sok was, to my dad, a mostly reasonable person to clock in for.

I remember Gou Sok for the chocolates he bought each of us children at Christmas. There were four layers of chocolates inside the cellophane-wrapped box and we each had our own box. One year, my box of chocolates had a big-eyed kitten on it, photographed with a pinkish halo. I kept the box for many years until its sellotape-reinforced edges finally gave in.

We leaned the boxes against our fireplace that did not work and where our tinsel-laden Christmas tree took pride of place over the holidays. The few small presents around the plastic, green spikes were now dwarfed by the decorated boxes. We nagged mom to let us open the chocolates ahead of Christmas day until eventually she folded under our pressure and said okay.

The four of us sat down together to open the boxes. We knew they were identical but we needed to be sure. We lifted off the lids to reveal sweet nuggets that looked like delicate jewels on display. At first we chose carefully, but after a while we gorged ourselves and then we felt sick. As the days wore on, we started all over again until at last only a few overlooked dairy gems remained and we were sorry that we had not paced ourselves.

With the chocolates came the present of having dad home a bit more for the holidays. We knew too well how little time we got to spend together when the school term was in full swing. Most days dawned with dad still sleeping while we got ready to catch the school bus. By the time his work day ended, we were usually tucked in for the night. Many nights I lay awake, waiting for dad to come home safely, only falling asleep when I heard the familiar squeak of the garden gate and the acceleration of the car as it thrust forward after dropping him off.

Before my father was a fahfee man, though, I remember him as a shopkeeper, with my mom working hard by his side. The shop was on Sauer Street in downtown Johannesburg. My mom called it an 'eating house' in English; it was like a canteen for the black workmen of the city. They also sold some *mageu*, traditional beer, behind the counter, along with provisions such as snuff, loaves of bread, a few slices of polony, some canned goods and bottles of cooldrink.

But it was mostly for the hot food that the men arrived each midday. There were stews made from cheap cuts of meat, cooked in hearty gravies and served with steaming *pap* or chunks of thickly cut white bread ready to mop up the gravy. These men were not allowed into white restaurants and there were few places they could sit down to eat a hot meal in the middle of the day.

Next door to the eating house was a butcher's shop. Both were owned by a woman we called Daai Jeh Jeh, literally meaning big sister. Her actual name was Ah Siu, meaning smile. My dad had known her since she was a young woman, and he was just a few years older. Daai Jeh Jeh's father and mother had first met my dad when he was a new arrival in the city of gold. I heard years later from my mother that my dad never forgot the kindness of this family when he first arrived. Then, when Daai Jeh Jeh's father died, the family struggled. At that time my father had the small butcher shop he ran in Alexandra. Many Chinese families lived around the township and they also used the butchery. Daai Jeh Jeh was among his customers. She told us that my father weighed out the meat they ordered but always added in a little more, without saying anything, and wrapped up the parcel for her to take home to her widowed mother and her sister and brothers. I guess she never forgot his kindness. And now she had my mom and dad running the eating house.

Daai Jeh Jeh's financial life had taken a turn for the better by the time she had married her first husband. The marriage, though, was less successful.

She was young when she started her family and her three children were nearly grown by the time we Ho children were toddlers. Daai Jeh Jeh's marriage did not last. It was still unusual for a Chinese woman to be divorced and a single mother, but she did both and started building her butchery business by herself. She eventually started and ran a successful franchised Chinese restaurant that still operates today.

Way before the restaurant business, there was the downtown butcher shop and the adjoining eating house. She wanted my father and mother to be the ones to manage and run this part of the business. When I was little, she always teased that she wanted to adopt me and I was unofficially her *kei neu*, her adopted daughter. She eventually emigrated to Canada, following her daughter and sons. Over the years we have lost touch, but I always remember her generosity, her big laugh, her independence and industriousness in a time when a clever and self-sufficient Chinese woman was not often supported for being so forthright and determined.

I loved the shop as a child. As the third-born of my parents' four children, I was the toddler between the older brother and sister in primary school and my baby sister at home being looked after by my granny. So I got to join my mom and dad at work. I played with the Coca-Cola tops as they popped off the hard-working bottle opener fixed to the wooden counter and I napped in a glass cabinet. It was painted blue on the outside for my privacy and foam-lined on the bottom half, while loaves of bread shared the upper bunk. I was called the bread-cupboard child in my family, something my mom still occasionally mentions, maybe disbelieving that I could have grown up from that small body that could fit inside the makeshift cot.

Mom and dad served the overalled workers who descended on the dingy shop at lunchtime. Mom got to practise her own brand of Fanagalo, a mish-mash of languages used for communicating mostly on the mines, years before it became politically incorrect and a part of the shameful past.

Today my mother slips into this language sometimes; she even throws in a bit of Chinese. Part of me wants to die of embarrassment, trying to shut her up, explaining again that it is derogatory to speak this way. But these days mostly I see people smile at the effort, laugh a little and understand exactly what she means.

In the shop, though, a bit of English, a bit of Zulu and bit of this Fanagalo was what got her by. Once the lunch-hour rush was over, the eating house would grow quieter until the end of the workday. Taking the gap, my father would drive to fetch my brother and sister and cousins from the Chinese school at the east end of Market Street. My cousin Sandra, who was the oldest of all of us, remembered that my dad would pick her up and the other two eldest cousins each morning and drop them all off in the afternoons.

'If your dad had won at the races he would treat us all to *won ton mein*, steaming bowls of noodles in soup with small meat-filled dumplings in Chinatown before dropping us off at home,' she told me.

Yolanda also remembered the treats. 'Most times dad would arrive with a treat for us. It was a drumstick or a sausage, something yummy.'

Sometimes he would not drop Yolanda and Kelvin at our Bertrams Road home for my granny to look after; he brought them back to the shop with him.

Then we could go out to play together at an open lot not far from the shop. There was a man who would take us out to the lot. It is sad that I cannot match a name or a face to him any more. I just know he lifted me up into his arms and bounced me along with his stride to get to the lot. Because I was the baby he always carried me, and my brother and sister ran along at his side. He probably worked at the shop or the butchery; I remember he always wore blue overalls. But he was the one who took us to the lot and kicked a ball around with us until it was time to go back, to meet the after-work rush when the other overalled men of the city returned. Some would have changed back into their ordinary clothes, some would still have their blue uniforms on. They bought the half loaves, the cans of pilchards and beans and whatever else they needed before heading for the trains and the taxis to go to their homes, far from the city where they were not allowed to live.

Behind the shop counter was my private playground that I did not have to share with any of my siblings. Sometimes Daai Jeh Jeh would pop around to pinch me on the cheeks or to talk to my parents. But mostly the two shops ran separately.

My mom remembered that once I saw a mouse run across the floor and scurry under some pallets. I screamed '*lou su, lou su*' (mouse! mouse!) and then I sat calmly watching the commotion that ensued, with Daai Jeh Jeh climbing the walls because of her enormous fear of rodents and everyone else either scrambling to catch the frightened creature or catch their breaths from laughing at Daai Jeh Jeh's hysterics.

I remember my personal intimacy with the space. This was my domain to watch these small dramas unfold. As long as the busy adults could keep sight of me, I was left alone in my corners to watch a mouse scurry somewhere, to make up games with the toys of empty cigarette boxes and matchboxes or to explore among mazes formed by goods for the store, towering stacks of bars of strong-smelling soap and canned food in bulk, plastic-wrapped trays.

I got to watch over the entire eating house but I was not really part of any of the transactions. Lunchtime brought the thunder of men, loud and noisy, ready to eat and to relax for a few minutes as they tucked in. The men sat down at the metal tables and their plates and cutlery clanked noisily as they ate with hungry gusto. They spoke to each other loudly and laughed and argued rowdily; it was their pause from driving pickaxes into the city's soil, from laying bricks in new buildings and shaping the city they were not allowed to live in, and from simply nodding their heads and saying '*Ja, baas*' (yes, boss) to their employers.

From my bread-cupboard view, peering through the small peepholes where the blue paint had flaked off, or sitting behind the counter on an upturned Coca-Cola crate layered on top with a few sheets of cardboard for some cushioning, I watched the comings and goings of these customers, but did not know anything about where they came from or where they were going to after they had put their change back into their pockets and mumbled a thank you or goodbye. The following day they would be back again.

Eventually I was enrolled in nursery school and there was no more sleeping in the bread cupboard or stacking bottle tops into the towers of my imagination. It was time for me to join the world of other four- and five-year-olds playing on jungle gyms, making Plasticine animals, doing paintings for my parents and sitting still for reading hour.

I hated nursery school in the beginning. I wanted to be back at the shop, happy among the commotion and noise of the eating house with my parents. I cried for weeks when I was dropped off each morning with Yolanda and Kelvin. I was so stubborn that I managed to keep up the waterworks until eventually the nursery school teacher would send for Yolanda at the primary school to console me. I refused to be comforted and it was many weeks before I settled into nursery school life.

My mom used to bribe me by giving me sweets to take to nursery school, also hoping they would help me to make friends and start to enjoy playing with other children. But still I cried and cried most days and probably ate all the sweets myself, not bothering to share with anyone.

Now I was stuck with the routine of a scheduled nap, a pigeon-hole that held my small suitcase and a jersey, and snacks of a glass of Oros and a Marie biscuit before home time. There were no more of my mother's lunches, treats from the shop shelves and nodding off in my cupboard whenever I wanted to.

The nursery school was in the basement of the Chinese school building, so we never saw out of the windows. Thankfully, there was a small library and this I did love. The stories were fantastic and almost as much fun as some that my granny used to tell us. The teacher would read to us about a flying car, Chitty Chitty Bang Bang, that could get his family to their beach destination before everyone else by flying over the traffic. There was the gingerbread man, gobbled up by the fox that was supposed to help him across the river. There were the pigs that got gobbled up by the big bad wolf with his mighty huffing and puffing. The teacher read these books to us, and I returned to them in my own time, working through the stories by looking at the pictures. I never tired of them.

While I thought about what sweets looked best as buttons for a gingerbread man in the fairytales I was being introduced to, my parents carried on working in the eating house for some years. Eventually, though, both the butchery and the eating house either closed down or changed hands, I am not sure which. Daai Jeh Jeh and her brother opened up a big butchery that became a booming success and she also started her restaurant businesses. My mother and father went back to what they knew: fahfee. My dad would be a fahfee man for the rest of his days once the Sauer Street eating house closed its doors for the last time.

I ended up working on Sauer Street as a journalist for *The Star* newspaper in the mid-1990s. My father and I both worked on the same Joburg street.

By the mid-1990s, the street had changed so much I could not make out exactly where the shop would have been as I got off the bus each day for work. Gone were the small shops, the dignified old Barclays Bank with its heavy revolving doors, and the giant unicorn that had flanked a building's facade further up from the main drag.

As children, we often waited in the Cortina as my father did his banking at Barclays. We even got money boxes once. I remember a solid steel money box fashioned like Cape Town's Table Mountain. It had a one-way slot so that coins could be slipped through the flat top that was the mountain but no coins could be shaken out of it. It could only be opened with a special key so it stayed full, heavy and unopened for years. It outlived other money boxes from the bank as they started giving out cheap plastic money boxes that would split even before you had filled them halfway.

As for the unicorn in town, I loved it because it was the only creature that started with a U, just like my English name. Unicorns were my special animals, even if they were the creatures of myths, or maybe because of this.

Even with changes to the area by the 1990s, I would still scan the street trying to imagine where the eating house had been and where we had kicked a ball in the open lot until Yolanda and Kelvin's black school shoes were covered in a fine dusting of red earth.

Fahfee was not my dad's first choice of occupation. Instead, it was a last resort. With fahfee you were harassed by the police and you ran the risk of actually being arrested. You were up against irritated betters most days and your profits were a seesaw of luck and chance.

By contrast, shopkeepers might have a bad month or two, but they did not face the blow that came with a succession of losses that could not be predicted or planned for.

But fahfee was what my father did, and being an employee was also one of the hard choices he had to make. Working for someone else meant he did not have to find the capital to float a sustainable number of fahfee banks; there were minimised risks and a fixed income.

Dad had tried to run a few small banks by himself before he worked for Gou Sok but they never turned out to be as lucrative as he had hoped. Throughout that time, my mom played a role, counting out the money and helping with the recording of the playing trends. As my brother and sister grew older, they also learnt how to transcribe the data from the betting slips to the record books. My mom was meticulous, neat and fast. Her accuracy and speed meant that when my dad worked for Gou Sok my mom occasionally took on work from other fahfee men who needed someone to keep their books up to date and ready for each day's *num ju*.

When my dad returned to fahfee after the shop, it was as Gou Sok's employee at the Doornfontein flat. Eventually Gou Sok and his wife moved to a bigger house in the suburbs that became the base for their fahfee business.

But we knew the flat in Doornfontein best as it was just around the corner from the other grey suburbs where Chinese families like us could live. In the flat building were a number of other Chinese families. Our school bus even stopped in front of the Robincrest flats that were a short distance from the concrete trunks that held up the noisy old Harrow Road offramp.

We sometimes went to the Doornfontein flat to drop off my dad, pick him up or fetch something during the day. We also visited the flats during the holidays for one of our family's favourite entertainment: Chinese videos.

An old man who lived there hired out Chinese videos on Beta and VHS. We had a Beta machine, and we liked his secret shop that was illegal for all sorts of reasons, including piracy and operating from residential premises without a permit.

The old man knew people in Hong Kong who recorded the various Cantonese drama series on TV there and shipped the tapes out to him. The old uncle had a slow drawl that was about as ponderous as his walk. He wore his neat, belted trousers pulled well above his waist to contain his bulging belly. He would lead us into one of the bedrooms converted into his video store. In metal cabinets lined up against the walls, there were rows and rows of hours of drama, period movies, kung fu movies and variety shows.

My mom read out the titles and asked the old uncle about them and he told us about the stars and the plots. Most series spanned four cassettes, sometimes six, and there were even epics over eight or nine tapes. We liked movies with modern-day plots but we also enjoyed the kung fu movies with the heroines with their perfect hair pinned back in black, shiny buns and hair clips dangling with beads and silk flowers. The heroes and heroines all had powers, special fighting magic. My favourites were the heroines who could strike a *kata* pose, then unfurl a bolt of flying ribbon from inside their beautiful, wispy Chinese dresses to reveal a deadly strangle of silk that would stop a baddie in his tracks.

We selected a series and headed home for one of the video marathons that marked so many of our school holidays. There was only one final wait: rewinding all the tapes so we could watch without interruption. People never rewound video tapes; we never did either. Then, with only the play button to push, we were in video rapture.

After the first three-hour tape, we broke for dinner – something quick and easy to prepare, like leftovers and a spinach soup or instant noodles, so we could get back to the TV. Sometimes we popped out to get takeaway fried chicken or pizza. For the pizza we went to a local café that had a wood-fired oven among its Pac-Man machines and the racks of canned goods, soap powders and newspapers that made up the rest of the store. It was a café and pizzeria in one, without any fancy Italian decorations, but the pizzas were delicious all the same.

During these video marathons, we were allowed to eat in front of the TV and our dinner bowls were stacked in the wash basin to be dealt with in the morning. We also neglected the chores that we were expected to do. Mom was as engrossed as we all were.

We kept watching until dad arrived home. He did not spend much time in front of the TV with us, but settled at the table in the living room. One of us made him a cup of tea and he often crunched on a few peanuts, one of his favourite snacks. He liked the nuts that came in sealed tins. Sometimes my mom cooked up kilos of fresh nuts in salted water before drying them in the sun. We would peel them and put them in little money bags so dad could snack on his treat without any effort.

Dad forced himself to watch only a few glimpses from his seat because later, when we had finished the second tape, said our goodnights and gone to bed, he would watch the first tape.

In this way, the family would all watch the series over two or three days, and then return to the flat, ready for the next release the video man had on offer.

By the end of the school holidays, we were dreaming about the handsome heroes and their beautiful counterparts and singing the theme songs sung by Hong Kong celebrities from two or three years previously.

Mah Jong and Ponies

Other dads may have had hobbies, from tinkering with car engines to getting stuck into DIY projects or playing and watching sports. These were not pastimes for my father. He was a gambling man and betting for the fun of it was his favourite relaxation. He enjoyed betting on the horses, playing *mah jong*, or *daa mah juk* as we say more commonly in Cantonese, with a few friends or others who gathered at private houses or in the back rooms of restaurants to play a few rounds. Years later, he also started to gamble at the casinos when they opened up closer to Johannesburg. He preferred one-armed bandits, roulette and the blackjack tables.

It was the best of both worlds for dad when we went on an outing that also involved gambling. Sometimes we went to Sun City, about three hours' drive from Johannesburg, in the former homeland of Bophuthatswana where a black man ruled. We knew this because there were lit photos of him in the dark, artificial spaces of pseudo-plush casinos and he wore an impressive sash and a lot of medals on his jacket. Only many years later would I learn about homelands and the poisonous concessions and trade-offs made by the National Party.

At Sun City we spent our day at the pools and waterslides, exhausting ourselves as my mother looked on. Occasionally she checked in with my dad and tossed a few coins into a one-armed bandit to try her luck as the sevens, cherries or bells lined up. Then she came back to soak up a bit more sun. She was never in a bathing suit, but she wore a sundress and a big peak cap to keep the sun from her face.

Photographs from those days showed us splashing at the poolside or clutching balloons and sitting on the velour seats where under-eighteens were allowed to wait as adults gambled in the casinos. We nodded off and goofed off, fiddling with the tops of the ashtrays and seeing who could slide off the seats with their velvety finishes, as our dad played just one more round, placed one more bet. There was always that one last try that stretched out our waiting and delayed the return journey to Johannesburg.

We mostly went to Sun City on day trips as it was too costly to stay overnight. But occasionally, usually in the Christmas holidays, we did stay at the hotel for a weekend or a few nights. There were perks to being a regular like my dad; the casino cut some deals and there were discounts designed to keep him at the tables a little longer.

No matter how it happened, the hotel room was a complete treat for us children. We turned the air-conditioning right up, then right down; we stroked the perfectly ironed and perfectly white linen; and we could not get over the miniature soaps and bubble-bath containers being replenished every day. We crammed on to two sofas and two camp beds in the space behind the folded shutters that adjoined the room that had a double bed. It was a squeeze, but we did not argue; the hotel was too much fun.

My dad allowed us to order room service. He knew we wanted to be like characters in the movies who lounged around on their beds, picked up the phone and had their meals delivered on a trolley covered with a silver, domed lid. Yolanda was in charge of ordering as it was unfamiliar to all of us. The first time she wanted to order bacon and eggs but was confused by the fancy-sounding 'continental breakfast' and asked for that instead. We all waited for our bacon and eggs but instead along came six baskets of toast, croissants and more baked goods than we knew what to do with.

Dad also loved betting on horses. In our house there was always a stack of racing magazines that had photos of horses and jockeys in black and white freeze-frame victory. There were also piles of betting slips that my dad kept handy. Betters were supposed to mark off their favoured ponies on the small rectangles printed on the betting slip and hand these over with their money at the tote. I sometimes went to the tote with dad. TVs were affixed with adjustable arms to shelves and betters tilted their heads to look at the horses cutting through the wind. Their arms were folded. Crumpled betting slips and old receipts lay abandoned on the tote floor, testament to changed minds and disillusion following loss.

We were not supposed to waste the betting slips at home, but we could not resist the crisp sheets to doodle on or to fashion into origami lanterns, folded paper cameras or aeroplanes we launched against each other. As long as we left enough in the stack of slips for dad's use we mostly escaped him noticing.

When dad was home on Saturday afternoons he listened to the racing results on the radio or he turned on the TV to the racing coverage if there was some live action happening. We kept quiet as the horses sprang free from the starting gates. It was exciting stuff for dad so we held our breath as the commentator rattled off one very long sentence, only taking a breath as the winning horse galloped past the camera and slowed down to a trot after a few paces.

On one occasion, dad made a family outing of going down to the horse track at Turffontein. We arrived and found a grassy, shaded spot outside the track on which to set up our picnic blanket. Dad left us to go and place his bets. We lounged around eating our snacks and listening to the radio that was on inside the car.

When dad returned to our picnic spot we told him the radio in the car had stopped working. He was already edgy as he turned the key in the ignition; clearly the ponies had not been kind that day. The car's battery was stubbornly uncooperative and because we were in a secluded spot it was not easy to find someone to help jump-start the car. Dad stormed off to find help.

It was a disaster of a day out. Even the novelty of a picnic of red jelly inside the shells of scooped-out oranges, which Yolanda had made especially, along with other itsy-bitsy picnic foods, quickly vanished. We never went to the track again with dad after that.

Dad also placed bets with a Chinese man who had a sideline business as a bookie. The Chinese bookie was a regular drop-in visitor but he rarely stepped inside the house. 'Oh, don't worry about opening the gate,' he would say, each time we invited him in, even though we knew he always declined. It was an expected exchange marked by good manners and pleasantries.

Then he passed a nondescript brown envelope to us. Written on the envelope would be my father's name in Chinese and a figure. Sometimes the envelope would be bulky and we knew that my dad had won money on the horses. Other times the envelope would be empty and the number written on the front was what my father owed the bookie.

I occasionally thought of hiding these empty envelopes when they were delivered week after week and I knew that receiving them would make my dad unhappy. But he would get doubly mad because the bookie would issue a second empty envelope and the shame of having to be asked twice would be worse. Instead, we received the envelope, greeted the uncle and said goodbye properly, then placed the empty envelope where my dad would see it when he got home later.

We propped up mail and other important things for my dad's notice against a 3-D picture of a Chinese pagoda that my mom displayed on the mantelpiece. On the other end of the mantelpiece was another 3-D picture of a doll-like Hansel and Gretel standing outside their magical gingerbread house with wafer biscuits for tiles and candy-striped lollipops for flowers.

Sometimes I swopped the pictures around, hoping that the smiling children standing outside their gingerbread house of deliciousness would lessen the blow for dad when the envelopes kept arriving empty and the ponies were not running the way he wanted.

Dad carried on playing and sometimes we even played along with him when there were big horse-racing meets. He got each of us to bet on our favourite horse. We crowded dad and his spread-out newspaper to scrutinise the colourful pictures of the jockeys. We did not read any of the text that came with each photo. We did not understand favourites, odds, places and all the other jargon of horse racing. Instead, we chose our horses by the colours and designs of the jockey's outfits. It had to be something pink or something flash that caught our eyes and we would point that horse out as our choice. Choosing in the random way we did was close enough to how gamblers mostly make up their minds anyway. Decisions are based on chance and fate, and the irrational and illogical are turned into imagined strategy.

It did not matter that they were usually no-hopers; my father made the bets for us anyway. Sometimes he said we had made a good choice and then after the big race he would come home and hand one of us a R10 note or even a R20 note because our horse had crossed the line first.

Mah juk was another happy merger of the social and the thrill of gambling for many men and women like my dad. It was also a party favourite for many Chinese families. *Mah juk* is not like a spontaneous round or two of the board game 30 Seconds after dinner. *Mah juk* at a party is second only in importance to the food that is served.

A couple of square tables are set up. Each is draped with brown paper as the four players at each table settle down to build up a double deck of the special tiles, building pairs, building sets, like a kind of rummy, I believe.

Unlike most Chinese children, I never learnt to play and neither did any of my siblings. It was something my mother was particularly proud of. 'I do not want you to grow up broken gamblers,' she said each time we asked to be taught how to play. My dad obliged her and he never taught us either, even though we asked regularly and insistently.

Instead, the *mah juk* sets we had were used to build towers and to make boxy animals from the decorated tiles.

Mom firmly believed that in our family the gambling gene skipped our generation. Maybe she was right; I have never had the desire to buy a Lotto ticket or to chase the supposed thrill that comes with a casino win. The sound of coins hitting metal basins, ringing alarms and flashing lights only remind me of how uncomfortable plush seats eventually became in the darkness of casinos like Sun City when we waited for dad as children. The flashing lights and mechanical ringing of someone's win would startle us awake from our already interrupted sleep. Then we would try to stay awake a little longer, fighting our eyelids that dropped like lead weights. We were not supposed to sleep on these seats and a security guard would walk by every now and again to make sure my mother nudged us awake.

I never wondered much about how gambling ran through my father's life, a thread of obsession that sewed up his life from work to down-time and even socialising with his friends. It was normal, the everyday of our lives.

This normal included my frequent trips with dad to *Ma Lay Gum*, the name local Chinese gave to Chinatown in downtown Commissioner Street. Today the locals call it First Chinatown, to distinguish it from the city's later Chinatown of newer migrants in Cyrildene. The old name, I am told, came from when the top end of Fordsburg was part of the Malay quarter. The Chinese were here, too, and they set up the old Cantonese Club and established a little Chinatown of a few streets under the gaze of the blue building that was the notorious John Vorster Square police station, where people the apartheid government despised slipped on bars of soap or threw themselves out of windows.

I would go downtown with dad to do the family shopping for our sacks of rice, the long grain fragrant variety, not the parboiled, never properly fluffed-up stuff on supermarket shelves. There were the wrapped parcels of dried sheets of bean curd that you could add to vegetarian stir-fries, bottles and bottles of soya sauce and fresh spinach, all dark green and spotted with specks of soil.

With my dad there were also treats to take home along with the staples my mom expected for the pantry. Dad chatted to the shop owners as they prepared his order, gathering from a tower of bamboo steamers soft buns filled with honey-roasted pork, *char siu*, and sweet lotus bean paste. There were also bite-sized *dim sum* and chicken drumsticks covered in a crispy batter.

Then we headed to what was probably the most important part of our downtown shopping trip. Our destination was one of the oldest and smallest shops in the strip of stores and restaurants along Commissioner Street. It was a small provisions store in which everything was imported from China by the old uncle who ran it. I swung my legs on his old wooden stools waiting for dad and the Ah Buk to finish their catch up. Boxes filled with egg noodles, bottles of black bean paste, Chinese bowls and pairs of chopsticks were packed right up to the ceiling. His miniature window display had porcelain figurines of Chinese ladies in flowing dresses, laughing Buddhas and ornaments depicting scenes of pagodas and rickety bridges all cut from cork. Ah Buk always treated me to sweets, the *saang jah beang* that are little discs of sweetened dried fruit rolled up one on top of the other. I loved that in one stack you felt like you had a roll of sweets to last you the whole day, or at least the whole trip home. He often passed me a few extra rolls to give to Yolanda, Kelvin and Unisda. He knew us all through the years.

Once I was sorted out with sweets, my dad and the Ah Buk would vanish temporarily to the back section of the tiny shop. My dad would walk out with a wrapped and sealed parcel under his one arm and a plastic bag bulging with odd shapes in the other. As I got older, I realised that the purchase was the printed stacks of fahfee paper, wrapped up so that cops who may stop the car would at first glance not know what they were looking at. The odd bulges in the plastic bags were the little wallets that would be numbered and distributed to dad's betters.

This was the norm of shopping with my dad. Also usual were the superstitions that were attached to gambling and to fahfee. One of mom's superstitions was about our shoes. If she found our shoes flipped over, she would get very upset. She believed this would bring bad luck to dad, that our flipped-over shoes were an omen about dad's car turning over in an accident. He spent so much time driving that one of her biggest worries was that he would be injured or even killed in a car crash. If my shoes were found in the crash position, I would not be able to sleep for nights on end, worried that I had willed the portents of death to dad's car.

Of course, I was not allowed to talk about the fear that filled my heart. There was another superstition attached to that. '*Choi, choi, choi!*' my mother would exclaim if we said something ominous or unlucky. The '*chois*' in triplicate were for countering the evil that would be made real as the thought turned into words.

She had other superstitions, too. We were told not to touch or bump the chairs of *mah juk* players when we were at gatherings and parties. Their losses and bad luck could be blamed on us, my mother warned. And lose people did, whether we bumped them or not. There would be a grand performance of mock rage, throwing down their *mah juk* tiles and letting out some angry exclamation, shaking their heads and pushing their chairs away from the table in disgust. But after a break, they were back at the *mah juk* table ready to have another go. And at other times, a player would ask us children to fill up a teacup or bring back a snack from the kitchen. For this small favour we were given a generous tip, a *dak jay*, so sometimes we were seen as a good luck charms, too.

For my dad, gambling was the adrenalin of a win, a high with rewards. But like all gambles, it was followed by the tumble of mood swings, desperate raging when Lady Luck turned her back on him and more of his chewed-up nails would be bitten down into the infinity of regret.

I knew dad's mood swings that came with the seesaw of wins and losses but I also knew that whatever gambling tempted him, it never consumed him enough to cloud his biggest priority of raising us properly. Dad and mom went without treats or new things for themselves to make sure we had rice in the pantry, money for books and even for the extras of a field trip or a treat at the roadhouse.

Mom moaned a bit about dad's gambling but she often said to relatives and friends: 'At least he is not a reckless gambler. He has never gambled with money that we needed for school books or to pay the mortgage and when he does win he gives the money to me for running the house.'

I separated dad's social gambling from the gambling of fahfee. One was fun and the other work. And while even social gambling had its fair share of superstition and peculiarities, it was fahfee that defined the codes and unspoken rules that came to dominate the Ho household.

Fahfee had an overwhelming code of silence. Its stigma and secrecy grew formidable in the silence. This stigma and secrecy became a striking emblem of my parents' existence of working and more working, but still being excluded from an economic mainstream and being labelled socially unacceptable outside the Chinese community. Fahfee stayed relegated to taboo, even though it was a strategy for economic survival.

As children, we kept quiet about fahfee, even to our Chinese school friends. They knew about this code of silence, too, because their fathers, mothers or uncles were also involved in fahfee. We dodged the truth on all official forms asking for 'Father's occupation' and for his official work status we piggybacked on the details of the one legitimate shop that a relative of ours had in Denver.

We knew to turn off the TV and hide, not making a sound, when policemen, both black and white, came knocking on our door. We hoped to fool them into believing there was no one home, but more often than not the knocking did not stop and my mother or father ended up opening the door and thrusting money into the deep palms of these cops.

There were also the times when the urgent ringing of the phone would bring a panicked call from some police station where my dad had been detained. But, ultimately, fahfee did not land anyone in jail for very long.

When there were court cases, they ended in suspended sentences. More often, there were simply warnings or money, bottles of brandy and bow ties changed hands. These were the weapons of agency and power when you were not part of the system.

I hated that dad sweated and laboured like he did and still had to suffer the demeaning injustices of someone else's laws. I hated that fahfee took so much out of him and that we had to pretend this was not what he did at all.

My dad was not a bitter person; he never took it out on us that he worked so hard and he never resented that there were so many of us to feed and raise. But I remember well the one day when his frustration with us, his surly ungrateful teenagers, overflowed. The house must have been in a mess and maybe he could not find something he thought we had misplaced and he exploded.

'I work like a donkey for what? For you?' he burst out as the four of us children scattered from his anger. He did not speak much English, but he chose to use this foreign tongue because he wanted us, his growing children, who had become estranged from the ideals of his imagination, to understand unequivocally that as much as he protected us from his pain, and spared us having to repeat his hard life as a child and young man, that old hurt resided in him still.

The Outside Toilet

The first dog I can remember having, I had for only one night. I was about five years old and I simply picked up the furry bundle of caramel from the street corner and carried her home. I was convinced she was a girl dog and I was also convinced we could keep her. She loved me instantly with warm licks and a wagging bushy tail and I loved her back so I figured such a certain bond had to be the start of a beautiful friendship.

But my mom said no. She said the dog probably belonged to someone who lived in the block of flats at the corner of the street. She said she had seen the dog in the garden there sometimes. At these words, I must have cried and cried and my mom realised I was not going to give up this new friend easily. She calmed me by saying we could keep the dog, so my siblings and I played and fussed with her the whole day until, exhausted, we tumbled into bed. Mom said the dog could sleep in the backyard and assured me we would be together again in the morning.

Late that night I was woken by a commotion outside our bedroom that was always lit by a night light of a lampshade with soft tassels and purple pleats. I heard my parents talking and I heard the front door opening. But I turned over in my lower bunk bed and went back to sleep.

Morning brought news that my caramel friend had escaped in the night, but of course my parents had returned her to her owner, saving me the heartache of goodbyes and saving them from having to go through another round of impossible explanations.

It was this incident, Yolanda said, that convinced our parents to get a family dog we could all grow up with.

Our pets were so-called pavement specials with no pedigreed pretensions, just big spirits and wagging tails and we fell in love with all the dogs and one cat who came to share our home over the years. We also came up with our own language. We 'furry' our pets, instead of 'petting' them. Even as grown-ups, the Ho-styled verb sticks as our own sentimental all-gooey doing word for loving pets and animals.

Our parents did not expect this when they finally agreed to have animals in the home. My parents believed dogs were for warding off intruders. They growled and barked to keep the dangers of the dark from the house. Cats caught mice and kept one eye open for birds that pecked at the spinach and prickly melons growing in the garden. Pets were not for being pampered at fancy parlours or for annual vaccinations at the vet. In our house, dogs had to have sturdy digestive systems; they ate store-bought food and scraps off the table, not the luxuries of scientifically designed and imported dog foods.

When we were much younger, Kelvin was allowed to keep silkworms when the craze hit our school. We collected mulberry leaves for them and Kelvin first kept the slim slithering worms in an old Mill's cigarette tin. As the worms grew fat, he put them into a shoe box. Personally I was grossed out by them and I hated it when other children took the worms in their hands and thrust their opened palms to my face for me to get a really good look.

When we looked again, the worms had disappeared, having woven their chunky bodies into tight, yellow cocoons. Mom told us that in China people would collect the cocoons, boil them and create silk from them. She even had a story about how she once used a few strands of silk to fashion an almost translucent slip knot to fish out a few freshwater prawns from a brook near her village.

I did not believe the story. I did not want to believe silk came from silkworms. Surely the worms, ugly as they were, did not have to be sacrificed to make silk and how could mom bear watching them pop the living, breathing worms into the vats of boiling water?

Nowadays I understand quite well my parents' attitude. It was summed up for me in a documentary I watched on TV some years ago that featured migrants' thoughts on the relationship between people and pets in the United States.

'I could not believe they let the pets sleep in their beds; they treat them like children or a member of the family and some of them even have toys,' said the subtitles as the newcomer to the US spoke to the interviewer.

Our parents loved our pets in their own way. Pets had their place – outside; being useful, functional. With each new pet that joined our lives, we used the opportunity to test the functionality rule; we also ended up testing our parents' ability to pronounce English pets' names that went from the reasonably-easy-to-pronounce Happy and Winnie to Figaro and Mozart.

'Please can Mozart sleep in the kitchen?'; 'Please can the dogs come in the house in the daytime at least?' We never convinced our parents but we tried damn hard.

The first pet dog to join us was a straw-white mutt called Lingo. She was a medium-sized dog with a pretty coat that curled in places and she had the sweetest face.

But it was in her litter of puppies a short time later that I met Happy. Lingo's tiny black puppy was the one my parents decided we should keep. I was about five years old when Happy was born. So we grew up together. We had been worried for days when Lingo did not want to come out to play and barely touched her food. Then suddenly there were all these puppies. I loved the happy face of the puppy we were allowed to keep and I called him Happy. He was coal-black like the charcoal backyard that was his domain, but he had the lightest, truest spirit. In our Bertrams house, Happy shared the backyard not only with pigeons, chickens and rabbits at various times, but also with Sophie, our domestic worker.

Sophie's room was in the basement beneath the kitchen. It had one small window and seemed to me always to be in pitch darkness, probably because there was no electricity in her room. She had a paraffin lamp for light and sometimes she cooked on a hissing primus stove when she wanted to make her own meals and not eat what my mother had put aside for her. On some nights, she took chunky slices of white bread with margarine and jam and her enamel cup filled with tea with three sugars and said goodnight for the evening.

Sophie wore canvas takkies without laces and with the tongues turned up. She tied a *doek* (headscarf) on her head and wore housecoats over her voluminous layers of skirts. In winter, a hand-me-down jersey, stretched and misshapen, might top her shwe-shwe fabric dresses that always smelt faintly of the no-nonsense green bars of Sunlight soap.

Sophie was a third parent to us in many ways, but in so many other ways she was simply a servant – never eating from our plates, living in a room separate from the house, where the pets were, where the outside toilet was. She was someone whose birth name or family name I did not even know.

In Chinese culture you do not address people who are older than you, strangers included, by their first names. You show deference by tagging on an honorific. Even Yolanda and Kelvin, my own brother and sister, I call names that translate as 'my family sister' and 'my family brother'; I do not use their names. But Sophie, this stand-in parent, was never afforded this respect.

When my parents were away and when, on many occasions, my mom helped out at relatives' cafés and eating houses in downtown Johannesburg, it was left to Sophie to keep order and look after us children. It was Sophie's discipline and judgements that we conformed to and her '*haibos*', the Zulu exclamation of surprise, that she used to keep us from mischief.

When we had it our way, we squeezed out the fun of each day in games that included sibling feuds ranging from irritating each other to physical fights involving hair pulling and punching. My brother exploited his bigger size often and it was to Sophie's skirts we girls would run, clutching the material in fistfuls as my brother reached around the skirt trying to swipe us and grab us, until Sophie put her foot down. Literally, it was an ankle she decorated with the woven woollen threads that represented her church colours. When she demanded that my brother stop, he would.

She never cared half-heartedly for us and sometimes she even stepped forward in our defence when we were being punished by our parents, knitting her brow, shaking her head and putting her hands out to ward off a slap destined for our behinds.

During the year, Sophie sometimes went on leave to visit her own family for weeks at a time. I never knew where she was going. In Chinese my mom explained she was going to her *ju kaa* (family home). It was far away in my imagination, in reality, too, I am sure. She would prepare big, hardy, crunchy plastic bags that stood like firm rectangles when they were filled. They would be bulging and neatly zipped up as she readied to leave. The housecoat would disappear and so would the *doek*. On her head would be a jaunty beret and she would wear a freshly pressed dress and short coat. We waved her goodbye at the gate and then she would be gone until a few weeks later.

Only years later did I even begin to wonder about her life away from us as a wife, a mother, a woman, a friend. At the time, I never thought much about Sophie's other life or the things that were important to her, like why she wanted us to bring her back some sea water when we once went on a family holiday to Durban. Why would anyone want sea water, I wondered? It was salty, it burnt your eyes and it was the gigantic toilet of all the sea creatures and holidaymakers, too, no doubt.

I only learnt about the spirit in those waters much later. In the meantime, my mother saved up the empty bottles, rinsed them and made sure they got stashed in the car boot as we headed south to the coast for our rare treat of a beach holiday together.

Sophie clapped her hands when we presented the water to her on our return. I knew it held a kind of magic, but just looking at the bottles, and the few grains of sand resting at the bottom, I was not convinced.

Years later, I got the chance to visit a cave in the Free State, a sacred site. The ancient mountain, and the river that runs alongside it, was a place of the ancestors and a place of the gods for those who know it. My friends and I found a small, hidden path and walked it until we reached the river. A few faithful were being baptised. They were dressed in church outfits that I remembered looked like what Sophie wore all those years ago when she went off on Sundays to her church meetings. Like Sophie, the women also covered their heads in a cloth tied neatly at the nape of their necks. And then they were plunged into the water as a preacher, knee-deep in the fast-moving water, prayed over the baptised.

No one asked why we had come; someone simply told us to leave our shoes and cross the river. Three of us made the crossing, without conferring with each other, without saying a word and barely feeling the sharp pebbles beneath our feet.

'You have come because the ancestors have told you to come,' one man said as he welcomed us at the top of the inclined path that led to the coolness of the cave. He pointed out a trickle of water that ran down the smooth face of the cave. 'You can wash there and be cleansed, then you can speak to the ancestors,' he said.

We washed and drank in the coolness, then sat quietly with him a bit, understanding a little of how the ancestors turn waiting into patience and surrender. Others had come before, decorating parts of the mountain, sweeping the sand smooth where they slept, dreaming the ancestors' message into reality.

On our way down the mountain we met two people who had been baptised. We congratulated them and made the journey together to the bottom.

The pair needed a lift in the opposite direction to where we were heading, but we were the ones with the transport. When we dropped them off in the small town, they said thank you and the man closed his eyes briefly. He raised his hand a little and prayed. Then he withdrew from a plastic bag a small Coke bottle filled with the water he had collected from the trickle down the mountain's face. There were other bottles he had carried all the way down the mountain.

'Put this in the baby's bath water,' he said, pointing to my friend's infant boy who had been part of our group. 'It will protect him.'

I stayed in my spot at the back of the canopied pickup where I had sat with the man we had given the lift to. I had offered up my seat to the older woman who had joined us. I cried quietly all the way back past the mountain. I knew then the source of Sophie's magic water.

Sometimes Sophie would arrive a day or two later from her leave than had been agreed on. My mother's grumbles started up as the sun set on the agreed-on return date. I hated those sunsets, because I knew heads would butt when Sophie walked through the door in the next day or two. Of course, my mother had the upper hand. Sophie would have to take the tongue-lashing and there would be no happy greetings for someone we had genuinely missed.

But eventually she would come back and as soon as she had removed her beret and her closed ladies' shoes, she was back in the role of the maid. The *doek* was back on her head and her spotless takkies with their turned-up tongues on her feet.

She was like a second mother but she remained a mystery. When she invited us into her room, we saw her bed raised on bricks and covered with neat layers of blankets. The bricks were to keep away the tokoloshes, she told us. The mythical creature with a man's face and a monkey's body that Sophie described terrified me throughout my childhood. Later, when I was in Standard Four and going through a government-issue history textbook, I remember coming across a drawing of what the artist imagined a tokoloshe to look like. It was probably some pejorative dismissal about 'native' superstition. My jaw dropped and my eyes grew wide – Sophie's devilish demon with its supernatural terror was indeed true because it was in my textbooks. I did not care what the words said, there was the picture of the tokoloshe! I wished for years after that my bed could also be elevated on bricks.

These days I still like to ask people what a tokoloshe looks like. I smile when, if they are South African, they do not say 'a what?' or 'huh?' but launch into a description as if they had seen the creature the night before as it bounced from the darkness across their bedrooms.

It hurts now that I do not remember Sophie's face well and I do not even know if Sophie was her real name. Back then, I did not question this relationship in the same way that I never asked questions about the outside toilet, a feature of so many South African homes.

Now I see the outside toilet as the ceramic bowl of national shame. There it stands, apart from the rest of the house. There are no sparkling tiles, no extras of a mirror to adjust a stray strand of hair, hand lotions in pump-action bottles to indulge freshly washed hands or two-ply toilet paper.

But it stands sure, apart, plain and basic; it is meant only for the maid and the gardener. And new generations have filled Sophie's shoes. They are still black women, still the women who wear overalls with matching aprons and *doeks*. They no longer have to say madam or eat from the enamel plate but they are still considered the primary suspects behind a missing brooch or the dipping sugar levels in the pantry. They are still paid a wage that is little more than the cost of some madams' pairs of shoes.

I get sad when I hear Chinese South Africans speak about their pain and humiliations at being treated like second-class citizens. Their faces burn with anger when they remember the humiliation of having to ask white people if their children could learn in their schools, or they had to carry documents like my dad had to, declaring them 'gentlemen of good standing' or they had to go from door to door with spring rolls and smiles asking to be allowed to buy or rent a house in a white suburb.

But their memories of racial injury were fuzzy when it came to their domestic workers or gardeners sometimes. Food that was past its expiry date was good enough for the 'girl'. There were still separate enamel plates and cutlery differentiated with a crude scrape of a sharp knife. This was for the woman who knew the exact amount of milk to pour into the madam's tea, how to coax their grumpy children to sleep and what underwear they kept in their drawers.

Sophie must have worked for our family for six or seven years until shortly after we moved to our house in Judith's Paarl, just a few kilometres away from our Bertrams home. I am not sure if she eventually had a fallout with my parents or whether she did indeed have to return to her family in that faraway *ju kaa*, as we were told.

We never had another live-in, full-time maid and I never saw Sophie again after she said goodbye to us for the last time outside the gate. All these years later, it is a shame that in some ways I remember Happy, the sweet, loyal dog of my childhood, better than I do Sophie, this woman who was also a stand-in mom.

The Hand that History Deals

As gambles go, it was a big risk for my parents and grandparents to have hedged a bet on a good life in Naam Fey, this country in the south of the world.

They could not have guessed, or maybe they did not want to know, about something like the Group Areas Act of 1950 that was already in place by the time they arrived in the country. Maybe they figured these were itty-bitty laws like 'keep off the grass' or something like that. I imagine they must have convinced themselves that things would be better for them. They would have believed that their hard work, their readiness to face up to whatever hurdles lay ahead, would see them through. As poor villagers not politically connected with the Communist Party elite, they were second-class citizens in their own country anyway; could South Africa really be worse?

Dad's older brother, whom we called Lok Buk and who lives in Macau today, cast his mind back over 60 years and remembered that his younger brother, my dad, as the uneducated orphaned teenager in China, had to survive as a scavenger when they had all left home and when his mother had died. Dad could lean only so much on relatives and on the kindness of those in the extended community of the village who themselves had so little to build a life. By going through other people's rubbish, he found things that could still be used or that he could sell or barter for a few coins or lumps of rice.

Lok Buk's story opened valves of sadness for me but it also gave context to why men like my father and women like my mother made the decision to come here. It was really about choosing to leave a broken China. Whatever lay ahead for them – racial persecution, being second-class citizens, starting from scratch – still held the possibility of being better than what they knew in those southern villages in Guangdong, especially for dad.

For my Lok Buk, who ended up in Mozambique, the years there gave him the life of a second family and the odd jobs and few years of shopkeeping meant he did get to save enough money. When the outbreak of civil war prompted him to leave, he returned to China, to his wife and three children, without empty hands. He chose to settle in Macau, which, like the old Lourenço Marques, was familiarly stained with its Portuguese colonial imprint.

In *Colour, Confusion and Concessions* Melanie Yap and Dianne Leong Man spell out how bad prospects were for the Chinese from their very first days on the African continent: 'From the 1870s [Chinese immigrants] settled in the Cape, Natal, and later the Transvaal only to discover that being Chinese limited their opportunities and made them outsiders in a land where race drew the dividing line.'

The South Africa of the 1960s that greeted my parents was already haemorrhaging. Protests against racial oppression had turned from marching to massacre; the bleeding from the Sharpeville uprising had soaked the streets with the blood of 69 people. It was the follow-on from the incendiary flare-ups that had started years before, including in 1956 when hundreds of women showed their steel by marching on the Union Buildings to protest the carrying of passbooks.

The campaign of public bombings by the armed wing of the ANC had started to crest and by 1963 it would result in the Rivonia Trial that would see Nelson Mandela and his nine ANC co-accused charged with sabotage. It made the National Party more resolute to keep the black man in his place, under its tyrannical thumb.

That thumb would press down on the Chinese and squash their hopes for a better life, along with all non-white groups. The Chinese may not have been part of the political melee, but they were still part of the dangerous non-white unknown, the *geel gevaar*, the communist yellow danger, as the apartheid government referred to them. Even though there were quotas that restricted the number of Chinese allowed into the country, the Chinese had been in the country from the early days of the Dutch East Indies arrivals in the 1660s. Back then, they arrived as slaves and convicts from what is today Indonesia. In later years, they would arrive as stowaways from the mainland, like my family. In addition, a handful of free Chinese had ventured to the southern tip of the 'dark' continent over the decades.

But long years here did not mean that the Chinese eventually gained the status of merging with the comfort and acceptance tagged on to being middle class. The Chinese of my parents' generation remained on the periphery. They were allowed to become traders, like the Indians, but they were prohibited from owning property or shops, from serving whites in white areas and they were not allowed to live in white areas.

Even those who became professionals, who got the same degrees and qualifications through quota systems, were forced to take lower positions than their white colleagues. But instead of uproar, protest or joining a union, they simply carried on working harder and becoming even more loyal to their companies, even when their employers checked first with white staff if it was okay for the single Chinese employee to use the same toilet.

Apartheid entered the statute books when the National Party came into power in 1948. Their plan was for social engineering for not just separateness, but for oppression of the black man. It was a methodical system that was terrifyingly efficient. It would reserve decent jobs, decent education and decent living areas for whites only. For my immigrant father, illiterate in English and without any financial muscle, his life in South Africa was always going to see him as a shopkeeper, a fahfee man or put to work for someone else who ran a small trade business like making security gates and fencing or selling spare parts for cars and other light industrial operations.

My father did not arrive here with the prospect of becoming a citizen; he was not the kind of immigrant marked for strategic assimilation by having to learn the chronology of a country's past presidents or being able to mumble through a national anthem and to eventually join the tax base. Dad had to survive in South Africa as the loathed trespasser, not someone who worked through the migrant milestones over a few years to eventually become a citizen. It would take decades before he and my mom were given the status of naturalised citizens.

Fahfee becames an allegory for the life the Chinese hid from polite white society. Fahfee, the transaction of hidden spaces, was known to some and hidden from others. It always bore a burden of guilt and shame yet it could not simply be abandoned because it had economic muscle. It played out in secret spaces, making it part fiction and myth.

Numbers for fahfee betting revealed themselves in synchronicity's peculiar visions and dreamtime revelations. It was a mystery that was completely rational and reasonable. But you could only see this if you were a fahfee insider. From the outside – the view from the white neighbourhoods of over-chlorinated swimming pools and 'garden boys' scooping up dog poop – fahfee cleaved to its impenetrable anonymity.

Fahfee stayed a secret because that was how it could survive as an economic lifeline. Fahfee was the way out of the paltry trade of selling half loaves of bread and giving change in Chappies bubblegum in a shopfront. The hush around fahfee protected and disguised it enough to keep mainstream white society from getting too nervous about the Chinese.

But officially the National Party's Calvinistic state made fahfee men like my father criminals, along with buying liquor on a Sunday or being in possession of skin magazines without stars on the centrefold's critical bits. Fahfee was a tax dodge, it was also sinful gambling and, perhaps worst of all for the apartheid authorities, it looked like collusion between the non-white groups.

For the fahfee man, there was always a cat-and-mouse game with the fahfee man evading and eluding the police and the police giving chase. Sometimes the fahfee man got away, sometimes he got caught. When the blue lights flashed him to a standstill, the game was up for the mouse. Then came the confiscations of the record books, betting slips and the day's takings or the day's cash floats. Their bribes and warnings came next and also the parallel exhibition of power and contrition all ending in the tacit acknowledgement that the next day the chase would be on again.

An uncle of mine ran a corner café for many years. It was not until I was an adult and asking questions about the Chinese under apartheid that he said that he was also a fahfee man at one stage. I did not know this. With four children to raise, he had to supplement his income from the shop. You could only sell that many cans of pilchards and loose cigarettes to that many customers, he said.

He drove out in the middle of each day to a few banks, while my aunt stood behind the café counter by herself for a few hours. One day, he was just about finished at his banks when in his review mirror he saw a cop car tailing him. He turned into a side street, hoping not to look suspicious but also hoping to shake them off. But the blue lights came on and the police gave chase.

'I did not stop immediately and all I could do was drive off, roll down the window and throw out all the money, the betting slips and everything,' he said.

'When I looked in the rearview mirror I just saw the money flapping around and the coins bouncing off the tar. It was really heartsore to work so hard for your money and then to have to throw it all out the window like that. But I had no other choice, there was nothing else I could do because when they caught up with me, they would have arrested me if they found all the fahfee stuff in the car,' my uncle told me.

The story stunned me. It stunned me that the memory of the day's loss was so distinct even years after his children had grown and years after he had put his fahfee days behind him. It stunned me, too, because I had assumed that a shopkeeper had a better, more secure, life than a fahfee man.

Fahfee tested the elasticity of laws and it was high risk. On the days the fahfee man's bribes did not work, he was hauled downtown and kept locked up for a few hours. Very few fahfee men were processed according to judicial procedure. I did not hear of a single incident until I was an adult about people who actually came face to face with a magistrate. Fahfee as a transgression did not warrant the amount of paperwork for most policemen and less so for a courtroom. The arrests and heavy-handedness were about a show of power and about the clout of threat.

Three or four times throughout my childhood I can remember the alarm of a late night phone call from my father or one of his colleagues telling us that he was being held at a police station. There would be a flurry of phone calls as my mother made more inquiries to make sure my dad was safe and that he would be released soon.

Longing and absence became normal for us. Wishing my father to be near more often and knowing that that was not possible was part of our lives and our childhood. Those nights thinking that he could be taken from us and put in prison would send me into an internal frenzy of worry. At the same time I knew we were all expected to be composed enough not to lose it even when we knew the dread of bad news loomed as a very real possibility.

I visualised my father locked up like an animal, shouting to be let out, ignored and harassed by the cops and also by other inmates. It was the Hollywood picture of imprisonment that stalked my imagination.

In reality, the fahfee men were probably made to sit in the corner of some grimy charge office or holding cell. They were deliberately not told what was going to happen to them and they were punished by the silence and the hell of looking over and over again at the oily Prestik marks showing through outdated posters or listening to the hum of fluorescent lights. The cop would move behind the counter and find some paper to drag his black ink pen across slowly. The show of officiousness was a very effective weapon of bureaucratic torture.

Even though we knew that my father would be let out with a bribe or a fine, we never took these arrests lightly. He could come across that one policeman who would want to make an example of my father and detain him overnight or force him to show up in court to face even stiffer penalties.

Years later, I met a fahfee man who said he was one of the rare cases who did end up being charged and forced to make his case in front of a magistrate.

I joined him on rounds for some fieldwork for an anthropology research paper I was writing. I used a pseudonym for him, Georgie.

He was unusual because he was younger than my father's generation of fahfee men, he had a high school education in South Africa and he had some technical training as a mechanic. Still, he ended up as a fahfee man, working for himself and taking on the mantle of a new breed of fahfee men. He was regularly able to use his English proficiency to talk himself out of an arrest. Sometimes, he offered the cops a bribe as low as R30. It was a very low bribe, full of scorn, meant to show disrespect and contempt in his own subversive way. Unlike my father's generation of fahfee men, he got to play the rebel a bit. He was still the mouse, but now it was a mouse with attitude. I liked it a lot.

Georgie was not reckless, though. He had been caught those years earlier and the magistrate gave him a five-year suspended sentence. During that time he was forced to change his livelihood and he helped out as a mechanic's assistant and the family had to rely more heavily on his wife's income.

Today he is back at his banks, still dodging the police, still threading his way through the secret paths between rows of shacks. In these places where he finds his betters, the roads look like they come to a dead end but if you drive a little further along the dusty streets they lead to more informal settlements, the contiguous overflow from ordered urban life.

It was 2007 when I met Georgie, but in some ways he took me right back to the life of the fahfee men in the 1980s and early 90s. Fahfee had changed very little: the same betting slips were there, even the purses numbered with thick markers. Also unchanged were the townships and locations. Now they had names like Chris Hani and Ramaphosa but there were still few trees to hold back the dust. Houses were still shacks made up of zinc sheets and salvaged pieces of scrap held together by wire. People still arrived home by foot, dropped of somewhere by a taxi or from the train station.

I asked Georgie how fahfee men still made a living. He now competed with the new government's Lotto and the explosion of casinos across the city. Bonus balls and the artificial interiors of casinos with controlled temperatures tempted players away from men like Georgie, surely?

'People still bet on fahfee because our bets are still so low and also because the *ju fah goung* still comes right to their doorstep,' said Georgie. And he was right. I checked his betting slips and people were still betting 10 cents or 20 cents. It was a shame to think that R2.80 from a winning 10-cent bet was still something the poorest of poor South Africans looked forward to.

I guess in the same way Georgie made his living adding up all those failed 10-cent bets. Fahfee is never a first choice to make an income. Georgie knew that more was expected from him because he had a shot at education and because he could speak English fluently.

'This is a mug's game, I do not want my boy to follow in my footsteps,' he said. He drove and smoked, his right arm, resting on a fully opened window, getting darker than his left, just like my dad's arms took on different shades from his endless fahfee rounds.

Georgie's fahfee life was a mystery to his family, the way he wanted it, like my dad and the men and women of his generation wanted it.

'My family only know the routes to the banks so that they can know where to look if something happens to me, but more than that I do not want them to be involved with any of this,' he said.

Later that evening we returned to his home. His wife had already arrived from her office job and was preparing dinner as we chatted a bit more.

'Maybe, I will do this fahfee business for another five years, maybe I can sell the banks to someone who wants to take it over and then I will call it a day. It is not a great life because it is not safe and it is bloody hard work,' he said.

From the stove, his wife turned around and said: 'That is what you said five years ago.'

The risks were real. When I arrived at Georgie's house earlier in the day, he was starting his work day with prayers to the ancestors and to the gods (Kuan Kong in particular) – for protection, he told me. Georgie said that Kuan Kong, wielding his mighty sword and a formidable expression, would cut down his competitors and the lurking dangers that he faced as he headed off to his fahfee banks in the west of Johannesburg. He told me, as he lit the incense, that since he started making the offerings and giving thanks to the gods and ancestors things had started going more smoothly for him. He grew up Catholic, but he said religion in the form of Hail Marys as absolution from sin just did not cut it for him. Praying to the gods and remembering the ancestors, he said, felt more like the right thing. It was a return to his roots somehow and it fitted in more appropriately with his life as a *ju fah goung*.

For my dad as a fahfee man of the 1980s, the risks came from the harassment of police rather than the threat of criminals and thugs in the townships. He was part of the township landscape after all. He knew its unwritten codes, the hidden streets and secret places. He was not of the community but he was expected, he was known.

In the suburbs, the Chinese also had to make themselves known, at least known entities. They had to be seen and heard, but only just. They had to be contained by what people could assume about them but they could not be too conspicuous either.

The Chinese intentionally flew under the radar; undetected, they could make their lives, make their money. Some Chinese did make money, some even got rich but they could not be too showy about their fortunes. Flashiness was not encouraged; it drew too many questions and frugality was what the Chinese knew best. The shadow of hard times remained, the memory of what life used to be like in the villages of China did not fade easily.

Many years later, I was reminded all over again of the frugality of so many of the Chinese of my parents' generation. We moved house for my mother. Her things were put in boxes and old plastic crates that she marked in Chinese. The boxes and crates seemed to come from a wellspring of things that were half-functional, worn out or on the wrong side of their expiry dates. My mother was not able to part with old clothes that she never wore anymore but which were too good to throw away or donate to a charity. There were spatulas with plastic handles that had barely survived the great meltdown from a hot frying plan, dusty ornaments bought from a trip long ago to Durban, along with toilet paper bought in bulk from an opening special years before.

I moaned about having to pack these things, unpack them and dust them off all over again. I told an old relative of ours I thought mom's things were better off in a rubbish dump or a charity shop. My aunty, who is a bit older than my mother, said: 'Yes, Ah Ngaan, it is a nuisance to have to move these things and to sort them now, but do you know how difficult it was for us to get these things in the first place? Sometimes I am still grateful that I have a decent meal to eat at night.'

I sighed and nodded, agreeing with her. Looking around her shopfront with its old newspapers doubling as placemats and a cigarette carton flipped over as scrap paper, I knew she was right about hard work and its disdain for waste.

By the late 1970s and early 80s, the Chinese were granted a few more concessions than other non-white communities in South Africa. One main concession was being allowed to live in white areas with neighbours' approval. There were a few children who managed to enter whites-only schools and sometimes school groups were allowed to take part in cultural activities reserved for whites, like watching a play or taking part in interschool programmes.

Our family did not live in a whites-only area even in the 1980s. Neighbourhoods like Bertrams and Judith's Paarl were grey areas, which meant Indians, Chinese and coloureds could live there. On our street there were a few Portuguese families and a single mom with a boy we watched grow up over the years. She was a white woman who worked for the trade union COSATU and sometimes we saw people from TV or the newspapers come to visit. Her parties were lively and there was a standing invitation for my parents and the other neighbours. Of course they said thanks and never went. We children peered over the wall into her windows and saw for the first time the racially mixed group of people dancing to Prince's *Raspberry Beret*, laughing and topping up their glasses. There were also the Isaacs and the Padayachees and by the early 1990s the first black family moved into the street.

Living here we did not stand out too much. No one had a pool, a remote-controlled gate or pedigreed pets; we still waved at each other and noticed when someone did not make it to the bus stop after a morning or two's absence.

But even here, the Chinese had to hold on to a carefully constructed public persona. It was too risky to confide in anyone who was not Chinese. We did not talk about what dad did for work; we stuck to saying he worked at a shop, even though he kept unusual hours that the neighbours must have noticed. But no one bothered us much about it; they probably knew anyway.

The Chinese community in South Africa stayed tiny. Even at its biggest, it swelled to only about 25 000, and their small numbers made them almost invisible, unseen and concealed. And it also made them less of a threat and helped get them 'special treatment' through the concessions but it entrenched a separateness and isolation. It meant having to defend themselves against the tag of being honorary whites, for instance, having to reassert the fact that it was the Japanese who were given honorary white status. The demeaning 'honour' was not afforded to the Chinese in South Africa.

At the Chinese school, we learnt some Chinese dances with feathered fans, chopsticks and elaborate moves with our heads turned at right angles and our fingers mimicking the flow of the wind through trees. We would perform not just at parents' evenings but also for visiting dignitaries, white school inspectors and the white mayors who came to visit the school every now and again. The principal of the school was a smart but stern woman who never showed warmth unnecessarily and who perfected the ugly art of fake smiles for parents and for dignitaries. She, too, was part of this perfect public display of what was polite and acceptable to the world outside Chinese circles. On the days of one of these visits, she would wear her beautifully patterned *cheung saam*, a mandarin-collared dress with a discreet slit up the side of her leg, to show the embroidered richness of the sophisticated Chinese woman in her gracious refinement. On every other day, she just wore her Woolworths outfits and stiff blazers with shoulder pads.

Being associated with somewhere else was a useful foreignness sometimes. It was an anomaly; it made the South African apartheid government less sure that the Chinese were part of the black community they despised so much. It demonstrated to the government behaviour that was the opposite of holding up scribbled posters of enraged dissent or burning tyres and hurling stones in protest.

The Chinese were not part of struggle politics. There were a handful of Chinese who did get involved in fighting apartheid, but mostly they kept to themselves, choosing not to rock the boat. If they remained pliant and yielding, they could carry on working. Maybe then they could send money back to China, or raise a child to celebrate a proper wedding with a traditional lucky eight-course dinner and even the adopted Western custom of a bottle of whisky on the guests' tables.

The Chinese had no political home in the underground, in the struggle of the black townships. But they also had no connection to the white government. The Chinese may not have liked being treated like second-class citizens but they could not associate with this nationalist thinking either. They did not see enfranchisement and freedom as a right but as something that would require more negotiation and sacrifice. It was sacrifice, especially, as was national conscription. Growing up I did not encounter one Chinese South African mother who recognised a cause that justified her son fighting for the *volk* (Afrikaans nation or people).

It was better to hold on to what little they had, to work harder, save harder and close in on the battle for economic freedom, rather than to take the fight to the political front. They would keep their concessions, the freedom fighters could keep their struggle.

Growing up in the post-apartheid era, I was sometimes uncomfortable with the absence of the Chinese in dismantling apartheid. Why were there not more Chinese names lined up in melancholic pride along the small plaques at Freedom Park in Pretoria, remembering the fallen of the struggle? Why were the few stories that were on record, or told by those who were in the struggle, about small roles of hiding comrades or driving people to banned protests or lining up in sober pickets at places like Wits University where sedate objection to apartheid hardly matched the anguish and coalface terror of those running for their lives, those forced into exile and those sent to prison?

The answers did come as I understood more about this state of in-betweenness, this small site of not belonging, so small it was almost invisible. I realised more and more that for the majority of Chinese, people like my mother and father, the mothers and fathers of my school friends and the relatives all around me, maintaining the fog of invisibility was the struggle they knew best. They could look on evil and not fight it in the instinctive way of a struggle fighter because they had little expectation of a good, easy life in Africa. They were never completely from here and even when they were born on this African soil, their umbilical cord was fixed to a placenta of a faraway mainland. They lived with the hardships and the wrongdoings, including racial oppression and the wickedness of apartheid, because they had never dared to hope too much for anything more.

The Chinese had traditionally not fitted in anywhere in racial mainstreams. Many early Chinese identified with China more than South Africa. And economic pursuit rather than political reform through struggle were what mattered to a community with immigrant roots. Like so many migrants, and specifically in racially divided South Africa, the Chinese never had the roots that knot and twist deep into the soil of a place and become an extension of identity. That goal of making good on the gift of life was to work hard, not draw too much attention to yourself, live frugally, save enough to build a home and to send something back to the family members in China. The first dream always would be about returning to the homeland, the motherland, reuniting with the filial piety of a grown child submitting still to a parent.

My parents did make it back to China, but they returned as visitors, more than twenty years after they first left. It was always a big deal to be able to make that costly journey back home but more importantly the journey back across the Indian Ocean, now on an aeroplane, was to be able to see family again and to be able to reassure them that they were fine, that there was enough money to make South Africa home, that the children were growing and going to school and that everybody was in good health.

The first time my dad went back to China he made the trip without my mom. I remember he came back with a little photo album of shots someone had helped him take. The rolls were already printed and inserted into small giveaway albums. My dad was finally the tourist. He was expected just to have fun, just to indulge in the frivolity of posing next to an impressive pagoda temple and also to stand for a family picture with relatives he had not seen for decades. Dad also had a touristy decorative plate made; it featured two old women in traditional Mongolian outfits as his tour group had made it further up north.

'All the pretty, young girls were taken so I ended up with these two old ladies,' he laughed at the picture, this prize of making it back, showing him with his arms around the shrunken, smiling grannies.

By the late 1970s and the 80s, the Chinese were granted the demeaning concession of acquiring permission from would-be white neighbours to live among them. They could attend white Catholic schools if they converted to Catholicism and some Chinese went to white universities on the quota system available to Chinese, Indians and coloureds.

The concessions, though, were nobody's free lunch. The Chinese had eaten of the poison fruits; it was a bite of the tainted apple that would stay stuck in the Chinese people's throats as the political seesaw started to sway. But in the 1980s, the option to stay in a white neighbourhood, even if you had to go cap in hand to ask for it, was a plum opportunity for a family. It was either that or live in an under-serviced township or in a grey area where the grassy pavements and verges grew into thick, weedy curtains before the council put them on the cutting rotation or where neighbours on drunken New Year's Eves pulled out guns and fired into the air at the stroke of midnight.

Even if you had to be 'good' by someone else's standards – not throw loud parties, not fight with the wife too loudly or not let the dog escape out of the front gate – it was all part of the price to pay to live in a better suburb, to make sure your children could have something better.

It was an unfortunate pay-off, but one about taking opportunities where you found them, choosing different aspirations and most importantly about looking out for your family first. A friend who happens to be white once said to me he could not understand the fuss about my being Chinese. 'It is like you are Italian or Greek or something,' he said, exasperated because none of it made any sense to him. As a friend, he saw me as the friend, not the person with history's complexity that becomes embedded in your skin colour. But I had to laugh a little, too, at his oversimplified version of where he placed me. If he could contain me somehow, then the nuance and subtleties did not have to keep bubbling messily over the top.

It was the same when I lived in my all-white residence as a student with its majority of Afrikaans-speaking girls. One night we were all up to a bit of mischief, as was the usual craziness of student life. A senior who was part of our group let out an ironic giggle and said '*gedra jouself soos 'n wit mens*' (behave yourself like a white person) as we hurled another cup of old yoghurt, specially prepared on a sun-soaked window ledge for days, from our first floor balcony on to some unsuspecting drunken person dragging himself back up to the residence steps. I was part of this joke as the stinky dairy missiles went flying. It was meant as a remark of acceptance and inclusion. She did not see me as anything other than her residence-mate after having lived with me for two years. I laughed, but at the same time I did not feel included – I was not a white person.

The Chinese community juggled its multiple identities to fit in as I expect I still do. I laugh at jokes, I smile to myself, I say nothing; sometimes I feel I should have an abridged history of the Chinese in South Africa tucked into a back pocket, just to set the record straight for the umpteenth time. For example, I have a special nod for people's sentences that start with 'But you Chinese people...' and it is filled in with everything from 'like to eat dogs', 'are good at maths' and so on. I have even listened to things like 'hey, I saw your "sister" yesterday'; but while I am thinking they mean Yolanda or Unisda, they go on to say, 'I met this woman, and she looked so much like you, she was visiting from Korea.'

The Chinese were caught again in this no-man's-land many years later as the new South Africa was born. Once again they did not fit in to other people's fables or made-up facts about Chinese South Africans.

As a young reporter, I got a job at *The Star* in Sauer Street, Johannesburg. I waited for a bus every afternoon to get back home to Judith's Paarl. On Fridays we usually knocked off a little after lunchtime and I waited as usual for the bus to arrive around the side of the old Library Gardens. Propped up against the building, with the impressive facade and moulded sculptures of Spinoza and gargoyles, I watched the minute hand tick along on my watch, willing the bus to arrive on time.

I looked up to see a slim swathe of red moving along Market Street, growing like a steady bleed, then getting louder with chanting and with pounding feet. It was a group of hawkers in red union T-shirts making their way up the street in protest. I stayed where I was, mildly intrigued by yet another Friday afternoon protest. But the crowd did not move past me. They stopped and screamed directly at me: 'Go back to China, go back to China'. This group of hawkers was angry that the growing presence of new Chinese hawkers in the late 1990s spelt doom for their own businesses of street trading in the inner city. They did not ask about whether I was paying tax to the current government or what my passport said about my nationality; all they could identify with was my skin colour.

I was a little shaken by being the target of their aggression, but thankfully the group moved on. Then the bus arrived and I went home.

On the journey home, I could not stop thinking about 'going back'. They assumed that I was from somewhere else, the only clue being that I had a different skin colour to theirs.

A few years later I visited Hong Kong. My sister Yolanda had fallen for a guy from Hong Kong and their long-distance relationship had eventually ended up with her moving to the fragrant city, strangely creating a loop back to the motherland for the Ho family. I was visiting my sister there.

An unusually chatty taxi driver quizzed me about my accent when I spoke to him in Cantonese. He had a brash manner, quite typical of Hong Kong taxi drivers, where Ps and Qs, polish and political correctness have no place.

I liked him, actually, as he delivered his cheeky presumptions loudly from the front seat. But his final conclusion was that I was a bamboo child, he told me. I was not sure what he meant. And he said: 'You are like bamboo, you look yellow on the outside but your insides are white.' I also hear the banana analogy applied often.

I wanted to start explaining: there are few Chinese in South Africa, I am a South African by birth and I fall into a Western and an African way of life simultaneously, but it was too much effort to make him understand on the short drive. In the end I just agreed with him. He was probably right but for reasons that he could not know.

What I did think about was that this was my reception to 'going back'. This China of my supposed belonging did not recognise my accent or my frame of reference. It could not make room for the fact that I shared my home country, my South Africa, with people with skins so pale you can see small veins line their faces or people who have skin tone the colour of brewed tea or the colour of charcoal.

But I was getting used to feeling like I did not fit in or rather that other people battled to fit me in. In my Chinese school everyone was just like me, race did not matter. It was as a student in Pretoria in the early 1990s that I got to see a very different world. I ended up in a residence with a majority of Afrikaans girls who had come from far-flung small towns to the capital city to be educated. Apartheid was about to expire, but it still managed a few gasps and it managed this especially well in the residences, which still did not admit black students.

I was only seventeen when I started at technikon and because I could not drive legally and I had chosen to study journalism in Pretoria my parents agreed that it would be best for me to live in residence rather than commute from Johannesburg daily. They preferred a residence for me because it was something vetted by the institution, the technikon, in the same way that school regulated our social lives when we were growing up.

At first, my application to residence was not successful. I did not have a spot and I would have to wait to see what came up. It did not dawn on me as a teenager in the 1990s that my being Chinese was an issue.

Yolanda and Kelvin had both been to Wits University and their experience of mixing with students of other races seemed to be such fun. They both had friends at residence and sometimes they envied their friends who got to live away from home in the newfound freedom of on-campus life.

I thought this was going to be my reality in Pretoria and I was excited and grateful that my parents had agreed to pay for me not just to study, but also to stay at residence, which would be a significant extra expense.

When I had not heard any news as each week passed before the academic year started I just assumed it was a shortage of space and that I was the unlucky student who did not get a place. Initiation week was underway and I still did not know if I had been given a room at one of two on-campus residences. Yolanda and I stopped at a CNA off Church Street to buy a map book of the city one Friday afternoon when she picked me up. We trawled the city, stopping at short-term accommodation, flats or other student lodgings because it seemed unlikely I would get a room in residence. Yolanda was given the task of doing the first recce of finding a suitable place that was safe and affordable.

I could not guess at the racial divisions on a Pretoria campus that was still very white and very Afrikaans.

Then to our surprise and the relief of Yolanda and my dad who were ferrying me to and from class most days, I did get a room to share as first-years are expected to do.

With my few things bundled into the divided room of built-in desk and shelves, bed and wardrobe, my family said goodbye and left me to settle into this strange place that I was to call home. I was to share the room with another first-year student, Bernadette.

I was nervous about meeting Bernadette. My closest friends were Chinese girls and the Chinese people I had grown up with. I heard a key enter the lock on the door, the handle was pushed down and in she walked.

Bernadette was an Afrikaans girl and she turned out to be a warm bundle of energy with grey-blue eyes and short, dark-brown hair. She had been told that I was Chinese and was asked if she would be okay sharing her room with me. She absolutely loved the idea, she said, because she loved Chinese food anyway and because I spoke English and she would get to practise her English. Only then did I realise that for my application the residence had to rethink their policies about letting a Chinese girl live there even in the last days of apartheid.

Bernadette and I turned out to be great roommates, apart from me being a night owl and her getting up when the sun was still new in the sky. She helped me navigate the culture shock of Afrikaans residence life, with its *sakkie-sakkie* dances, a half-sweep, half-shuffle movement that went with just about any kind of music it seemed. For my part, I snuck out plates of dinner from the canteen when she could not make dinnertime because of an aerobics class or a date with a boyfriend she met after our first few months as first-years. It was Bernadette who calmed me as I cursed the initiation rituals like having to play dress-up at all hours of the night. She would paint exaggerated lipstick circles on my cheeks when an intercom announcement would wake us up from our sleep with giggling seniors instructing the first-years to dress up as clowns and get down to the recreation hall in ten minutes. Other times we dressed up as whores, as church-going aunties and other times we had to make cups of Milo for the men's residence that we would serenade with whatever pop ballad the seniors thought appropriate.

Mostly, the house committee members did not know how to deal with me as the only Chinese first-year. We had a particularly wicked house committee member assigned to first-years. Wanda the wicked also did not know exactly what to do with the Chinese girl from Joburg, so most weekends when first-years were forced to stay in residence for closed weekends, I was excused and could go home. They could not fight my legitimate excuse of having to get back home to my weekend job as a waitress in a Chinese restaurant. Anyway, it was easy to keep me away from mixing too much with their 'cultural' activities.

Still, I was initiated into the strangeness of Afrikaans student culture. There were firm gender roles and expectations that women did things like entertain their male friends in the lobby with doily-decked tea trays and neatly arranged plates of homebaked goods. It was proper, it was ladylike and that was what was expected from good Afrikaans *meisies* (girls). But even so, there were some scandals and a few 'good' girls vanished from residence unexpectedly and later we would hear that they had got married or had returned to the farm. There was the getting drunk all weekend, throwing up in the flowerbeds and streaking across the residence forecourts, then dressing for Sunday lunch with a tie and saying grace with pious performance.

In my time at residence, my Afrikaans improved immensely, my dancing did not. I did become less of a novelty and more just a person to the people I came to call friends.

But there were collisions, too. I was an outsider even as my Chineseness became less and less of an issue; it came from my being a journalism student rather than because my skin colour was different. Not a single journalism student had managed to survive at one of the on-campus residences. These residences were notoriously repressive with their exaggerated austerity meant to 'break down, then build up' first-years. The fussy and often nonsensical rules and regulations were anathema to the idealistic journalism students who wanted to use writing to change the world, fight the establishment's censorship and denial of the truth that was still choking the country. Many journalism students could not deal with rules like having to wear white stockings, learn residence anthems and be called by a nickname the whole of the first year. But, being the good Chinese girl I was, I never thought too much about putting up resistance or refusing to participate. I was not about to kick up a fuss that would mean my parents would have to make alternative arrangements for me. I did use the student newspaper to criticise residence policies but I still wore the white stockings, turned to look if one of my seniors called me 'Tweety' and I did not resent that as just another lowly first-year student I had to do switchboard duty.

Still, there were students who experienced institutionalised bullying. There were students who simply crumbled under the drawn-out initiation process and with the added pressure of studying they were often pushed really close to the edge. An opinion piece I wrote for the student paper criticised the failure of initiation to recognise that this intensive period, followed by a milder but still persistent form of the so-called rite of passage just before year-end exams, had a destructive and humiliating edge while masquerading as team building. There were silly punishments and chastisements for transgressions like being caught not wearing your residence badge on campus or around town.

My piece brought on the wrath of the student representative council for the technikon. The SRC called for a meeting with me and the paper's editor. The editor and I arrived dressed as typical students in shorts and T-shirts only to be met by the SRC men all with crushing rugby-boy handshakes dressed up in their SRC ties and blazers. They laid the piece I had written on the table; it had red rings and underlined sections everywhere. Part of what they battled with was that I had the right to write an opinion piece in the first place.

It was the final throes of apartheid but there were incidents of journalism students' rooms at other residences, the supposedly more open residences, being raided for having the 'wrong' books such as political literature that was pro-democracy, pro-labour, pro-struggle or anything that looked too socialist, too communist. When I heard about the raids, it felt like it came from twenty years earlier. Although I was never questioned for any of the many books, pamphlets and essays that I amassed as a journalism student, I did take to keeping some of the more 'sensitive' political material inside my padlocked wardrobe.

In the meantime, our reading list for political science, to create more rounded journalists, our lecturers believed, included knowing the once-banned works of books and films like *Fanny Hill, Lady Chatterley's Lover* and *A Clockwork Orange*. For a sheltered seventeen-year-old, it was like being let in on the biggest secret. The world opened up to me with full-frontal male nudity, institutionalised violence, infidelity, lust and prostitutes.

While I was a student, there was a massive march to the Union Buildings by ANC supporters. The government was no longer able to stop the waves of protest and a sea of people, close to 60 or 70 000 strong, was going to descend on the Union Buildings.

We journalism students were excited to attend the event that was set to bring the capital city to a standstill and convey a message. At the residences, though, a kind of panic set in as the march date was announced. It was decided that the residences would be locked on the day of the march. The men's residences went into testosterone mode and vowed to protect the women's residences. Students who had lectures on the inner-city campuses were advised to abandon classes.

When the house committee member on my floor heard that not only was I going to go to class as usual but that I intended being part of the march in the city centre, along with the other journalism students, she was shocked and agitated. She pleaded with me to reconsider for the sake of my own safety. I tried to explain that the march was about making a political point, it was not war. She was not convinced.

I went to the march, while the rest of my residence friends were barricaded behind closed doors, too frightened to attend lectures.

We were all so young; many of us were just teenagers. But the world was changing; democracy was just around the corner. History was reshuffling its deck. For some of us, it was the dawn of the new world we believed we could finally be part of. For others, the candle lighting the dim view of the world that mattered so much to them was about to be snuffed out forever.

I remember one afternoon a fellow journalism student, who was a black person, asked if he could borrow a book from me. I had to fetch it from my residence room and invited him to walk with me to get the book. Men were not allowed inside the rooms so Vusi took a seat in the lobby and waited as I ran up the stairs.

I came back downstairs with the book and saw one of my seniors in the lobby. I greeted her warmly as I always did. Instead of her usual friendliness, she glared at me and then at Vusi.

Only then did I realise that I had unwittingly violated a code, a code that almost said that I would be tolerated as the Chinese girl they had come to know, but Vusi would not and if I was with Vusi then I, too, was not going to be tolerated. I was shocked and hurt. I never said a word to Vusi about it but as we walked back to class, my cheeks burnt.

The Dark Night

I was still a student in the capital city as the seat of power in the Union Buildings was about to get shaken up. On the streets there were whites-only buses and it was still unusual to see a black person in a restaurant, unless he was a waiter. Change felt like a distant rumour but the portents started to creep into consciousness.

One of them was the announcement of a national referendum. It would be for the white voting public only and they would be asked to say yes or no to the ruling National Party proceeding with talks with the recently freed Nelson Mandela.

In my class, there were about 40 journalism students. On the day of the elections, those who were white and old enough to vote headed for the biggest recreational centre on campus that had been turned into a voting station.

One girl said: 'I am going to vote yes today for you Ufrieda and Vusi and Mpho and Kenneth.' I was not sure what response I was supposed to give her as she called out the names of the few non-white students whose lives she was going to change. But I knew what she meant, so I smiled. I walked with a few of them from our lecture room down to the voting station. I knew I was not allowed inside. It was a whites-only affair, a yes or no vote to see if the white minority was ready to cosy up to the unbanned ANC and its leader who had already walked free from prison in 1990.

I walked to the entrance of the hall. I was intrigued to see how a vote took place. But before I got through the door I was asked to leave.

Politics still mattered to me then. My naive student self was convinced that political shifts could make the world a better place and that it could respond with decisiveness to the lives of vulnerable people. Political science was the holy grail of our lectures. We had a demanding political science lecturer. He was impatient with teenagers who could not grasp Immanuel Kant and Rousseau or who were still whingeing about his prescribed reading lists that went on and on with everything from *Alice in Wonderland* to Gramsci, Marx and the Bible. There was an urgency in what he wanted us to know about the world, about how it was going to change and what role we were about to play in a new world. I was not quite ready and definitely not so when it came to reading Homer's *The Odyssey*, which was part of the reading list. I had duly started wading through the wicked list of literature as I regarded it then. I eventually chose *The Odyssey* because it had adventure and multi-headed sea monsters. But I was drowning rather than managing to stay afloat reading the dense text. Eventually, after about the third time of renewing the book from the Pretoria library, I realised I was not progressing past about the first 40 pages every time I sat down to read from the old tome. I approached the librarian and asked for a simpler version, maybe an abridged version, or one with a bigger font at least. She nodded and told me to walk with her to the shelves. But she walked beyond the dusty hardcovers and instead we carried on straight to the children's section. She handed me a copy with colour pictures and bigger text and finally Homer started to make sense.

Politics and learning about what bought us to where we were did matter then. Our lecturers urged us on with their hurried anxiety. We had to rage and be victorious over things like our reading lists, we had to know the world and what had shaped it to this crossroads in our history. We would be the first generation of journalists not to be threatened by the notorious Section 205 that compelled journalists to rat on their sources or face being imprisoned; we would be the first generation to work in an era of democracy, they hoped.

It was weighty stuff, but I was still trying to master another serious task: I had to learn to drive. I was still a learner driver at that time, confused about hand signals for failed indicators or how to do an incline start.

Without my licence it was up to my dad or Yolanda to do the Sunday night trek up to Pretoria for me to make it for my week's lectures. To get home on Fridays, I caught the train. People were being pushed off moving trains and carriages were being set alight, all in the angry uncertain days of the early 1990s. But for a few extra rand, which I was lucky enough to have, the first-class carriages were an option. First class was just simple padded seats and racks for luggage, but it kept us immune from what could be happening at the tail of the train. More of the separateness of two worlds so close together. One Sunday night, as dad, mom and I were driving back up to Pretoria, we glimpsed the throbbing labour pains of the world that was about to come and it would come into sharp focus as the traffic lights changed. Waiting for a red light to blink to green as we neared my Pretoria campus, I saw three white men putting up banners on a street lamp. At first I did not notice that they were all khaki-clad and in shorts. This was not particularly unusual, as it could have been the uniform for many men in Pretoria. But then my gaze dropped to the posters they were putting up. They were Afrikaner Weerstandsbeweging (AWB) members, the far right-wing group, whose ideas of self-determination extended to thinking that a white supremacist worldview was ordained by God. Then one of the men turned and saw us.

He glared at us, then from his lungs he released a deep, venom-filled 'Heyyyy!'

His friends turned and they all faced us as our car was paused at the light. Without taking my eyes off them, I said, 'Just drive, Ba'. He did not say a word and put his foot on the accelerator.

Rumours of change were in the air, I reassured my father and myself. Theirs was a lost cause and all they had now were posters to hang and rage to act out on passing motorists.

The world was changing.

At home, though, dad and mom were unconvinced that a black government would be any good for the country, or more specifically good for the Chinese.

'The Afrikaner is an arrogant oppressor who has no morals and the black man is a lazy fool' was the kind of sentiment that circulated in my community and it was also the thinking that seeped into our house. I was not sure what to think about that. I had met and lived with Afrikaans people and a Sotho-speaking student who moved into residence for a semester during my second year. I was not sure I agreed.

197

My parents worried that a black president would run the country into the ground. They had never heard of this Mandela anyway, until just a few years earlier. My granny worried that the small pension the state gave her now as a naturalised South African would be taken from her with all the talk of a change of government. They all felt that whatever happened at the Union Buildings, it would have little positive impact on the Chinese. They knew they would just keep on working, detached from politics as always and just trying to find their way among the big men, white or black, who would call the shots.

Under the apartheid regime, the Chinese South Africans wanted what was entitled to the whites but they did not want to be regarded as white. It was part of why in the early 1980s when the Chinese South Africans were offered representation on the President's Council, with a seat on an advisory panel, the Chinese community rejected the offer. They did not want to be in the white camp, not when the same offer had been denied to all other non-white groups. These were just scraps from the master's table. But at the same time, there was no sense of brotherhood between the Chinese and other non-white groups either. The Chinese regarded them as inferior, with no culture and with no moral centre.

On TV, it was clear that whatever was to come for our country would not come easily and it would make its demand in the price of lives. News reports used words like 'massacres', 'faction fighting' and 'necklacing'.

But things were shifting. For some years, *The Cosby Show* presented a version of normal that was not about an all-white family. Into our own living rooms came a black family we loved, from the big-hearted, funny doctor to his wise wife. I thought Lisa Bonet's older sister character was so cool. She always looked funky and there was something individual and free-spirited about her that made me want to be like this black girl.

For the first time, TV advertisements showed a few black people, not as 'Philemon' the gardener or the tsotsi for a security gate company, but just people cracking open a few beers together.

I went back home to Johannesburg for my final year of study. We had to do an experiential year of training as part of our qualifications and I had managed to get a job at a community newspaper in Edenvale that was not too far from my home.

My family and friends rallied around to help me get my driver's licence that I was required to have for the job. While I was at the residence, my friends turned their beat-up Datsuns and old bakkies into my fleet of cars with the learner driver's 'L' stuck on them. When I learnt to alley dock, as the K-53 test required, my friends lined up as poles as I navigated past their legs. They let me drive on the quiet streets of Pretoria to test my clutch control and to see whether I was checking all my blind spots and mirrors properly.

My dad took his turn to teach me how to drive at home. He was a good, confident driver but I think even he was shaky about getting through to me to co-ordinate my body enough not to stall and to figure out when you changed gears before the engine started to squeal for it. At least, unlike Kelvin, my father never sat in the passenger seat with his hand on the handbrake, just in case. Kelvin's style of teaching did little for my confidence and each time I would return from the driving lesson with my nerves as raw as theirs.

Even though everyone tried to be patient with me, handing over a set of car keys to me was like looking over a cliff with a frayed bit of rope as a bungee cord. One time, after a Sunday afternoon of driving up and down the streets of the city with the big homemade 'L' sign on the car, we finally made it home. I remember dad, who had volunteered to give me the lesson, walking into the house and going straight for the back rest of the sofa. He held on to the textured fabric for a while, like he had to steady himself before taking a few more steps. I think he thought then he would be driving me around for many more years because it would be unlikely I would ever get the thumbs-up from the clipboard cops at the testing station.

But teaching their children to drive is what dads do, even fahfee men who have little free time. Dads have to let their daughters burn some rubber unintentionally and stall more than drive. It seemed like just a few short years earlier when he had taught me how to ride a bicycle without training wheels in the old Bez Valley park near our house. I could only balance for a few metres at a time, then I would squeeze too hard on the brakes and fall to the side of the bike, refusing to try again.

Dad would urge me on. He even ran alongside me, holding the back of the seat as I pedalled and as my grip on the brake eased up a bit. 'Keep pedalling, keep pedalling, *chai, chai*,' he said, until the day I turned my head to see that I had cleared a whole stretch of park and dad was now standing still, waving me on.

I started work as a reporter just a few days after my final exams. I arrived in the Edenvale office of the newspaper that had advertising representatives and a tea lady, all in an office small enough for me to hear the receptionist singsong her standard greeting every few minutes when the phone rang.

But I still did not have a driver's licence.

Embarrassed to have to ask for anything on my first day at work, I had to approach my editor for a morning off the following week. He raised an eyebrow.

'It is for my driver's test,' I told him (my fourth attempt).

'What, you don't have a driver's licence! Well, you better get it,' was what he said after agreeing to my request.

I did, thankfully, and much to the relief of my family who was fed up with carting me around.

At the Edenvale community paper, I was given the crime beat and the responsibility of covering local council news for the town of Bedfordview. And, of course, being a community newspaper it involved covering all the general reporting expected on a small local paper. One of the first stories I had to cover was a children's art competition, followed by a Barbie show, with a tall blonde dressed up to be the toy doll in real life. I went along with my notebook and took the photographs, remembering the tight cropping we were taught and remembering to ask people to spell their names always. Importantly, it was remembering that a rosette on a child's drawing was more than a silly first prize, it was a big deal for that child and everyone connected to the making of that crayon image.

My grandfather loaned me his tomato-red Mazda that he only really needed at weekends to get to church and mostly he preferred the minibus shuttle anyway because glaucoma had caught up with his eyes and he did not like to guess at robot colours and people crossing the streets.

I was grateful for the old car that my grandfather secured with a padlocked length of chain from the brake to the steering wheel. It was a second-hand car and the red on the bonnet did not match the rest of the car. It broke down often and over time I learnt its little quirks, like how to get the windscreen wiper going if you manually gave it a shove to get it into action. It was why I sometimes arrived at an assignment with a wet right arm, as I had leaned out of the window to yank the wiper just once before it squeaked into action and sloshed the raindrops to the sides so I could drive off.

The policemen I met at the four police stations that made up part of my beat thought it hysterical that I bothered to lock the car that I stuck bumper stickers on. There was one sticker that said 'No to Animal Vivisection' and another about clean air and clean rivers. They said that if my car got stolen they would replace it. The also made jokes about the car being held together by its bumper stickers.

'Do you leave your car outside at night, Ufrieda?' asked one of these cop contacts one day.

'Yes, why?' I asked.

'You must be careful,' he warned, 'the mosquitoes could puncture those tyres.' He would burst out laughing and even I had to smile about the beat-up car that I loved so dearly.

But even as I loved the car, my Ah Goung loved it more. Once or twice when he did need the car, he would drop me off, or wait for me at an interview, then pick me up afterwards.

One rainy day, we were together on one of these first assignments of mine and the Mazda cut out. It started to rain but we got out and flipped up the bonnet. My grandfather fiddled a little, but there was nothing obvious to him or to me that was wrong with the car.

As the rain came down harder, I went to retrieve an umbrella from the car. My grandfather was always prepared and the car was an extension of a storage space for all the emergencies you could think of. But instead of an umbrella, Ah Goung took out a Checkers plastic bag, unfolded it neatly and placed it over his head with the handles drooping around his ears. As the raindrops fell, the centre of his plastic hood started to sag, leaving the corners of the bag looking like bright yellow Batman ears. I urged him under the umbrella and he dismissed me.

'Shush, this is fine,' he said.

'But please, Ah Goung, you are going to get sick and then what?' I tried to scare him a little.

He still ignored me. Eventually another car stopped. It happened to be a Chinese man who greeted us warmly, calling my grandfather the respectful Ah Buk, uncle, and I called him Ah Gor, my brother. Then he started to do fiddly things to the car. I died of embarrassment at my Batman grandfather with his plastic bag hat. This was how I was going to start my journalism career, I thought, in the rain, with a car that was going nowhere and my grandfather with a canary-yellow plastic bag on his head. But in my other life, I was still the granddaughter of this frugal, practical man, whose Batman ears may just have been what caught enough attention for someone to stop and help.

Work was a window into a strange new world for me. I was allowed into strangers' homes as I interviewed them and took photographs. It involved everything from telling the stories of those fighting the council over illegal dumping near their homes, to letting surviving family members devastated by a violent crime speak about their loved ones or telling me about celebrating 50 years of marriage. These were homes without the Chinese altars for the ancestors or the *fai cheun*, the four-character lucky poems that are so typical of Chinese homes. There were people who lived in shacks where swept dirt stood in for carpets and where sunlight never penetrated once a makeshift door was closed. I also entered into mansions that had staircases leading storeys and storeys upwards to where chandeliers dripped from the ceilings. None of them was the home of the fahfee man or the Chinese shopkeeper that I knew so well.

My job was letting me see a world very unlike the one I grew up in. There were so many ways to live a life, so many variations on family, on relationships, on success and failure and on what people held close to their hearts. I was happy to be working at the little knock-and-drop that was always jammed full of advertisements and inserts. My job meant I was actually getting a pay cheque, too. Even though it was still a study year, we had to complete a training year to qualify. The newspaper paid me a junior reporter's salary and expected me to deliver like any rookie on the beat, not a student.

After a few months, I decided I wanted to pay my father back for that year's fees that he had already paid upfront. I was living at home, driving my Ah Goung's car, and apart from keeping his car running I really did not have many expenses and I wanted to be able to give back to my father.

I handed over a wad of money to my dad one day. He refused to take the money. He said it was his duty as my father to provide for my education.

'Just keep on working hard, do your best at work and learn everything you can, then I will be a satisfied father,' he said to me.

Proving yourself in my parents' books meant doing more than what was required of you. 'Sweep the floor if your boss asks you to, do not say it is not your job and do not put on a sour face when you do it. Help your colleagues, help them carry the load and be ready to learn from them.' It was the kind of advice that my mom and dad always gave to us. Do more, moan less and the hard work will pay off. It was also about working with dignity. 'You can be the street sweeper or the president, it does not matter as long as you have pride in your work and you do it with dignity,' was another of my dad's oft-repeated sayings.

I was happy for his advice; I was happy that my dad saw more dignity in sweeping a floor well than in complaining about a raise or stomping all over others to get to the top.

Most of all, I was thrilled to be working, my writing was being published, people were reading my articles and responding and even though I was still a student I was indeed starting my journalism career. I had an editor who believed you earned a byline, you did not get it just because you typed a few sentences on a computer screen. But soon, in that small office, I was getting my byline on the big stories and I was pulling my weight. And now I had a salary and I had some money that I wanted to give back to my parents.

My father still refused the money I had offered to him, but I insisted.

'Take it, dad,' I said. 'Take the money and go bet on something or whatever.'

I wanted him to be able to do something absolutely frivolous with the money and enjoy it even if it was on gambling. Maybe especially if it was gambling because it was the guilty pleasure he enjoyed so much. He finally relented, happy, I hope, to recognise that he had a child becoming an adult. He had worked hard enough.

A few nights later my dad was dead.

My father was shot somewhere in Boksburg on Johannesburg's East Rand. He was on a fahfee round and he was with two other colleagues, wrapping up the banks before heading back to Gou Sok's house. My father was in the driver's seat that cool April night. He had a younger colleague who had done most of the driving in the few years since he had started working for Gou Sok. That day, though, my dad volunteered to drive because the younger man had obviously had a rough night and my dad pitied his youthful excess. The gunman came up to the driver's window and the one shot he fired into my dad's face killed him instantly.

He may have been a soft crime target for the car or the cash they associated with the fahfee men. My dad's shooting may have been a revenge killing of some aggrieved gambler or maybe it was part of how violence was starting to become a way to settle things, that dark shadow that is a seductively convenient solution in South Africa. Those of us who loved him had no answers; we never will.

The news came to our house like a dark cloud moving over the tin roof and it began with a ringing phone. I was working that night, covering a council meeting that was one of my monthly night-time jobs. When my dad was shot, I was sitting in my little press gallery seat in the Bedfordview town council's chambers. The mayor would walk in with his chain and his robe and we would all rise until he took his seat at his special, raised seat. There was a lot of ritual and ceremony, then the toing and froing would start as we worked through an agenda and each councillor muscled for his or her personal wants and desires for the small East Rand town.

While the storm tore into my family home as the news came from someone with the telephone message, I was still sipping on a drink and snacking on the food that was always the way monthly council meetings ended.

After the meeting, I drove Ah Goung's Mazda back home and turned into our street as the night's quiet deepened. I usually parked the car in a neighbourhood garage. The old lady, who lived a few houses from us, let us use her parking spot for a few rand a month. We could not park on the street; we had already woken up one morning some years earlier to see an empty space where our second-hand car was the night before. I could see Unisda walking up the street to meet me from our house. She did this sometimes so I did not take much notice of her as I started wrapping the metal chain-link around the two gates to padlock the gate for the night.

Unisda walked slowly like she could not bring her feet to me. Her arms were folded and she was gripping her forearms, hugging herself tightly. Maybe she thought she could squeeze away the news she was about to give me.

I started chatting immediately as she got within earshot. I was nattering about my day and the council meeting.

'Ngaan, dad has been shot,' she stopped me.

I looked at her for a few seconds; the words sank in, but they did not make sense.

'Oh no, no, where is he? Is he alright? Oh my God, no,' I was pleading. I could not imagine that my dad, my precious, precious father, could be dead, surely he was only hurt and the doctors would be able to make him better again. The seconds she did not confirm his death dragged out in slow motion for me. She had made a mistake; it was Unisda's idea of a cruel, cruel joke; this was just a nightmare and I was going to wake up. 'He has been killed, he is dead, Ah Ngaan.'

My silent scream ripped through the night. Nothing came out of my mouth but my body was trembling; my skin instantly felt like it did not belong to my body as the tingle of tragedy crawled all over me. My head was spinning. I ran back to the house with Unisda following my pace. Even before I made it inside the front door, the weeping and the desperate sobs from inside the house rushed at my solar plexus and I knew then that a part of the sun would never rise for any of us ever again.

My dad did not live long enough for his 60th birthday – that would have come just two months later in June. Years earlier, we as a family had settled on 26 June as my dad's birthday. Of course, we had no way of knowing for sure, it was just following the data made up for this paper son.

Sixty is the first counter for an old-age milestone in Chinese custom. Dad also missed his 25th wedding anniversary that we would have celebrated that year, too. He did not get to mark those 25 years of intimate partnership. Together he and mom had watched us grow out of shoes, learn to drive and be tall enough to help them bring something down from a top shelf. They opened up our presents of ornaments, crazy ties and soaps through the years. They endured us slamming doors as teenagers, then finally were rewarded when we came home with a driver's licence and a university exemption.

Now no longer would mom and dad turn to each other in bed in the comfortable silence of a dark night talking about us, about hopes and dreams, anxieties and fears, the to-do lists and even the gossip; all those basics that glue two people together as lovers.

Yolanda had been thinking ahead about ways to celebrate the wedding anniversary and she thought sitting for a family portrait was the way to honour my dad and my mom. We could hang the picture in the lounge. It was a la-di-da thing to do for our family but it was precisely why she thought it would be appropriate. It would be a salute to our hard-working parents who had stayed together mostly in happiness and were there for each other and for us.

Now his side of the bed would never be slept in again. My mother would fill the space with a teddy or two he had bought her a few years ago, but it would stay empty. She put a picture key ring with dad's face on it on her keys. He had had it made many years earlier. He had a playful snarl and grin when the photograph was snapped. The key ring stayed in a drawer until then when my mother needed him closer.

My sadness was multiplied a million times for mom. Her life partner was gone. The man she cooked Jungle Oats for, with just a sprinkle of salt when he was sick, was gone. She would not sit up front in the passenger's seat of the car any longer, she would have to drive herself.

I breathe in my longing for him; it is involuntary, reflexive. I miss talking to him, watching him pore over the horse racing pages while his cup of tea, with milk and two sugars, cooled alongside the paper. I miss asking dad's advice, not in the ways of serious discussion, but just hearing his thoughts about all the grown-up stuff of life.

Just before he died, we had watched and talked about the night-time broadcasts of the O.J. Simpson trial that played out in the weeks before. Dad chewed on some peanuts or cracked open the Chinese melon pips that he liked as we talked and watched as O.J. wiped his brow. Dad had stopped smoking for some years and he liked to keep his hands and his mouth distracted with the melon seeds. I liked that he had stopped smoking. Every day dad smoked I reminded him to smoke less. When doctors gave him the ultimatum to quit, he had no choice.

I miss that he is not part of my future or the conversations we will have, the boyfriends he will or will not approve of, having my own home to invite him into. I will miss him asking me to drive him somewhere, to read through a letter for him or to make him a cup of tea.

For years after he died I listened for the squeak of our little front gate, waiting for it to announce that my dad had made it home and was safe.

But the nights would just grow darker and quieter and the gate stayed silent and I would eventually fall asleep. Sometimes I still wake up crying, having had him visit my dreams.

By the late 1990s, we moved out of our house and into the little suburb of Judith's Paarl that had once been welcoming to a Chinese family and also to the Padayachees and the Isaacs. We were leaving the house where a peach tree that started off by dropping its sticky offerings to the ground, had turned to a dried-out stump. The old lucky conifers that my mother had planted as short little plants on either side of the house when we first moved in, stood tall on the lawn that was only a few square metres wide. It was here that my brother and his friends sunk an old tin can to play their rounds of 'golf' and where my mother grew sprigs of spring onion in between sweet peas and snapdragons. It was the house my father had saved enough to buy for us and we had grown up with the plants and the pets, watched coats of paint start new and flake off over time and get refreshed to start all over again. This was my dad's castle and it was our home. He bought that house for us really. He knew his responsibility was to secure my mother's future and ours, whatever happened. Now we were moving out of the house he bought and had managed to pay off a year or two before he died.

I closed the squeaky gate for the last time.

A New Day

Almost exactly a year to the date of my dad's death the new South Africa was born.

Getting to that day was a year of parallel hells. I watched the country tear itself apart with violence and death. On TV and in newspapers, people bled to death from gunshots, they screamed and dropped to the ground as they were burnt alive in flames from petrol-doused tyres around their necks. Rocks and Molotov cocktails were flying everywhere.

In that year, the man many believed would be president was murdered. Chris Hani was slain not even three weeks before my father died. Far right-wing fanatics plotted his downfall and killed him outside his home in Boksburg, the same place where my father was shot. I sometimes wish that I could go back to those days and beg dad not to go into the burning townships at the time. Gou Sok's banks were just not worth it, I would have said. I know, though, that dad and his colleagues would have been cautious; the shooting came anyway.

Another right-wing movement, the AWB – the same crowd that had scared us enough to jump a red light in Pretoria – were intent on derailing multi-party negotiations at Kempton Park's World Trade Centre a few months later. They smashed tanks through the buildings, terrorised everyone and thought they could bully people into not going ahead with forging a new country.

So-called black-on-black violence, third forces and other nefarious evils were also at play like an anonymous army commanded to destroy everything. People went to sleep at night and woke to find their neighbours' throats slit. All the time, it was put down to the elusive third force.

It seemed there was no refuge. People were slaughtered in churches. Schoolchildren were being fired on and people were killed by 'friendly' fire as the South African Defence Force's bullets proved to be indiscriminate.

As we edged closer to the autumn of April 1994 and the date for the first-ever democratic elections arrived, canned foods became the highest commodity. The same went for candles and batteries, bottled water, dry biscuits and all the things you would have on your bomb shelter checklist.

Even my granny stocked up on canned viennas and bloated soggy bits of spaghetti preserved in fake tomato sauce. She never ate the stuff ordinarily but she was terrified that war was coming and no matter how I tried to convince her that things were going to be fine, she still kept building her stash.

Hope tamed the anxiety and there were more ordinary people who believed that a new day was coming. Radio stations played John Lennon's *Give Peace A Chance*; people stuck bumper stickers on their cars representing peace with blue and white doves.

Political sentiments were shifting. The US was talking about lifting sanctions, diplomatic ties were being made thick and fast with our former pariah state and in the coming months there would be a joint Nobel Peace Prize for two former foes, one white, one black, who would now form a government of national unity and set in motion a constitution for a new country everyone could call home.

That rumour of change that I had spoken to my father about was no longer an uncertain whisper; now it was being shouted from the rooftops, and no one could help hearing it, not even if you blocked your ears.

In our house, silence fell into the places where he used to be – the chair he sat on as he tapped his foot impatiently looking at the fahfee record books every night; his clothes that still hung in the wardrobes that he shared with mom; his reading glasses ready on the mantelpiece; the half-used bottles of Vitriol still in the mirrored bathroom cabinets. I used to watch dad shake a few drops into his hand, smooth them into his hair, mess everything up a bit as he stared purposefully at his task in the mirror. His brow would furrow as he combed everything back into place and formed the all important comb-back to cover his bald spot. He would turn a little to each side, checking that the strands were in place. Then he put the comb down.

Immediately after dad's death, we entered into seven weeks of mourning. It is an old-fashioned observance that is undertaken as a sign of filial piety. It would be a mourning that my mom and us four children would observe: 49 days with no entertainment, no socialising, no red or bright things in the house or on your body, no visiting people and just following a routine of lighting incense and candles at an altar where my dad's photo, in black and white, stood. For those first nights of the vigil of incense and candles, Kelvin moved into our bedroom and slept on the floor. Not one of us wanted to be more alone than we already felt. Some nights Unisda crawled into mom's bed, cradling her as she cried for the man she loved.

We carried on with work or studies but we were dressed in black most of the time. We had on a black ribbon attached with a safety pin to our clothes always.

We children knew what was expected of us for those 49 days. We knew the austerity of the severe mourning regime but our broken hearts did not know what else to hold on to.

My grieving grandparents, my dad's in-laws, felt they wanted to carry this burden of mourning for us. They were not part of the official mourning but their hearts did not stop bleeding. I had never heard my grandfather weep until the morning after the murder. Daylight had not ended the nightmare as I held my grandfather who had arrived at our home. He was wearing a well-padded suede jacket and as he arrived at the door, he collapsed like a bear on to the sofa, held on to me and sobbed in my arms. Exhausted from tears long minutes after, we parted.

A part of my Por Por died along with my dad. She buried some of her soul with him, and until the day she died, she would find her way back to a worn pleading to the gods. They should have taken her and spared her precious son-in-law from the bullet. Dad was her champion; he held her heart in safe hands; he stood up for her when my mother wielded her cruelty and unkindness.

I felt betrayed, angry and bruised. A new world was being made and this, too, my father would miss out on.

But we had to survive, like the country we lived in, and we had to make it through the uncertainty, believing a new tomorrow would bring a better day.

After the 49 days of mourning, we ceremonially burnt the small black ribbons that we had pinned to our clothes for the long weeks that passed. My mother also wanted us to burn the piles of sympathy cards and notes affixed to sympathy bouquets that came to our house. To her, they were messages for my father, not for us.

Although the mourning period came to an end, our sense of loss did not.

People stopped asking after a while how you were doing. Even my closest friends did not know that I perfected a split life. I cried silently into my pillow at night, then I would wake up and have to remind myself that the rest of the world was not responsible for my dad's murder and I would have to learn to tame my rage.

But death can be unsentimental. Life throbs on.

I returned to the crime beat. At the time of my dad's death, my editor had decided to give me a buffer from having to look through crime dockets and police reports about shootings and also having to talk to family members about losing their loved ones to bullets tearing through their hearts and heads.

Mostly, I fought him when he tried to stop me covering certain stories, like the time he refused to send me to cover an AWB meeting. I insisted on doing everything the job required, be it wearing a skirt and proper shoes to sip tea at the ladies' club (they had handbags that matched their shoes) or watching police process crime scenes as bodies laid like lumps before a mortuary van arrived. Now I did not fight him; I was just grateful to sip tea at the ladies' club, and I still did not bother about a proper handbag.

Weeks passed and I realised that my colleagues were doing acrobatics around me to try to share out a big chunk of my workload, the crime beat. It was the old-school way of working in a small newsroom. It involved watching each others' backs, not hanging anyone out to dry, not insisting their byline came before mine if we shared the workload.

They deliberately worked around me, shielding me. They went through a convoluted process of getting someone's telephone number instead of just asking me to flip through my contact book. When I walked in on a conversation about a crime lead they were working on, they shifted the conversation and walked off to their desks.

I cottoned on that they were trying to protect me at any cost, so I told my editor I was ready to get back to my old beat. I was still finishing my last year of study and my lecturers were happy that I had come to this decision. They had been supportive and careful not to push me too soon in the weeks after the murder. But they showed enough leadership not to capitulate to sympathy. They had to separate my loss from what lay ahead for my career.

And more than covering the crime beat, the most amazing story was about to unfold: the democratic elections were going to make front-page news everywhere. The new day was finally dawning.

I got dressed up on 27 April 1994. It was an occasion. I wore a dramatic black dress that fell to my ankles. It had a beaded top with plastic beads of stars and hearts and some other shapes full of colour and spectacle. I called it my witch's dress. On my head was my favourite black hat and on my feet a pair of Doc Martens. Unisda had embraced the grunge scene and I had tagged along. Among our most treasured items were our eight-eyelet Docs that we wore to alternative night clubs like The Doors where they played the anthems from Nine Inch Nails and The Smiths. We wore our Docs to work and now also to the elections.

Phone calls started early in our house on election day. I was making arrangements with friends to rendezvous and to check on the election station queues. From the TV and radio coverage, we knew we were in for the long haul even if we were just going down to the local recreation centre in Bez Valley.

My Por Por was in a panic. She phoned us, scared and confused. People in her block of flats were saying that all the old people living there had to vote for the National Party or they would not receive their pensions. My gran hardly spoke English and she had no grasp of the political situation. Months before she had decided that she would be in no position to make an informed choice and we agreed with that.

But a minibus was on the way to fetch the old people from her flats to take them to their voting station. I phoned the Independent Electoral Commission (IEC) twice. I was so angry that I was put on hold and when

I finally got through to someone all I could do was lay a complaint. The IEC had warned the nation about intimidation and had urged people to report any incidents. But before I could get to my gran, the minibus had arrived. The old Chinese people who lived in the building were told to bring their IDs; they were shown where to make their mark, next to the face of F.W. de Klerk, their supposed guarantee to receive their pensions. My grandad was one of the only old people in the flats who ignored the general hype of the election. It was not something he felt connected to, he did not know what all the electioneering was about and he did not get into the minibus.

I could not get to my gran in time, though, and Unisda and I still had to vote. We had decided to go to the voting station together and later that morning we arrived at Hofland Park recreation centre, not far from our home. The excitement was palpable; I was glad we had gone bold with our outfits. There was the sense that something special was happening and we were going to be part of it.

The queue was long, though, very long and as the minutes ticked by we realised that we were not going to get anywhere for hours; people had already stretched to the perimeter of the park. We decided to return in the evening. In the end, it was third time lucky for us and we came back for a third time, on the extended voting day of the 28th, to finally make our crosses.

People lined up to make history. All the burning tyres, flying stones and armoured vehicles had not crushed the hope of this huge snake of people waiting patiently, smiling a little and shifting their weight from one foot to another.

I missed my dad so much that day. The paper son, ruled by pieces of paper all his life, was not to take ownership of a ballot sheet. His identity was made up on a piece of paper; someone's stamp of approval and signature on a piece of paper declared my father 'a gentleman of good standing'; and it was an A5 piece of paper that held his death certificate.

Each April, as autumn starts to give way to winter, it clocks up another year without my father. Just as the weather chills, I feel the frost of loss grip my heart all over again and I am taken back to the April night when things did fall apart, when the centre did not hold and Yeats's blood-dimmed tide was loosed upon my world.

But that April day in 1994 I could not help being moved. A cross on a piece of paper mattered to all who stood as links in this slow-moving meander of humans.

The Under-catered Party

One of the biggest social sins you can commit is to under-cater at a Chinese function. Chinese are not shy about eating and enjoying their food, lots of it.

There are eight courses plus dessert at a wedding. The tables must groan with symbolic luck, fertility and happiness for the couple. The number eight is chosen because it is auspicious and guests leave with a reciprocal box of biscuits from the bridal party.

An appropriate present for someone celebrating their 80th birthday is noodles and whisky, presented in pairs, and half of the gift is returned to the guest. The unbroken strands of noodles symbolise long life, and the alcohol represents abundance and enjoyment.

For a baby's *mun yut*, its 'first full moon' or full month party, there are dyed red eggs and parcels of ginger as take-home gifts.

It is all about celebrating with food as well as sharing the bounty and prosperity presented at a dinner table. At any function, you want people to say the food was good, the 'mushrooms were so silky', 'the pork was unbelievably crispy' and, of course, a resounding 'I have had way too much to eat'.

The new South Africa started out excitingly enough. Like a happy wedding, everyone was given an invitation and just about everyone RSVPed. They all wanted to witness it, to be there to cheer on the new union, to celebrate for all the right reasons. Like any party, a few disgruntled uncles and aunties stayed away; they never spoke to anyone anyway. Some guests fought to sit at the head table, some were drama queens and sulked on a stool at the bar. But mostly, an extra chair could be pulled up and an extra place setting could be made, even at the head table.

South Africa's reinvention as a democracy saw everyone arrive in their finest high heels and aired-out suits. We found our seats, the music played and we clapped politely through the many speeches. Then came the part that should have crowned the occasion: the food. But in the new South Africa, there had not been enough to go around.

The head table had grown bigger than we anticipated and they kept calling for more heaped plates. Some tables had received their food and they were tucking in. But other tables were still waiting. All the time fresh plates headed to the top table and the tables tucked in the corners stayed empty. And when their plates did arrive, the kitchen had done some creative plating-up and there was more garnish than meat. Those at these tables were going to eat what little had been offered but they were going to leave the party with hollow tummies, while the top table and those near to them were calling for another bottle of whisky.

The Chinese South Africans felt they were among those who had not eaten well at the South African party. They knew others had gone hungrier, but they thought of themselves first. Someone had withheld the crispy duck from them and given them stir-fried bean curd instead.

Under apartheid that was what they expected – they knew that even scraps were hard to come by – but the Constitution in the so-called rainbow nation promised that if they came to the party they would get a bite at something else. The Chinese still felt too black for some, too white for others and economically, socially and politically they were still pushed up against the margins.

Years before, when there was a census in 1991, I was young, aggrieved and ignorant of computer data-capturing techniques. There was no box for Chinese where it asked for race. There was a box for white, black,

Indian, coloured. I did not feel like I fitted in anywhere, so I drew in my own box and wrote 'Chinese'. For so many official documents, for years I have had to tick the 'other' box, whatever that means.

I looked at interviewee comments in Yoon Park's *A Matter of Honour*. One comment reads: 'I call myself a South African Chinese because I see myself as South African first and then Chinese.'

The more accepted way to identify yourself is with your ethnic origin first and then your nationality, like African American or Chinese Canadian. But in South Africa the Chinese who are South African have inverted this deliberately to show where their identity and their allegiance lies. There are even those who call themselves 'SABC 1' or 'SABC 2' or 'SABC 3'. It stands for South African Born Chinese, first generation or second generation and so on. It is a deliberate and sure way to avoid confusion about where you place yourself. And, ironically, it is so aptly South African, playing on the names of the national broadcaster's TV channels.

Through the years I have caught myself saying, 'I am a South African Chinese,' also feeling that the soil under my feet is where home is and so I should state that bit first. I do not belong to an imagined motherland of China. Home for me is not the place where my grandmother remembered the pears to be so perfect they collapsed with tender juiciness in her mouth. She often told us this as she lamented the 'dud' pears that showed up again and again in our supermarkets. As a child, I did wonder about these scrumptious pears; they were like magical fruit. But eventually I realised that it was not about the pears or the homeland they were supposed to represent, but the lush fertility that springs from memory and nostalgia.

Now I have lived long enough myself to remember some things to make comparisons and to reflect a little, too. I remember when things seemed like they were right, but only because a sinister order of being became our brainwashed normal. Shopping centres' metal detectors were symbols of anxiety and fear of the terrorist that lurked behind every black skin. You would never see a black woman driver on the roads and the only Sotho we learnt was from the dubbed version of Spider-Man, *Rabobi*.

At the same time, I feel duped and stupid that I believed the spin about equity, diversity and tolerance. Instead, we are in George Orwell's *Animal Farm*. Every day more pigs are at the trough, there is more rewriting of the rules and more people are discarded like old horses sold off for cheap pet food.

Sometimes I wonder what my life would have been like if my parents had headed off to another golden mountain. If they had ended up in

Melbourne or San Francisco, would they have worked off their label of migrant more quickly? Would they have been able to run a noodle den or a Chinese takeaway and not stress about having to find someone to front for them so they could register their business with a surname like 'Ho'? When they saved enough money, would they have been able to move into a better neighbourhood without having to consult with neighbours first? Would I have been raised to say 'I am an American' or 'I am Australian', unlike in South Africa where I say 'I am South African' and then have to tag on an explanation.

I am exasperated sometimes by having to present a CV of belonging before I can be considered South African, or African. If skin colour is the marker of belonging, how shallow and insincere, but also how convenient for those closest to the feeding troughs. I met an artist a few years ago. He was born in Cameroon, grew up in Paris and now lives in Switzerland. He speaks French and English mostly and declared, 'I am an African.' There was no hesitation as he claimed his identity without a burden of explanation. But eyebrows are raised and there are derisive snickers when lighter-skinned South Africans or white people claim the same affirmation. They are born on this continent, they know where the Southern Cross will appear in the night sky. They even know the Southern Cross has other indigenous names, they know the time of year the rains will come and when the sardine run will hit the Durban coastline. Yet they do not belong, because their skin colour is not dark enough.

Of course, my rational mind reminds me that our racialised present is a by-product of our history of segregation. Years of isolation from a bigger world picture made us all wear blinkers. A lack of access to quality education and the opportunity to cultivate critical thinking must be factored in. Then it is easy to understand why assumption, pigeonholing and stereotyping for this nation waving a frayed and faded rainbow flag is valid and logical to so many people. One day, far into the future, when the rainbow nation flag has faded sufficiently, maybe then we will find a truer colour, all blended into one colour, one unity for one country.

The Chinese community in South Africa has not remained static either. Change and adaptation is the natural human condition, just like tweaking those public and private portrayals of themselves.

The South African Chinese mostly fight off too close an association with newcomers who make up the recent waves of Chinese immigrants to arrive on Africa's shores.

People in the community repeatedly complain to me: 'Please Ufrieda, you have to write in your articles that we are not like the *daai lok jays*.' It is a loaded term for the newcomers from the mainland, meant to imply someone who is uncouth and uncultured: the kind of person who does not lift her feet properly when she walks, shuffling instead; she talks with her mouth full and shouts across the street to get someone's attention.

'They are the ones who spit in the streets, they push you out of queues and they are so loud,' I am told.

Other people will tell me that they are pulled over by cops and the cops automatically start the 'What can we do about this problem' routine, which is a code for bribe money for a licence disc that is no longer valid or because a driver's licence has been forgotten at home.

'It is because "these people" always give bribes, just like they cannot be bothered to put up a curtain in their homes and they will just make do with stringing up a sheet across the window. Because of them, all Chinese people must suffer.'

The local community has short memories. Just a generation ago they were bribing their way in and out of a system to which they did not belong. Only by tempting someone into the realm of illegality did they have some agency.

I know the scale of things is different now. These days, the crimes where migrants are concerned make headlines. I also cringe when simply because of my skin colour people think I am somehow responsible for poaching rhinos, smuggling perlemoen, running brothels and prostitution rings with trafficked women and for flooding the markets with fong kongs, the knock-offs of every big brand out there.

The newcomers do things differently. Georgie, the local Chinese fahfee man who showed me around his banks for my anthropology research, also told me this.

'It is not like in your father's day. There are no gentleman's agreements about territories or banks. These people [the *ju fah goungs* from the new Chinese communities] use this.' He made his hands into fists and crunched his face into a snarl.

I know in my dad's day *ju fah goungs* stuck to their banks; you did not go muscling in to other people's territories. Betters were free to bet wherever they wanted to, and many played with a few ma-chinas in their areas every day, but you did not take over entire banks. If you did sell a bank, there would be a proper negotiation, a fee and a handshake at the end.

The newcomers do not abide by any of these established codes. They do not have to face anyone at a social gathering or a family do and they cannot be identified as so-and-so's uncle or cousin. They exist outside the community web and therefore outside the circle of common courtesy.

'You should hear how some of these guys treat the betters; they shout at them and treat them like rubbish, they talk down to people. It is not the way to do things, you do not have to scream at people like that, especially not when you also rely on them to play your banks,' said Georgie.

He mentioned the armoured bakkies that are now used in the townships. The fahfee men do not take any chances and there is none of the 'buy cooldrinks for everyone' from my father's day or even the attitude of Georgie whom I overheard offering more seedlings from his garden to one of his runners who had moved into a new Reconstruction and Development (RDP) house. This no-nonsense fahfee man who told me you had to be made of hard stuff to survive was talking about new sprouting flowers that he could share with his betters.

When I have covered stories in the townships as a journalist I have seen the modern armoured trucks with their plated bodywork and windows that do not roll down. There is just a small circle cut into the opaque bulletproof material, just big enough to pass through a bag full of fahfee wallets and for a few curt words to be exchanged.

'There was a really sad story we heard some time ago,' Georgie told me.

'One of these guys [the newcomers] had parked his armoured bakkie to do his round at the bank. When he finished he drove off as usual and returned at night for his evening round to be surrounded by cops. He thought he was being bust for the fahfee but he had actually killed a child earlier in the day. The kid had been playing around the car and he ran over the child without even knowing it because he was in such a tank of a car.'

Georgie felt little kinship for the newcomers. He did not trust them.

While the locals, even the fahfee men and the shopkeepers, worked to be accepted and to raise the generations of SABCs, the new migrants could not be bothered to be South African was what he felt. And why care when you are not a tiny minority, relying on what you are given because you can take all you can grab? They are part of the fiery breath of the mighty Chinese dragon and they are scorching the African soil as they like.

In 2007, when I interviewed an official embassy spokesperson, the number of Chinese nationals in South Africa was estimated at between

125 000 and 250 000. The official said it was a very small number compared to diaspora figures in other parts of the world. What struck me more was that there were potentially 125 000 people the Chinese embassy could not account for. It meant that for all those in South Africa with legal papers there were about the same number who had to negotiate their being here by flying under the radar, still being paper sons and daughters.

Some new migrants are involved with businesses and dealings of organised crime, but many are not. Many are simply here to make better lives for themselves. It is the same old migrant story.

I met a young woman called Ah Mooi in Chinatown some years ago. She and her husband arrived in South Africa in 2006. She worked as a waitress, trying to improve her English by explaining that chicken's feet, *fong jeow*, are a delicacy and that loofah sponges are not only for drying out and bathing with but can be turned into bites of vegetable heaven with the right amount of garlic and *wok hei*, literally the breath of the wok.

'The competition for work is just too intense in China,' she told me in Cantonese. When I met her, her husband was working as a chef and kitchen hand at another Chinese restaurant in Sandton. They saw each other once a week on their day off. They had left a little girl back in China who was only a voice at the end of the line or the little one growing up through photographs that arrived in the post. They had not been able to go home for more than three years at one stage. Like my parents, a year in Africa had turned into three and then more as the calendar kept flipping over. I kept thinking of the little girl, like my mom, who was not getting to be with her mom or dad because they were far away in a place they called Naam Fey.

Ah Mooi also told me that when they first arrived, her husband had started out as a fahfee man. She had fought his decision, even though she knew he could do better financially with fahfee than working in a restaurant. She thought it too risky and that his life was not worth the chance of making a bit more money and eventually he agreed.

In 2010 they did manage to return to China. But it was not because they had made their fortune. It was because her husband, whom I never met, was involved in a car accident one night. He was given appalling care in the government hospital, waiting for months for medical procedures and being ignored by nurses who could not be bothered to try to understand his few mumbled words of English. Eventually they decided to return to China where he could get access to better state care and there would be family on hand to nurse him back to health.

Ah Mooi phoned me before she left. 'I will be back, Ah Ngaan,' she said, 'and my husband will be, too, once he is better.'

I really liked Ah Mooi's attitude; she was always cheerful, always wanting to try a bit more English out on me, as I did to her with my Cantonese. She never asked for anything, not even a lift somewhere, and I knew she did not drive or have access to a car. The only time she asked me for help was to translate for her to the man she was talking to outside the restaurant one day. No problem, I thought, and left my friends at the table where we were having lunch and followed her outside.

I greeted the man in a big black 4x4 with a Swaziland number plate. He grunted a greeting.

'Please tell him that I need my passport back,' said Ah Mooi.

I waited for a bit more of an explanation.

'He said he had connections to someone at Home Affairs who can renew my working holiday visa. I have already given him R5 000 to do that and he has not come back with my passport for months now. Tell him please that I just want to get my passport back. I do not care about the money or the visa,' Ah Mooi said, her expression now showing her agitation.

I faced the man and translated for him exactly what she had told me.

But he started swearing. 'Tell her that I have been contacting Chookie [or Chuckie?] at Randburg Home Affairs and she will get her f-ing passport when he gives it back to me.'

I could not believe this man. Now I was getting agitated.

'Listen, just bring back her passport. When can she expect it back?' I demanded.

'Don't you speak English? What's wrong with any of yous [sic], hey? She will f-ing get it when I am f-ing ready,' he said. He actually learnt out of the window of his car as if he was going to slap me for telling him what was expected from his end of the deal.

I was ready to have a full-blown confrontation with Mr Delightful, who did not let up with his threats or his swearing. But as Ah Mooi tried to pacify me I realised that I could retaliate and walk away from this man, but Ah Mooi would still have to deal with him – he had to bring back her passport.

I was embarrassed; I should have known better, sooner. As always, Ah Mooi was not too fussed. She said he always spoke to her like that; he spoke to all Chinese people like that.

'He comes here and just says f*ck, f*ck, f*ck all the time to us,' she used the English expletive. She had learnt that word just fine.

It was an illegal transaction that she had entered into, buying papers, hoping someone would come through for her and skirting the laws to get by. Ah Mooi was exactly like my parents all those years ago, a paper daughter trying to buy herself some freedom, some time and some opportunity in the promised land.

Then, one winter morning in June 2008, I woke up black – legally black that is. The Chinese South Africans had a won a nine-year legal challenge to have the definition of black, as it is applied in the Employment Equity and Broad Based Black Economic Empowerment Act of 2004, extended to the Chinese community.

The challenge started in 1999, even before Black Economic Empowerment (BEE) legislation was enacted. A pair of Chinese architects in Kimberley had applied for an affirmative action tender only to be told they did not qualify. With the rejection, a wave started to ripple through the community. South African Chinese were classified as 'coloured' under apartheid South Africa, but then were deemed not black enough in the new South Africa, once again caught in the no-man's-land of racial limbo.

When I initially heard of the representations to parliament and the pending legal challenge that the community was instituting, I did believe the Chinese were jumping on to the BEE bandwagon. So was everyone else who was not white. To me, it was an infected policy not really designed to level the playing field or fast-track people who were previously disadvantaged.

I had no respect for the 'we have struggled/suffered, now we must eat' mentality. It was myopic and unsustainable and a pact with the devil. I saw the devil cutting his deal: you can gorge yourself today, take on the labels and titles of fame and higher designation, drive the government car, use the company expense account and watch your share portfolio mount. You can have this because apartheid stole it from you. All you have to do is answer one question truthfully when the devil returns. One day, the devil will re-appear and he will ask: 'Did you live up to your full potential to create this success?'

Without the correct answer, he will take the prize that even apartheid could not wrest from you; he will take your dignity.

It seemed to me that the Chinese were dancing with demons. Then the chairman of the Chinese Association of South Africa (CASA), Patrick Chong, quietly chided me. He said: 'Ufrieda, you and all the Chinese children were protected from the worst of what apartheid dished up. This challenge is about political affirmation, recognition that as non-whites we, people like your mom and dad, were treated like second-class citizens. We were discriminated against like all other non-white groups in South Africa. We could not go to white schools, to cinemas or get on to certain buses reserved for whites. If you wanted to go to university you had to make it on to a quota system.'

I was at Pretoria High Court the day the ruling was eventually handed down. I saw Mr Chong shed a tear as he embraced those who had come out to support CASA's fight. Among them was George Bizos, the celebrated human rights lawyer who, through the Legal Resources Centre, had taken up the community's case.

I knew then that the long years of the court battle were not about being able to buy preferential shares or about pulling up a seat at that head table to gorge; they were about setting the record straight and about reminding other South Africans that the Chinese were part of the South African story.

But still it was not over. A court's ruling is fiction for some people. It does not change heads or hearts. Immediately after the ruling, I walked into work and colleagues, who happen to be black, gave me hugs and said: 'Yay, Ufrieda, now you are really one of us, sisi.' I laughed and shrugged, not sure what it all meant.

Then, about two weeks later, fury over the ruling exploded among organisations such as the Black Management Forum. How dare the Chinese South Africans claim a piece of the BEE pie? They never suffered as much as blacks did and they had more opportunities. It was like saying losing your legs is more serious than losing your eye. The Forum was going to challenge the High Court ruling. At that time, it was estimated that there were between 10 000 and 12 000 Chinese South Africans in South Africa – the sum total of people who would qualify for any BEE or affirmative action because the ruling did not apply to the Chinese who had only arrived in the country after 1994.

Coincidentally, there was at the time a preferential share option for a state-owned oil and petroleum company. Now that the Chinese were legally black they were allowed to buy shares at a very good price. And when newspapers snapped pictures of the Chinese in the queues it was the confirmation that the Black Management Forum needed to say: 'See, they are eating our pie.'

I was not thinking environmentally or economically when I decided to buy these shares; I was motivated more by anger, precisely because there were those who said I was not allowed to and who were challenging a court ruling.

When I went to buy the shares, there was a man in the queue in front of me who looked as white as any other white South African. He said he was buying shares, and that he was black. The lady behind the counter at the post office looked him up and down once or twice but in lieu of pulling out a pencil to administer a post-apartheid version of the infamous pencil test, she processed his transaction. I had to laugh at the insanity of it all but it was not a laughing matter.

The Black Management Forum and eleven other black associations were ready for court action. It was Patrick Chong who flew from Cape Town to address the Forum, ironically at one of their sit-down dinners in swanky, swish Sandton.

He knew it was going to be a hostile crowd, but he stood up and started his speech with words to the effect of: 'Not one of us in this room needs BEE.'

That was the truth, whether they wanted to hear it or not. When I interviewed him some time after that dinner, I said I was confused and irritated by all the labelling that had occurred since the ruling on 18 June. The legally black ruling made me 'a sister' in one of the newsrooms where I work, but a few weeks later I was a *'lekgoa'* to the same person, the Sotho word for a disrespectful white person that has its derogatory origins in the word for the white scum that rises on the top of waves to crash against the shores. I wondered what had happened to simply being Ufrieda, as I had always been.

Patrick Chong had more wisdom for me. 'Ufrieda, you have to realise that this ruling is not your right, it is your responsibility. You, like every Chinese South African, has to work even harder to make sure everyone around you who truly needs BEE will benefit from it.'

He was right. There was enough food to go around, less so generosity of spirit.

I will always be someone's 'Ching Chong Chinaman' and someone else's *'lekgoa'*, *'kaffir sussie'* or 'banana'. I grow more detached from these labels each time I put my mind to it. I see more context for past hurts and old injuries and I try to be patient for peace that cannot come just yet. In the meantime, I know I can choose who I want to break bread with.

Dear Ah Ba

The world has changed so much since you left. I want to tell you everything and share so much that is in my heart. But let me tell you what matters here.

Some of your worst fears for the country did happen. I could tell you about crumbling infrastructure, about manholes waiting to swallow small children because they do not get fixed by councils that do not bother to spend their budgets. They use the money instead for the big men with small hearts; you can spot them in their over-the-top imported suits or by the way they seem umbilically tied to so-called blue-light brigades.

I could tell you about rising road death tolls because no one has a proper driver's licence. Sometimes I wonder why you bothered to take me out on all those driving lessons. And when we are on the roads we are all so angry. Now they have a term for it. They call it road rage. It sounds all new, dad, but sometimes I think it is old anger. We are angry because we have all lost so much in this country and we cannot say it.

Crime has not improved since you were taken as a victim. South Africans and newcomers have even burnt people for having a different accent, for not being able to say 'elbow' in Zulu. I have said goodbye to many more people from violent crimes than I care to count. I am angry and tired of saying 'my condolences' to people who have lost their mothers and their fathers. Too often I hear people say, 'At least you got away with your life,' when thieves have ransacked their homes and invaded their privacy and the things they hold sacred. All those who do not die, keep paying the price in terror. It wakes them in the middle of the night and grips tightly in their hearts, making them cold even towards someone begging at the side of the road.

But you were wrong about some things, and I am glad for that. The black president who first came to power did just fine. He did better than fine; he was part of a miracle. We came to respect him, to love him even, and he reminds us of what is good and what is possible, even now.

Some things got bigger and better; some things just got bigger. Chips in a can made it to South Africa, and Kodak came back after isolation. They make cars with bum warmers these days and some even have little alarms to guide you into a reverse parking. Just imagine, dad, you would not have had to hold your breath sitting next to me, waiting for me to clear a pillar or a pole in a parking lot. There are American fast food burgers everywhere; you can even order straight from your car – that is part of the bigger, not better, bit, I guess.

The little roadhouse on Louis Botha is still there, the one you took us to for 'puppies'. It is fighting for its share of tummy space with the big franchises. I have not been back since you took us there. I think I am overdue for a parfait, one for you, dad!

You will be glad to know I fry my own egg noodles, not the two-minute variety we used to eat after burning crackers at midnight on New Year's or when we had played cards, 13-card rummy, doh daai dee, until late into the holiday nights and you thought a midnight snack would be a good idea. I actually soak the mushrooms and I cut the vegetables finely. I have even mastered Ah Goung's steamed eggs recipe; the right proportion of cooled boiled water to beaten eggs and just the right minutes for the wok to work its steaming fury. I get it right almost all of the time!

The Chinese have adapted and changed, too, here in this golden mountain. No culture stands still and survives. We keep what is useful, we discard the rest. You were never big on the fussy bits of traditions, even though you demanded that we show respect and personal discipline. Some things we hang on to a little longer and some things we know we have to let go of. The five-cent lei see, the lucky coin wrapped up in red paper at a funeral that is meant to restore the luck after the sadness of final respects, has been replaced by a bowl of sweets. It is still a reminder of the mercy of healing after loss but no one has time to wrap up all those five-cent pieces today. They even sell watermelons all cut up and packaged into chunks; they call it 'convenience'.

Remember when we would dunk a watermelon in a tub of ice-cold water, waiting for you to come home on a Saturday afternoon? You would bring out the big Chinese chopper, run it quickly along that sharpener from Ah Goung's butcher days, and we would all head to the backyard for the big watermelon slaughter. Mom said it was better to do it outside; 'too much mess for the kitchen'. You would cut it up into those big wedges and our chins and cheeks would get cold and wet as we ate. We spat the pips into the garden and laughed at each other because as hard as we tried, the juices slid down our elbows and the fronts of our shirts.

There are still dragon boat festivals and kung fu demonstrations but they are not reserved for only Chinese people any more. Dressed up in traditional outfits, beating drums and straining muscles as oars plough through the water, are all those who want to take part, regardless of their skin colour. There is even a monastery these days and monks from across Africa greet you with a bow and a nee how, in the Mandarin that all novices are taught.

We do not nod our heads in greeting to all the Chinese people we see in shops and on the streets any more. It is not like we are being rude or we have forgotten our manners. These Chinese do not even look twice at us; we are not part of a community, we simply have the same skin colour. Some come from as far as the Siberian border, some are tanned so dark or have facial features that mark them clearly as being from some far-away geographical origin. If they do speak to me it is in dialects I do not understand and accents that my ears do not register.

But there are the Ah Buks and Ah Mous, the uncles and aunties, that look familiar. I greet them as you and mom taught us: 'Jou saan, Ah Buk, jou saan, Ah Mou'. They greet me back with 'good morning' in Cantonese and then they ask whose child I am and I say I am your daughter, I am Ah Kee's child.

The Chinese foods are different, too, now and there are two Chinatowns. Your beloved Ma Lay Gum survives barely but you hear Cantonese here still, the kind we spoke with our bastardised words, the Chinese that mellowed into its South African distillation. And locals still make the journey downtown to bring donations in lieu of flowers for someone's family in mourning.

On our dinner tables are more than the speciality of the crab you used to cook up in the wok with your alchemy of garlic, spring onion and a splash of oyster sauce. Now there are spices so hot they numb your tongue before they land on your taste buds. We eat beans and vegetables that no one ever bothered to plant here in South Africa before the new waves of Chinese brought the seeds from afar. I wish you could taste these, although maybe you would still prefer a bowl of fried rice.

Pinky is still here. She has lost an eye now and mom had her bow replaced with a green spotted one. Mom holds on to you in so many ways. Pinky's head is a little floppier. She has been through more washes than an old bear can handle maybe. She is not the giant of my childhood any more, but I remember bringing her home that day with you. She sits on mom's bed sometimes, like she has done so many days since you have been gone.

We have grown up, too, dad – Kaatch, Kaa Heng, Ah Saan and me. We grow into our lives like you would have hoped for us – making mistakes, choosing more wisely a second time around, learning, loving and living each moment, whatever it brings. You have two beautiful granddaughters, Kaa Heng and Jo-Anne's girls Alexandra and Jordan; Ah Yee and Ah Jaan are their Chinese names. They test their tongues around calling mom 'Ah Mah' and the Chinese rhymes we used to sing: dum dum jun, gok fa yun... 'spinning around and around the rose gardens'. They stand to attention for our national anthem with its meld of languages proving that we can mix and match, we can compromise and make room for more; it still creates a song. Alex and Jordie hold our hope; maybe yours, too.

They are the branches and new leaves you left behind when you put your roots down here on this southern tip of the world, when you and mom built our lives for us. And me, I can only know my roots and breathe in the wide potential of the open sky, one breath at a time.

I love you dad,
Ah Ngaan